The
Lost Gift to the
ITALIAN
ISLAND

BOOKS BY BARBARA JOSSELSOHN

LAKE SUMMERS SERIES

The Lilac House

The Bluebell Girls

The Lily Garden

SISTERS OF WAR SERIES

Secrets of the Italian Island

The Cranberry Inn

BARBARA JOSSELSOHN

The
Lost Gift to the
ITALIAN
ISLAND

bookouture

Published by Bookouture in 2023

An imprint of Storyfire Ltd.
Carmelite House
50 Victoria Embankment
London EC4Y 0DZ

www.bookouture.com

ISBN: 978-1-83790-844-8
eBook ISBN: 978-1-83790-843-1

To Sarah, Bessie, Ida, and Rose
Forever and ever

ONE

SEPTEMBER 1943

There's something not right...

Giulia murmured the sentence to herself as she steered the *pattino* toward the approaching shore. She'd been rowing for hours, ever since she'd been awoken by the searing sun, its rays warming the flat, slatted plank where she sat. She was exhausted, having slept only briefly last night. She'd tried not to sleep at all, knowing it was dangerous to let herself drift off, but ultimately she'd been unable to keep her eyes open. The night sky over the Mediterranean had been like a soft blanket, its color strangely light for that hour. "Why is the sky that color?" her younger sister, Emilia, had asked when they'd left the main-land five weeks ago on their way to the Castello del Poeta, the grand, legendary castle at the summit of Parissi Island.

Their older sister, Annalisa, had praised Emilia's curiosity, but Giulia had shushed her, impatient with her chattiness. How she longed right now to hear her younger sister's nagging ques-tions so she could respond more generously. She refused to think about where Emilia might have ended up. But what she couldn't shake from her mind was the look on Annalisa's face when the two of them said goodbye to one another, aware that the Nazis were fast approaching and Parissi Island was about to be stormed. They'd been forced to separate and flee, with no way to know where Emilia was or whether she was safe. They'd had no choice but to take their chances and hope they'd all reunite in America.

There's something not at all right, Giulia said to herself once more, adding the "not at all" for emphasis. Because it was clear that the land mass ahead wasn't Anzalea, the port town on the mainland, as she'd believed earlier that it was. No, it was just the edge of another of the small islands that dotted this section of the Mediterranean. The boat must have strayed off course during the night as she slept. She would need to reorient herself and aim for Anzalea again. But could she make it to the mainland before sunset? It would be too dangerous to spend another night out on the water.

She wiped the thick coating of sweat from her forehead with the back of her hand. The *pattino*'s oars seemed as resistant to her efforts as the stone wall bordering the castle would have been, had she tried to push it across the wide courtyard. Her arms were so tired that she didn't know how much longer she could continue moving her little boat through the choppy water. She'd finished all the food she'd been able to snare on her way out of the castle—some chunks of bread and cheese and bunches of grapes from the vast kitchen. She'd finished the carafe of water she'd grabbed from one of the beautifully set dining tables, with crystal goblets poised to the right of the large plates and heavy silverware laid neatly on lace napkins. The settings hadn't been touched. No one had eaten lunch that day.

And maybe worst of all, the toe of one of her thin shoes was stained with blood, which was seeping through the leather and onto the floorboards. She'd sliced her foot, right through the shoe, on a protruding piece of wood on the castle's rear dock as she was fleeing. Nobody used that dock much, and it needed repair. She'd been the only one who'd run in that direction. The only one who knew there was one lone *pattino* moored there.

With a sigh, she dropped the oars near her feet and studied the island ahead as she tried unsuccessfully to clench her fists, fighting the swelling and stiffness in her fingers. She had no idea who lived here or what they might make of her. Or maybe the island was uninhabited, although that was unlikely, as she could see some kind of structure, maybe a house, on a hill behind the line of olive trees a short distance from the shore. It was risky to pull her boat onto the sand, but she had no choice. She was lucky to have made it this far. The *pattino* was designed for short fishing expeditions and occasional trips to the mainland. Though elegant and easy to handle, it was old and not particularly seaworthy, her friend Vincenzo had warned her. With each hour she'd been out on the water since leaving yesterday, she'd been testing fate.

She lifted the oars once again and maneuvered toward the shoreline, thankful for the times she'd snuck down to the rear boathouse and Vincenzo had taken her out on the water. They'd been having fun, the two of them, but she was glad now that she'd been attentive to the way he'd handled the small craft. Even though all she'd wanted to do on those afternoons was enjoy their silly banter, their childish flirtations. Annalisa thought the two of them might be falling in love, but Giulia knew that wasn't the case. Yes, she and Vincenzo were in love— but not with each other; no, they were in love with the castle, the sea, the sky, the simple reality of being young, carefree, and full of youthful dreams. The days had been sweet, the air filled with the scent of the oranges Vincenzo had brought for them to share. What fun they'd had, two lighthearted friends aboard the little boat, sailing on the translucent blue water.

She thought now about her friend. Where was he? With Emilia? Had he found her, as he'd promised to do?

Please be safe, she whispered. *Please get to America with Emilia.*

She hoped so much that they'd be there when she arrived. Because she *would* get to America, too. To New York. Her stopping here was merely a delay and not an irreversible change of plans. She had to believe that they were each as determined as she was. Emilia and Vincenzo. Annalisa and her beloved Aldo; and Uncle Patricio. They all intended to be together again, and they would, if everyone remained steadfast.

The boat reached the shore, and she placed the oars down again. Then she stood and lifted her injured foot in the bloodied shoe. It had hurt more yesterday; now there was only a dull, rhythmic throb that somehow felt more dangerous than the previous sharp sting. Slowly, she lifted her foot past the rim of the *pattino* and placed it on the sandy shore. She paused, straddling the edge of the boat, one foot in and one foot out. She didn't think her bad foot could hold her weight, so she leaned over to grip the rim of the boat with her hands. Her fingers—those once-smooth, slim fingers that had always garnered compliments—were inflexible. Her finger pads were white and wrinkled from the water that had splashed fiercely as she rowed. Her dress was soaked, too, and seawater dripped down from the ends of her honey-colored hair. She swung her good foot down next to her bad one and stood up straight.

What island was this? Who might live in that house she'd spied as she approached the shore? She hoped she hadn't spent these hours fleeing the Nazis only to end up in another Nazi stronghold. With any luck, the Nazi forces were only interested in one island in this region, Parissi Island, because of the magnificent castle where she and her sisters had been living for the past five weeks. The castle's head housekeeper, Signora Russo, had asserted a few nights ago as she supervised the preparations for dinner that the Nazis would struggle to maintain control over Rome while fighting the Allied forces coming up from the South. So presumably they had no resources available to go after other islands in this part of the Mediterranean.

Giulia felt a fresh burst of blood ooze from her toe. Trembling and dizzy, she sank down to the sand and folded her legs in front of her. Annalisa would scold her if she could see her now. She'd tell her to get up and pull herself together. She wouldn't understand how hard that could be when you were scared and in pain. Annalisa would never sink down onto the ground. She was too strong, too driven for that. Giulia closed her eyes, missing everything about her older sister—even her bossiness. Things weren't meant to have ended up like this. She and her sisters always stuck together. How had they come to decide that the best route forward was to head out independently and regroup in America? She'd never felt so abandoned and alone.

Opening her eyes, she looked toward the sea in the direction from which she'd come. There was no castle in the distance. It was as though it had disappeared, and the last five weeks had been a dream. Had it ever existed? All that luxury and brilliance? And the luscious foods and desserts and wine? Balls and concerts in the evenings, with an orchestra playing and couples dancing on the gleaming marble floor, the men in tuxedos and the women in gowns—she and her sisters included. Gems sparkling in their upswept hair.

And now she was all by herself. She knew she should keep trying for the mainland. That was where she'd be safest. But she didn't have the strength to get back into the boat and row on. Should she risk taking a rest? She could hide among the nearby bushes along the shore. She could try to hide the boat there, too. But what if the mainland was still quite far off? She could never survive another night in these wet clothes with no water—

"Hello!" sang out a young female voice, its tone confident and musical. "I'm Marilene Ciani, and I'm in charge of this island. Who are you, and what are you doing here?"

TWO

MAY 2019

Tuesday

"There's something not right…"

Tori studied the sleek white gown hanging in the center of her workroom—or, more accurately, the walk-in closet behind the showroom of Deirdre's Home Decor, where she worked during the day as store manager. Narrowing her eyes and resting her hands on her waist, she circled the dress form, taking in each of the gown's parts one by one: the strapless neckline, the shirring on the bodice, the layered folds along the hip, the ankle-length hem, and the small train that puddled on the floor.

"I think it's perfect," Brianna, the store's part-time sales associate, said, and she crossed her arms over her chest for emphasis. Tori gave her a sideways look. A student in college majoring in fashion merchandising, Brianna was endearingly puppy-like: raring to chime in, desperate to learn, eager to please. Her eyes always looked intent behind thick tortoiseshell glasses and beneath long, dark-brown bangs.

But she was wrong, Tori thought, shaking her head. She

scowled, knowing she'd never be able to leave for the evening if she didn't figure out what was off. Positioned once again in front of the dress, she tilted her head and walked backward, one slow step at a time, now viewing the garment as a whole instead of as individual parts. She tapped her bottom teeth with her index finger and pictured the bride she was designing for. That didn't always work, of course. The dress had to stand on its own, no matter who wore it. But sometimes thinking about the bride helped.

She turned to Brianna. "It's the hemline," she said, her tone triumphant, as though she'd found the answer to a seemingly unsolvable math equation.

Brianna's eyes widened. "But it's a normal hemline."

"Exactly," Tori said. "It makes the whole shape of the dress... too predictable. And Sheree is so sophisticated, she told me she wanted something a little edgy and unexpected. An asymmetrical hemline, that's what it needs. With a gentle drape from knee to ankle. It'll play off the straight neckline and be a dramatic counterpoint to the softer style of her hair. And the sheen of the fabric will enhance the surprise of the design as she walks down the aisle. That's the answer."

"Oh, wow!" Brianna enthused. "You're so right. How do you do it?"

Tori chuckled and walked over to pat her arm. Brianna was like a younger sister. Or even a daughter. Well, not quite a daughter—if Tori had a daughter Brianna's age, that would mean that she'd given birth when she was fifteen. But sometimes Brianna seemed barely older than Tori's actual daughter, Molly, who'd turned eleven a few weeks ago.

"It's so cool, watching you work," Brianna added, tousling her bangs with her fingertips. "When is Sheree coming back? I can't wait to see the look on her face when she sees it."

"I'll give her a call this week." Tori unbuttoned the dress

and transferred it from the form to a hanger. "Now that I know what I want to do, it won't take long. I'll bring it home and work on it a bit tonight."

"Tonight?" Brianna asked. "Isn't tonight the big anniversary dinner?"

Tori took a sharp breath, embarrassed that she'd forgotten. Then she rolled her eyes. "So I'll do it tomorrow. And by the way, it's not a big deal. It's just dinner."

Brianna fetched a garment bag from a nearby shelf. "Jeremy seemed to think it was an important anniversary. He was so cute, the way he came here last week with that huge chocolate wrapped in gold foil... so fun, shaped like the number five..."

Tori left her to her musings and went through the arched doorway and into the main part of the shop, which was crowded with slender maple writing desks, golden-oak farmhouse dining tables, tall distressed-walnut curio cabinets, and other vintage pieces of furniture, some dating back more than one hundred years. Deirdre, the owner, had a great eye for home furnishings. She spent most of each year traveling around the country, finding beautiful items at antique shows and estate sales that she'd have shipped to the store—which was why she needed a full-time manager. Deirdre loved that Tori designed wedding gowns on the side, and was happy to let her use the store's huge closet as a workroom and meet with clients in the showroom before and after store hours. And Tori was lucky that Brianna felt she had so much to teach her. She was happy to pay Brianna for an hour or two of work each week as a fashion assistant, scheduling appointments and ordering fabrics and supplies.

Walking toward the front of the store, Tori rounded her back and stretched her arms forward, feeling the strong, late-afternoon sunshine as it streamed through the plate glass window that abutted the sidewalk. The warmth bathed her arms, which peeked out from her sleeveless navy-blue sheath dress and glowed like toasted marshmallow. Clasping her hands beneath her chin, she gazed at the empty storefront across the street. It had formerly been a sneaker shop but now it was empty. She could almost see the sign she'd been dreaming of atop the front door: *Tori's Originals*. She longed to open her own dress shop, where she could create one-of-a-kind wedding gowns and carry formal dresses by emerging designers. She wanted to give talented people a way to shine, a place where they could take risks as they honed their technique and vision and developed their clientele. Everyone needed a platform. Everyone deserved to feel wanted somewhere. She'd been socking away money for years now, but still couldn't bring herself to take the plunge.

Behind her, Brianna approached with the garment bag that held the wedding gown, and she draped it over an upholstered armchair on the sales floor. "Wow, this is filling up fast," she said and Tori turned to see her pointing toward a waist-high white carton tucked into a corner that was overflowing with garments. "I'll inventory this batch and put them in my car so I can stop by the shelter in the morning to drop them off."

Tori nodded. Eight years ago when she'd started as store manager, she'd convinced Deirdre that they should collect gently used women's professional clothing to donate to shelters in the area.

"If you don't need me for anything else, I'll be heading out," Brianna said. "I have a date tonight. Seems like a nice guy. He's in tech."

"So, maybe a super-sophisticated one-shoulder look?"

"I'm thinking mermaid, with a V-neck..."

Tori nodded her approval. It was a running joke: whenever Brianna had a date with someone new, she liked to imagine the style of her wedding gown.

"And what about you, Tori?" Brianna said.

"What about me what?"

"What about... I mean, where are you and Jeremy having dinner?"

"Chez Pierre. On the water."

"Oh, Chez Pierre!" She tilted her head. "So many people I know have gotten engaged there. Sooo romantic! Don't you think there's even a chance he might be surprising you with a ring tonight?"

Tori shook her head as she went to the front counter to shut down the store's computer for the day. "He knows better."

Brianna looked at her doubtfully, her eyebrows converging. "You really don't want him to ask—not now, not ever? You never designed a wedding gown and thought, 'Gee, I'd like to wear this'?"

"Nope."

"How can that be? Don't you love him?"

Tori sighed. They'd been through this before. Maybe it was strange for someone who felt the way she did to design wedding gowns. But her creativity, her passion, had to do with fabrics and textures, structure and line, closures and trim, and harmony and shape. The interplay of tiny buttons with long, luscious trains or a plunging neckline with a full, luxurious skirt. It had nothing to do with marriage.

"Okay, okay, I'll shut up. I'm going," Brianna said and picked up the carton of used clothing.

"Have a nice evening. Have fun," Tori said and watched her leave.

Then she walked back to the window. The sun had dropped even lower in the sky and now seemed merely inches above the empty storefront across the street. It wasn't that she didn't believe in love. No, love was the best part of her life. She loved Molly, her daughter, and she loved Marilene, her grandmother, who lived with them in their cozy house on the other side of town. She had loved her parents, who were taken from her way too soon.

And she loved Jeremy. Utterly loved him. He was an amazing person. Kind and considerate, romantic, smart and funny. And talented. There was little she enjoyed more than stopping in at Danny's Pub, the local spot where Jeremy and his band played for kicks on Tuesday nights, and seeing him up there on the stage. She loved when he glanced out toward the tables and spotted her, and suddenly he looked happy—a warm, enveloping type of happy. She loved his large, pale-blue eyes set deeply below his broad forehead and his tousled, caramel-brown hair, and his smile, which was always so real, so genuine. Even after five years together, she still felt that tingle of infatuation when his eyes locked with hers. At moments like that, she knew she wanted him in her life forever.

She just didn't want to marry him.

There was a clamor at the door as Molly bounded in, still wearing her leotard and tights from ballet class, her feet in sneakers. Marilene walked in behind her, favoring her right leg.

"Mom! You are not going to believe it. We're doing *Alice in Wonderland* for the recital—that's exactly what I was hoping for," Molly said, sounding as though she were planning the town's next budget. Wisps of her honey-colored hair had escaped from her ballet bun and gathered around her forehead and temples, and Tori could see the glistening of sweat beads around her nose. The students worked very hard when they reached Level Four.

"I think I have a shot at being cast as Alice, although I could be the Queen of Hearts," she continued. "Except that Melissa is probably better for that because she's taller. I could be the white rabbit, I guess, although that's a comical part, and I'm not that kind of dancer. And Charlie is a really funny kid, he could make it work. So if I were Mademoiselle Diana, I'd put Melissa as the queen, Charlie as the rabbit, which leaves me as Alice, unless she thinks I could be dance captain and lead the group dancers, which could make sense, because I can help the others learn, but it's not what I want—"

"Hello, Mom, here's your hug. Did you have a nice day?" Tori said.

Molly came closer and wrapped her arms around Tori's waist, and Tori drew her close. Molly had grown a lot this year and her face had become more angular, her cheeks not nearly as round as they used to be. Tori was proud of her daughter, who was a smart and motivated fifth grader. But she did miss the little girl Molly had been as recently as... as last week, it seemed.

"She has the whole cast worked out," Marilene said, chuckling. "She even asked to stop on the way here to buy a notebook so she could write out her plan to give her teacher."

"I want to help with my ideas," Molly said. "So it can all be decided soon. I hate when things are so unsure. I like to know where I stand."

Tori kissed the top of her head. She had been thinking the same thing, when she'd been looking across the street, imagining the store she wanted to open. Like mother, like daughter. "I know the feeling," she murmured.

"Molly, sweetie, we can talk more about this later," Marilene said. "Your mom has to get home and get ready for her big dinner. I said just a quick hello because I've been starving myself all day so I can enjoy my fill of pizza—"

"Can I just look in the back and see the new ribbons with the zigzag edges? Brianna told me they were coming this morning for a dress you're working on, and I wanted one for my hair—"

"Okay, go, but just for a minute," Tori said. "Marilene's right, you need to get dinner soon so you can do your homework before it gets too late."

Molly took off for the workroom, and Tori walked over to give her grandmother a hug. "Hi, Mar," she said. She'd never called her grandmother Grandma or Nana, anything like that. Molly didn't either. Her grandmother had always preferred to be Mar, because she said "Grandma" felt too limiting. Marilene took pride in being her own person. Plus, she'd always thought the word "Grandma" made her sound old, and she didn't want people to think of her that way. In her smart capris and cap-sleeve blouse, and with her short silvery-blonde bob, she looked nowhere near eighty-eight years old.

"Hi, darling," Marilene said. Though she was Italian by birth and had what Tori believed was a beautiful Italian last name, *Ciani*, she had come to New York decades ago and lost nearly all of her accent. All that was left was a slightly throaty and elongated way of pronouncing vowels, which Tori found deliciously elegant.

"What time is Jeremy coming to get you?" she asked.

"Seven."

"That's only an hour from now. You've got to go home and get dressed."

"I will. It won't take me that long."

"But it's a special dinner. A big anniversary, he told me. And Chez Pierre! I think maybe…"

"Oh no, first Brianna and now you?" Tori went to pull her bag out from the bottom drawer of a nearby cabinet. "I left the mail over there," she said, pointing to a small stack on an antique bookcase, aiming to change the subject.

"Thank you, love," Marilene said as she headed that way. A bookkeeper who'd had a thriving business for decades, Marilene still kept the books for a few retailers on the block, including Tori's boss.

"Honestly, I don't know why you don't do all this online, the way the rest of the world does," Tori said.

"Because there's something satisfying about writing a check," Marilene said absentmindedly as she thumbed through the envelopes. "Something you barely did, something Molly will never know...

"And say," she added. "This isn't all bills. Here's something for you. A postcard from Italy it seems. With a picture of a wedding dress, and... oh my..."

"Italy?" Tori walked over to look at the note on the over-sized card. She guessed immediately who had sent it: Kelly Danforth, a graphic designer who had come to Tori to design her wedding dress but had been ambivalent about every silhouette Tori had proposed. After their last meeting, Kelly had embarked on a three-month vacation to Europe and had promised to send Tori any interesting ideas she came up with. She'd warned Tori that she would probably use regular mail, as she was going to remote locations without good internet service.

Tori read what Kelly had written:

Tori, I know you're not going to believe it, but I have found the perfect design for my wedding dress! We took a day trip to Parissi Island, this tiny place in the Mediterranean. Wedding gowns were the furthest thing on my mind, but they have a museum in this old castle, and it has displays from the 1940s including the beautiful wedding gown on the other side of this card. It was designed and sewn by this woman, Giulia something, who once lived here. Look at the little pink buttons, they're actually pebbles sourced on this very island!

Her curiosity piqued even more at the mention of the 1940s —she loved 1940s fashion—Tori turned the postcard over. On the back was a photo of a wedding dress on a pedestal, shown from the front and back. Tori was impressed. Ambivalent as Kelly usually was, her enthusiasm here was well-placed. It was a stunning dress.

Stunning in so many ways, even in this small picture, Tori thought as she studied it closely. The bodice was covered in hundreds of tiny glittering beads, and the scalloped neckline and sleeves featured lace appliqué. The skirt seemed to be constructed of layers upon layers of fine tulle, and the hemline and train were subtly scalloped, mirroring the neckline and adding a satisfying note of balance. The back had a slender column of tiny buttons—no, pebbles, according to Kelly—that shone with a faint, opalescent pink hue. She couldn't help but marvel at the thoughtfully rendered piece and wonder who the designer was and how long it had taken to make.

"So interesting," Tori said to Marilene, as she reread Kelly's words. "She's on some island in Italy and there's a museum there, and this dress is on display. She's right, it's quite beautiful—"

Glancing up, she stopped speaking mid-sentence. Her grandmother looked distressed. Her hand was pressed against her mouth, and the color had drained out of her face.

"What's the matter?" Tori asked.

"W...what?" Marilene's voice trembled.

"Come sit down." Tori took her arm. "Is your hip bothering you? I noticed you were limping a bit when you came in, and now you look pale—"

"I most certainly do not!" Marilene shook off Tori's hand. "Or if I do, it's from hunger. I need to eat, and you need to change." She looked in the direction of the workroom. "Molly!" she called, more harshly than Tori would have expected. "Molly, please! Let's get to the restaurant! Hurry up now!"

Molly came back from the workroom, holding a spool of white ribbon, and Tori nodded that she could take it home. Marilene was already at the door, and Molly waved to Tori and trotted after her.

Tori followed them out of the shop and watched them from behind. Marilene hadn't even said goodbye or told her to have a nice time at dinner.

Something was wrong, she thought as she went back into

the shop to close up for the night. Marilene's face had turned so white. And it couldn't have been because she was hungry; that kind of paleness doesn't happen in a split second. No, she thought. Marilene's color had drained when she saw the mail.

It had turned white because of the postcard.

But why?

THREE

MAY 2019

Tuesday

Back home, Tori surveyed the options in her closet and chose her new favorite piece, a short-sleeve, swingy black dress with decorative side pleats and a slim silver zipper running down the back. She had ordered it from the website of a young Philadelphia designer—the kind whose pieces she'd carry in her own shop if she ever had the chance. Looking at the dress now, she tried to imagine what the designer must have been feeling as she envisioned the dress—that playful urge to shape fabrics and trims in a way that produced a garment full of personality, conveying elegance, whimsy, professionalism, or unadulterated drama. Designing was about giving free rein to your intuition, so you could turn raw materials into a coherent piece that told a story. Tori loved to scrutinize all the components of an appealing garment in her head: Were the fabrics silky or stiff, flimsy or thick, smooth or textured? Were the buttons chunky or flat, shiny or muted? Did the zipper stay hidden and discreet, or was it visible and impactful? And how about the belt—slim and subtle or shiny and loud? To her, garments were a window into a person's heart, a visual representation of the unique individual who'd conceived it and brought it to life.

She slipped into the dress and then gathered her shoulder-length brown hair into a low bun. She stepped into a pair of cute and surprisingly comfortable low-heeled black sandals, which she'd found online from an up-and-coming footwear company that crafted all its styles from recycled plastic.

Then she turned to Albie, her three-year-old white mini schnauzer, who was stretched out on his belly on the rug, his head on his front paws. She and Molly had seen a picture of him in the local paper, in an article about rescue organizations. It described how white mini schnauzers were historically considered less desirable than gray or black ones, and in the past were often euthanized. They'd called the organization right away, and Molly had been close to tears as they'd brought Albie home, horrified that some breeder probably had sold Albie's brothers and sisters for a lot of money but then abandoned Albie to a kill shelter. Tori, too, felt sad at the thought that this little guy had been unwanted. As far as she and Molly were concerned, they'd ended up with the best dog ever.

"How do I look?" Tori asked him.

He wagged his tail, then jumped onto her bed and rolled to his back, and she tickled his belly. He was the sweetest little boy, and totally irresistible when looking for a good scratch. "Okay, you, that's all for now," she said. "Come on, Jeremy will be here any minute."

Downstairs, she sat with Albie on one of the bottom steps of the hardwood staircase, waiting for the sound of Jeremy's car. Yes, Chez Pierre was a fancy place, but Brianna and Marilene were wrong—there wasn't anything so special about tonight's dinner. She was willing to admit that five years was a long time to be dating, and perhaps for many couples, marriage would be a reasonable next step. In fact, many couples their age—she was thirty-six, he was thirty-eight—might have become engaged long before now. And, as Marilene often reminded her, Jeremy would make a great husband and stepdad. He was wonderful with Molly and very aware that she was Tori's top priority. Always patient and understanding when Tori had to cancel plans at the last minute because Molly needed help with a book report or had come down with a bad cold and wanted her mom around.

And he never seemed uncomfortable or overly concerned about Molly's father. Although, truth be told, what had happened was not particularly interesting. Tori and Molly's dad were two people who'd realized that they didn't belong together after Tori learned she was pregnant. He now was living in California and sent Molly a birthday present every year.

But still... the whole situation had left her firmly resolved to stay single.

The wheels of Jeremy's car crunched on the gravel driveway, and Tori opened the door just as he appeared on the front porch, looking so handsome in a tailored gray blazer over a black pullover and gray pants. She realized anew, as she always did when she saw him, that he had the best smile on the planet: it spread across his face, accentuating his square chin and producing a subtle series of smile lines on either side of his eyes, which made him look both slightly vulnerable and totally charming. He was holding a bouquet of wildflowers in shades of yellow, lavender, and white. He'd learned what she liked long ago.

Stepping inside, he handed her the flowers, then leaned down and grazed her cheek with a kiss. She loved how he smelled—a little woodsy with hints of leather and a tinge of citrus. So inviting.

"You look beautiful," he murmured. "Happy anniversary."

She kept her cheek pressed against his, enjoying the feel of his body, his breath, so close. "Thank you," she said. "You look beautiful, too. But come on. It's not really an anniversary."

"Of course it is," he said, pulling away to look into her eyes. "It's the anniversary of your singing debut."

"Something I'd prefer not to be reminded of," she teased, remembering the evening they'd met. He'd been performing with his band on the rooftop patio at Danny's, and she and Marilene had been there celebrating Marilene's recent birthday. He'd pointed to her and invited her to come up and sing a chorus with the band—he'd told her later he'd done it because she was the most beautiful woman he'd ever seen, and he needed to find a way to meet her. She'd been taken with him, too, which is why she'd agreed to go up, although she couldn't carry a tune, and her amplified voice made his bandmates wince.

"You were cute," he said.

"It was embarrassing. I was terrible. I can't believe I let you do that to me."

"We wouldn't have met if I hadn't brought you up on stage."

"Still." She stood on her tiptoes to kiss him, feeling good as she always did when she could follow her heart, do what felt right, and know it would be welcomed and appreciated. She loved that Jeremy let her be her. She squeezed his hand, then went into the kitchen to put the flowers in a vase, as he kneeled to give Albie a good scratch behind the ears.

"Quiet house," he said, standing back up.

She nodded as she placed the vase on the console table near the front door. "Marilene took Molly out for pizza," she said. Then she paused, remembering how pale Marilene had looked in the shop. The postcard and Marilene's face were still on her mind.

"Something wrong?" Jeremy said.

"Um... I don't think so. I hope not. A client of mine sent me a postcard from some island in Italy with a picture of a wedding dress made there in the 1940s. And Marilene saw it, and... well, I know it's a cliché, but she literally looked like she'd seen a ghost. She just stood there. I tried to talk to her, and it was as though she didn't even hear me at first."

"Did she tell you why?"

"No, in fact she yelled at me for saying she looked pale."

"Well, she did grow up in Italy during that time. The war. Maybe it reminded her of something. Do you want to stop by the pizza place and check on her?"

Tori shook her head. "She'd kill me if I did that. You know she hates being fussed over or questioned. And besides, if anything was wrong, they'd have called me or come home by now."

She reached for her phone by the wildflowers, and when she saw no messages, she shrugged. "I guess everything's fine," she said, as she patted Albie's head and then led Jeremy outside.

The fresh spring air lightened her mood as she made her way to his car, a gray BMW sedan he'd bought from his brother a few years ago, wanting something nice to drive in addition to the van that he used when heading to a gig. As they started for the highway, he mentioned that he'd received a phone call that afternoon from a Broadway producer he knew, and the guy had offered him the job of musical director for a new show opening next year.

"Jeremy... wow!" Tori said. It took her a moment to realize how big this news was, as he always tended to be matter-of-fact, even low-key, when talking about himself. "That's amazing. I'm so excited for you."

He nodded as he turned onto the exit ramp. "I'm pretty pleased," he said, and she knew that for him, such a comment meant he was ecstatic.

He glanced at her, his smile a mix of gratitude, humility, and elation. "I've spent so many years trying to break into this world," he said. "And it's finally paying off. Things are coming together. Really coming together."

She touched his arm, happy that he recognized how much

this offer said about his talent and reputation. While he enjoyed being a professor of music and orchestra conductor at nearby Hofstra University, a job he'd held for several years now, his true passion was musical theater. No wonder this offer had made him so happy.

And yet, she felt a bit uneasy with the way he'd described this position. The idea that his life was coming together—he'd never talked about himself that way before. As though he was starting a new chapter and seeing himself in a new way.

They reached the restaurant, and the valet opened her door. Jeremy came around to take her hand, and they made their way up the steps to the entrance. Tori had read about this place in local magazines but she'd never been here before, and she was excited that Jeremy had picked it. The night was breathtaking, with a full moon and a star-filled sky. The host led them to the patio and over to what had to be one of the best tables in the restaurant, with an expansive view of the ocean.

Jeremy ordered champagne and Tori caught her breath, hoping this wasn't his way of working up to a proposal. It seemed like hours, weeks even, before the server returned, and she shook her foot nervously. But when the champagne was poured, Jeremy simply lifted his glass to clink it with hers. She sipped, glad she could relax, confident that if the champagne hadn't signaled a proposal, then she was in the clear. She realized she shouldn't have worried. He knew how she felt, and he cared about her too much to go against her wishes. She was sure he agreed that their relationship, their life, was fine as it was.

They chose a burrata appetizer, followed by a pasta dish with spring peas and pecorino cheese, and a branzino entrée prepared with broccoli rabe, tomatoes and capers. They finished their first course and watched the server expertly split the portions of hot food in half and set a beautifully arranged plate in front of each of them. In between bites, Tori caught Jeremy up on her clients, adding that it would still take several more months, if not a whole year, for her to have enough saved to lease the shop across the street.

"You really shouldn't wait," he said, as he speared some sauce-laden pasta and then wiped his mouth with his napkin. Tori liked that he enjoyed eating good food as much as she did.

"It's a great location," he added. "And you know the land-lord's going to rent it to someone else if you don't step up. I'd be happy to—"

"No, don't say it—" she interrupted.

"But I would. I'll lend you the money. I know how much this means, and I want you to have it—"

"But I wouldn't want it that way. I don't want to depend on you like that. I'll get the money. And if I lose out on that space, there'll be another. Let's not even talk about it," she said. "Tell me more about the Broadway show."

He went on to name the others who were signed up for the project, and to describe what the musical was about. The evening flew by, and before she knew it, the server was clearing their plates.

Jeremy nodded when the server described that evening's dessert, a flourless chocolate cake for two, with whipped cream and fresh strawberries. He returned and placed the dessert in between them, along with two forks wrapped in fresh napkins. It looked delicious. Tori loved dessert—she was like a child that way—so she snatched one of the wrapped forks and unrolled the napkin.

A little velvet box tumbled out of the napkin and onto the tablecloth.

She looked at Jeremy, feeling stunned and foolish for letting her guard down. "What are you doing?" she demanded, more forcefully than she'd planned.

"What am I doing?" he repeated, sounding confused and defensive. "What's that supposed to mean?"

"You know I don't want this," she said, pointing to the box, which was resting on its side near the table's edge. "Why would you set all this up?"

"Because I want to marry you," he told her.

"But why?" she asked.

"Because I love you—"

"And I love you too—"

"—and we've been together for five years, and it's time." He watched her, then sighed and shook his head. "I'm thirty-eight years old, Tori. My career is good, and my life is good. I want to share it with you—"

"You already do—"

"I want to settle down. I want to be established—"

"You are established—"

"Okay—stop," he said, holding up a palm. "This isn't so hard. Everyone else in the world would understand what I'm saying, you know that. I don't want to live like a kid anymore. I want a family and a home. I'm done with this life, this way of life we have. It's been great, but it's time to move on. Don't make me feel like I'm crazy. You have to understand—"

"I love you," she repeated, taking his hand with both of hers. "Isn't that enough?"

"Not anymore," he said, pulling away. "Why are you surprised? You had to know this was coming—"

"And you had to know what my answer would be. Why ruin everything? We're happy, aren't we?"

"I have been. I was."

She sat back in her chair. "And you're not now? But you said you love me—"

"I do," he said. He moved his chair closer to her, then looked straight into her eyes. The votive candle on the table made his irises sparkle. "Look, you're a mom," he said. "A parent. I want to be a parent, too. I want all of it. Birthday parties, soccer games. Getting woken up early on Sunday mornings."

"Molly doesn't do that. She sleeps in on Sundays." She

paused, feeling her eyes widen as she got his meaning. "Wait, you're saying you want to have kids? Not just Molly but... more?"

"I don't know... maybe..." He looked at her, then rolled his eyes and tossed the napkin from his lap onto the table. "What are you scared of anyway?" he said.

"I'm not scared—"

"I know Molly's father left—"

"He didn't even stick around for her birth. But that's not the point—"

"But that's not who I am. I'm here for the duration. I *want* this. You don't have to worry—"

"I'm not worried." She heard her voice become higher and louder as she protested. She didn't want to sound defensive, but she hated feeling this way, as though she were cornered. She took a deep breath and lowered the volume of her voice. "I just know who I am and how I want to live."

"Without letting anyone in, right?" Jeremy pressed his lips together and looked toward the water. Then he turned back to her, leaning forward and pressing his hands onto the table. "And how do you think that makes me feel?" he said, his voice tense. "You won't even let me lend you the money to sign a lease on the space across the street—"

"I don't want to use you like that. I don't want you to feel obligated to help me."

"But we are obligated to each other!" He breathed out heavily and shook his head, as though she were speaking a language he found incomprehensible. "We choose to be, that's what people do. How can you say all this anyway? After what we've become to each other? I love Molly, you know that. I'll be a great dad to her."

"You're already great to her."

"Exactly."

"No, I mean, it's good the way it is. I like my life. I have control, I have order. Why make a change? Why do something so uncertain when we know what we have right now?"

He let out an exasperated laugh and looked away again, this time up at the sky. "Tori, this is ridiculous. Don't tell me you don't believe in marriage. You dress brides, for God's sake."

"It's fabric. That's what I work with. And art. Design. I'm not the one who connects the dress with happily ever after. That's on them."

"That doesn't make sense. You have to believe that people are doing something positive when they come to you. You have to believe that marriage is a good thing. You couldn't do that kind of work unless you did. How could you take their money if you thought it was all a big mistake..."

He leaned his elbow on the table and rubbed his eye with the heel of his hand. Seeing him so defeated, she looked away. To her right, she noticed an older couple at the next table glancing at them, the woman pouting sympathetically, and by the wall, two servers were eyeing them and smirking at one another. Tori felt horrible. Jeremy had engineered this whole surprise. He had even evidently included the host and the servers in his set-up. And she had ruined it. She knew how embarrassed he must feel. She had emasculated him, right here in public. And she never intended to. Why hadn't she listened to Marilene? And to Brianna, too? Why hadn't she admitted what was obvious to them—that he was planning a proposal for tonight, the fifth anniversary of the day they met? She could have declined the dinner invitation. She could have told him that she knew what was on his mind, and she didn't want to let him go through with the whole rigmarole here at the restaurant. She could have done a lot of things to avoid this moment.

Although this was also his fault, she reminded herself. He knew how she felt about marriage. She'd never made it a secret. Had he been so caught up in his wants and plans that he didn't even contemplate what he should have known—that she'd turn him down? She'd set him up for this sad outcome, but he'd set himself up for it, too. For two people who had gotten along so well for five years, how had they gotten tonight so wrong?

She reached out and touched his arm. "Let's go home," she said. "We'll figure this out tomorrow."

He stood and she watched him put the velvet box in his pocket.

They reached her driveway and Jeremy got out of the car to walk Tori to the door. As he always did. He was too much of a gentleman, too nice a guy, to have her walk to the door alone. She was glad to be home, as the quiet ride from the restaurant had given her too much time to think. About why she was being so stubborn. About how she didn't want to put her trust in anyone but herself. About how unfair she was being to Jeremy.

At the front step, she looked up at him. "Talk to you tomorrow?" she asked.

"Sure," he said. Although she wasn't sure he meant it. Probably he'd answered that way because all he wanted to do was go home. He leaned over and kissed her cheek. She wanted nothing more than to kiss him, a long, deep kiss, smooth as honey. But she knew that would give him the wrong message.

"Actually," he said as he took a step away. "I think it might be better if we kept our distance for a little while. Let us both deal with what happened tonight. I could use some time to clear my head. I'll call you when I can. In a few weeks, maybe."

Before she could even answer, he'd turned and walked back to the car. She understood now that his last kiss had been a goodbye kiss.

She watched the taillights of his car grow smaller until she couldn't see them anymore, then fished her keys out of her bag and unlocked the front door. Her chest felt tight, and she knew she was on the verge of falling apart, of crying harder than she ever had before. She loved Jeremy so much. Was he going to stick around in the end? Was she going to lose him? How could she go on without him? But how could she give in to him? How could she do something that felt so very wrong?

She went inside and saw the glow of a table lamp shining in the living room. It was puzzling, as she'd expected Marilene to be upstairs asleep and the lights in the living room to be off. But there Marilene was, on the sofa, leaning over with her elbows on her knees and her fingertips pressed to her mouth. She was wearing her glasses and staring at her laptop computer on the coffee table. Next to her was a half-empty teacup on a saucer.

"Mar?" Tori said. "Are you okay? Molly okay?"

Marilene kept her eyes fixed on the computer screen. "Yes, she's fine. Did her homework and went to sleep."

Tori let out a long sigh. "I'm glad you're up," she said as she dragged herself across the room and sat down next to her on the sofa. The bottom of the dress she had chosen so carefully earlier tonight draped over her knees. It didn't look nearly as pretty to her now as it had when she'd first put it on.

She put her head on Marilene's shoulder. "Oh, Mar," she said. "What am I going to do? I think I just ruined everything..." She paused, waiting for Marilene to stroke her cheek or pat her knee. But there was no such response. It was as though Marilene hadn't even heard her.

She lifted her head to see what was so captivating on the computer screen. It seemed to be the website for the museum in Italy that Kelly, the indecisive bride, had visited. On the screen was the same picture, the same wedding gown, that had been on Kelly's postcard.

Tori looked at Marilene, who was now shaking her head. "This dress again? This is what made you go pale at the store. Mar, what is it? Why has this dress made you so upset?"

Marilene turned to Tori. "Sweetheart, we have to talk," she said. "Oh, my goodness... Where do I begin?"

FOUR

SEPTEMBER 1943

At the sound of the young voice, Giulia scrambled to her feet, remembering to keep most of her weight on her good foot and off the one that was oozing blood. Holding her hand just above her forehead to shade her eyes from the sun, she surveyed the line of trees on a slope set back from the curved shoreline, trying to spot the source of the question. A moment later, a figure emerged between two of the trees and made its way toward her, skipping among the bushes and rocks. It was a girl—not quite as old as Giulia's younger sister, Emilia; more like twelve or thirteen. Although she wasn't dressed like a regular twelve-year-old girl. She was wearing boyish blue overalls cuffed at the ankles and a short-sleeved white shirt. Her feet were bare. Her long hair was loose and cascading over her shoulders. A row of golden-brown bangs lined her forehead.

A moment later, two little boys also dressed in overalls, no more than five years old, emerged from behind the trees and stumbled along behind the girl.

"I'm..." Giulia stammered. She felt too tired and weak to formulate a sensible response—and besides, she didn't know how to begin to answer the question. What *was* she doing?

"Who are you?" the girl persisted. "Is my father expecting you?"

Giulia shook her head. "No..."

"That's okay, don't worry," the girl said, as though concerned that she'd come across as mean and had unintentionally frightened Giulia. "Sometimes people come who aren't expected. He's okay with strangers."

"As long as they're not bad people," one of the little boys put in. "Daddy hates bad people. Like German people—"

"No, not all German people," the other one said. "Just the bad ones. The ones that don't belong here—"

"Quiet, both of you!" the girl said, waving a hand at them, as though she was the sergeant and they were her infantrymen. "Now, like I was saying," she said, turning back to Giulia. "Sometimes people can get a message to him ahead of time to tell him they're arriving. But sometimes they can't. And that's okay, he will allow people ashore he doesn't know. But he likes to know if you're expected or not. And if not, he likes to know who sent you. And then you can remain here.

"So... who sent you here to our island?" she demanded.

"I'm... I..." Giulia stammered. Nobody had sent her, and she had no interest in staying. "I came here by mistake. I only..." She paused, thinking it wouldn't get her very far to go back and forth with these children. "Is there a way for me to speak to your fath—"

"We're the guards!" the stockier of the two boys exclaimed, his hands on his waist. "You can't see him until we let you through!"

"Yeah! We let you through!" the smaller one agreed.

"Don't worry, we don't think you're dangerous," the girl said, waving a stick. "We've been watching you. From behind there." She pointed to some trees halfway up the slope.

"We like to spy on people," the first boy said, and the other put his fist over his mouth and giggled.

The girl waved them off again. "We weren't even sure if you were coming here or not because of the way you were steering. The boat was going all over the place. It was pretty funny to watch. That's why we didn't get our dad. Most people come here directly. And at night. Most people who come to see us don't like to travel in daylight. You must not be very experienced with boats."

"No, I'm not," Giulia agreed. She wondered who the people this girl typically greeted were. And why they only arrived after dark.

"But here you are," the girl said. "And we want to know where you came from and why you came here."

"Yeah, we do!" the first boy said.

Again, Giulia couldn't answer right away, which surprised her. She was usually good with kids. With all people, actually. Sociable, that's how people described her. Like her mother had been. But right now she felt too light-headed and foggy to hold a conversation. Eventually, she responded with the only words that came to mind. "I'm... I'm lost. I've... I've escaped..."

"Escaped? You mean, from Parissi Island? We heard everyone was running away because the Nazis showed up. Mama is scared that our island might be next, because Parissi Island isn't very far. You can even see the castle from the other side of the house. Papa shushed her but I think he was thinking the same thing, since everyone knows that the Nazis love capturing places. I think Papa just shushed her because we were there—"

"Papa's not scared of anyone!" the larger boy exclaimed.

"He's braver than any old Nazi!" the littler one added.

The girl scowled and turned back to Giulia. "Did you come face to face with any Nazis? Where's the rest of your family? Are they still back there or—oh, no! You're all bloody!"

Giulia looked down. The dark spot on her shoe had spread, and the sand in front of her foot was spotted red. The sight made her stomach roll. She felt herself sway, feeling another spurt of blood emerge from her toe and a wave of nausea jolt her. Her line of vision was narrowing. It was like a change of scene in the picture shows she used to go to back home, the way darkness would overtake the screen, leaving a circle of light that grew smaller and smaller until it disappeared. Her arms trembled, and her head started to spin.

"Are you okay?" the girl said, coming closer, the boys scrambling alongside her. "My dad's in the house. He's a doctor. But you don't look like you can even walk."

"No. I'm okay," Giulia said. She didn't want to scare the girl, but the word "doctor" felt like a gift. She needed a doctor. Someone to stop the bleeding. Then she'd be able to get back in the boat and continue to the mainland.

"The house is up the hill," the girl said, pointing. "It's not a very steep hill, but it is a little bit." She came closer and nudged her body under Giulia's elbow to support her. She waved the little boys over, and they both approached and grabbed her opposite arm.

"I'm Marilene," the girl said.

"I have to get to America..." Giulia mumbled.

"You what?"

"I have to..." she started.

The darkness grew larger.

When Giulia opened her eyes, she was lying in a large bed, her head on a soft pillow. There was a quilt sporting a joyful print, with lemons and white frangipani petals streaked with pink, pulled up to her chin. The sun was streaming in at an angle from one of the tall windows lining the room; the triangular ray pierced the air in between two fluttering white curtain panels, its edges as sharp as a shard of glass. Next to the bed was a small wooden nightstand, and by the near wall was a round wooden table and a white writing desk with a ladder-back chair. An additional bed, which appeared freshly made, was against the opposite wall. Lifting the quilt, Giulia saw that she was wearing a simple white nightdress, even though it was still daylight outside the window.

Her foot no longer hurt, but felt warm and cradled, so she pushed aside the quilt fully to see what had happened to it. There was a huge round bandage covering all her toes and most of her instep. The sight of it jogged her memory, and she pieced together all that had transpired since meeting those children on the beach. She'd been helped up the hill to a large house and then carried up a winding stairway to this room. A tall, lovely woman in yellow slacks and a tan button-down shirt, her sleek brown hair gathered at her neck, had helped her bathe and change, and an elegant man with a full head of gray hair, eyeglasses, and a salt-and-pepper beard had dressed and bandaged her foot.

The woman had then brought in a tray holding some clear soup, a glass of water, and slices of toasted bread. She'd set it on the table, and Giulia slowly ate and drank a bit, until her stomach felt that it couldn't handle anymore. Then the woman had helped her sink down into the cushy mattress. Giulia remembered feeling a little scared but mostly relieved and safe. Hopefully, she'd thought before she closed her eyes, she would feel stronger later, and be able to get some more food and water to take with her as she resumed her trip. With any luck, the people in this house—whoever they were—could point her in the right direction. If she could just get to the mainland, she could soon find the ship she needed to board and be on her way across the ocean.

"You're finally awake!" said a voice at the doorway. "You slept all day!"

Giulia looked up to see the girl she'd met at the beach. Marilene—that was her name. She'd changed out of her overalls and into a pair of white pants and a clean shirt with small blue polka dots, her long hair in a ponytail. She was carrying a glass of water, which she handed to Giulia.

"My mom says to drink more water," she said. "And she also wants to know how you're feeling, and if you want to have dinner with us. I'm Marilene, by the way. I told you that down at the beach, but I don't think you heard me."

Giulia nodded. "No, I remember. Hi, Marilene."

"And those boys? They're my brothers. They're twins and they're only five and so irritating. And your name is Giulia? I heard you tell that to my dad when he was taking care of your foot."

Giulia sipped some water. "That's right," she said. "I'm Giulia. And yes, please tell your mom I'd be happy to come downstairs." She actually was feeling stronger; it was amazing what a little sleep and some food could do. And she didn't want to spend any more time by herself in this bedroom. She was curious about where she was. Who were these people, who had taken her in and cared for her? Why had they done that? She remembered now how Marilene had talked about her father often hosting strangers. Why would strangers come here?

But even more than learning those answers, she wanted to be on her way. If the mainland wasn't too far off, maybe they'd give her supplies for the boat so she could be there before nightfall.

Marilene pounced onto the opposite bed, clearly in no hurry to end this private time with someone she apparently saw as a fascinating new friend. "Giulia, that's such a pretty name," she said. "And you're so pretty, too. I mean, you need to fix your hair and stuff, but you have such pretty hair. I wish I had golden hair like you! Tell me, did you really live on Parissi Island? What was it like?"

Lying on her back, she lifted her arms toward the ceiling. "Was it splendid? Did you wear jewels and pile your hair up in a bun and wear a tiara? Were the men handsome and did they ask you to dance? Did they twirl you around and around, so your gown floated and spun out all wide and everything? We heard so many stories, and I always wanted to go there! Sometimes I would lean out my window so I could see the castle. I want to wear a long gown and a tiara and have a handsome man twirl me around and around!"

She stood and twirled herself around a few times. Then she sat back on the bed and faced Giulia. "Do you remember how you came upstairs?"

Giulia shook her head. "Not so much," she said. She had a memory of being held by someone strong, someone who smelled like wood and vanilla. "A little. I think I was carried."

"Not just carried!" Marilene said. "Carried by Luca! Oh, you are so lucky! And then you were sitting on this bed and when he sat next to you... you put your head on his shoulder while my father bandaged your foot! Oh, I'd give anything to be carried by Luca! An...ny...thing!" she added.

Giulia felt herself redden at the thought of putting her head on a stranger's shoulder. "I did? Who's Luca?" She didn't even remember what he looked like.

"Only the most beautiful man in the whole world," Marilene said, twirling again, her arms outstretched. "I'm so in love with Luca! I want to marry him someday. His family owns a vineyard and I'm going to marry him and drink lovely wine with every meal. And eat delicious food and have a lovely life!"

Giulia couldn't help but laugh. This girl was so entertaining. Life had been sad and tense at the castle in the days before she'd left. A lot of awful news had come their way. It was nice to hear the musings of a girl who apparently knew no danger. Who approached strangers on the beach with her younger brothers as though they were playing some spy game.

"Is that so?" she said.

Marilene nodded. "His papa grew up with my papa. He

came back today after a long time away. He comes here pretty often and stays sometimes for a few days, sometimes more. But he always comes back. And when he does, he brings presents, lots of presents! Flowers and pretty fabrics and wines from his family's vineyard. I hate when he leaves. I want to be his wife so much!" She threw herself onto the bed, face down.

Suddenly there was a knock on the slightly ajar door. "How is the patient doing?" a male voice said.

"Luca!" Marilene exclaimed. "Come in! She's much better! See?"

The door opened wider, revealing a tall man in a black long-sleeved shirt and gray slacks. His close-cropped hair had some tousled curls on top, the color an ash brown that reminded her of embers, cool but with the scent of smoke still lingering from an earlier flame. His broad forehead and long straight neck struck Giulia as very regal, and his cheekbones were pronounced beneath large, green eyes, which made him look elegant and strong. He had a square chin with a gentle smile that seemed to indicate approval more than happiness. As though he approached the world with distrust so was relieved when it turned out his surroundings were more pleasing and agreeable than he'd expected.

His open collar reminded Giulia that Marilene had said she'd rested her head on his shoulder. Aware that she was in a nightdress, she sank into the mattress and pulled the quilt to her chin.

"Ah, yes. You do look much better," he said. "I hope you will join us for dinner. I brought you a little something to help you walk. It was here from the time I injured my ankle a few months ago." He came into the room holding a black wooden cane and leaned it on the wall.

"You've got a huge bandage there on your foot, in case you haven't noticed yet," he said. "It may be sore for a time, but it will heal. Marilene's father is quite a skilled doctor. People often come here injured, and he sews us up and sends us back out. Isn't that right, Marilene?"

Marilene giggled. "That's what he does!"

"Anyway, Mar," he said. "Your mother wanted me to tell you that dinner is almost ready, and she needs you to finish helping with the table."

"Okay, Luca! Thanks, Luca!" Marilene said, and he gave a small wave and left the room. She scrambled off the bed and ran to the door, then turned around toward Giulia. "Wasn't I right?" she asked. "What do you think? Isn't he so dreamy?"

Giulia loosened her grip on the quilt.

He was beautiful indeed.

FIVE

MAY 2019

Tuesday

Tori sat up straighter and turned on the sofa so her whole body was facing Marilene. She'd never seen her so agitated. What could be so upsetting about a wedding dress in a museum display? Marilene hadn't even changed yet out of her clothes into pajamas. It was so strange, seeing her grandmother here in the living room at this hour. And what she'd said—"We have to talk"—in that serious tone. Tori couldn't remember the last time she'd sounded like that.

"What is it?" she said. "You're scaring me. Why are you staring at that picture?"

"Nothing's wrong—I mean, no emergency or anything. It's... my goodness, I never expected this..."

Tori breathed in as she sat back on the sofa. "Is it... about Italy?" she asked softly. She wondered if the museum's website was the trouble. When Marilene was willing to talk about her childhood, she spoke only of pleasant things: candies and sweets, birthday cakes, and wonderful visitors coming and going, often young men she'd develop huge crushes on. Tall grass swaying in the breeze behind her house and the cool feel of the aqua Mediterranean water on her toes when she went to the shore with her brothers to welcome newcomers, the three of them pretending they were in charge. Evidently her father had been a doctor from a wealthy family and had inherited a small island in the Mediterranean. The rise of fascism had infuriated him, and he'd retreated to the island to wait for the homeland he loved to come to its senses and reject Mussolini as prime minister. That was where Mar and her family—her parents and two younger brothers—had spent the war years.

When Tori was young and studied world history in school, she'd asked about how it was to live in Italy under fascism. Marilene had said she didn't really know; living on a tiny private island, she'd grown up removed from the major events of her childhood and teenage years: the reign of Mussolini, Italy's alliance with Germany, and the surrender to the Allies followed by the Nazi occupation of Rome.

She and her family had it easy in the beginning, she'd said, other than the occasional delay in getting food or supplies from the mainland. They had an inventive cook and household staff who knew how to make do with less and keep the household cheery. Visitors came, and many stayed for a while or returned often, having no safe home. Tori imagined these so-called visitors had been displaced because of the war. Possibly they were Jews trying to flee Italy, or anti-Fascists like Marilene's father. If Marilene had known anything more, she wouldn't say; she'd only talk about how fun it was to welcome guests.

But Tori knew that things had gotten worse after the Nazis invaded Italy. Marilene had occasionally mentioned a time when she and her brothers were forbidden to play by the shore. Apparently her parents were concerned about the Nazis setting foot on their little island and destroying the life they had made for themselves. Tori wondered, too, if maybe they feared being punished for harboring Jews or engaging in some other anti-Nazi activities. And then, of course, Marilene had come to the United States all alone, a young, single mom with a five-year-old daughter, Tori's mother. Tori had never met Marilene's brothers. She didn't even know if they were alive now, or what had happened to the island where they'd all lived.

She thought now that the picture of the wedding dress in Kelly's email had triggered bad memories, and wished she'd separated the postcard from the other mail so Marilene wouldn't have seen it. Her grandmother had started changing in the last year, slightly but noticeably. She had a bad hip and an unsteady gait, and worsening eyesight. She appeared to be entering the twilight of her life, and Tori was determined to make it as stress-free as possible.

Marilene rubbed an eye underneath her glasses, and Tori wondered if she was crying or had been crying earlier in the evening. She knew the best thing to do was to give Marilene time. She wondered if she should encourage her to put the computer aside until the morning, when hopefully her mind would have cleared and things wouldn't look so dire. After all, it was after ten, and they both needed to get to sleep. But Marilene seemed wide awake and probably had no desire to turn in anytime soon.

"I'm sorry you had to see the postcard, if that's what led to all this," Tori said. "I knew something was wrong at the shop, and then you left so quickly the moment Molly came back from the workroom with the ribbon..."

"No, it's good that I saw it," Marilene said. She looked small and weary. "It's for the best. The picture. Even though..." She went quiet again.

"Even though what?" Tori insisted. This mood was so unlike Marilene. As old as she was, she was practical, a doer and a go-getter. She wasn't the type to wallow.

"Mar, please tell me what's upset you," Tori said. "Maybe I can help."

Marilene sighed. She clicked on a button on the screen that brought her to an English-language version of the museum's website. Then she navigated again to the wedding dress. The page had a text box beneath the image. Tori glanced at her grandmother, and when Mar nodded and murmured, "Go on," she read the English words aloud:

A talented artist and dressmaker, Giulia Sancino apprenticed with Savio Peralta, an Argentine painter, at Parissi Castle. She designed and sewed many beautiful garments while living there, including this spectacular wedding gown.

Tori looked up. "So?"

"Keep reading," Marilene said, and Tori continued.

For years, Giulia Sancino was thought to have been killed in the Nazi invasion of Parissi Island. But historians now agree that she survived the invasion and waited out the war on a nearby island. After the war, she made her living as a seam-stress in Rome until her death in the mid-1990s.

Tori turned to Marilene. "What about her?"

Marilene pointed to the screen. "What it says there—the island where she waited out the war?" She clenched her fists and rested them on her knees. "That was my family's island. She showed up on our shore in a little raft-like boat, all alone. She'd escaped when the Nazis stormed Parissi Island."

"You mean the person who made this famous dress... was someone you knew?"

"My father didn't say it, not to my brothers and me, but I knew he was worried when she arrived," Marilene said. "She'd come from Parissi Island, and he didn't know if the Nazis would follow her and destroy our home, too. But she was so weak and badly hurt. We had to take care of her."

She pressed her lips together, clearly distressed by the memory. "She had this deep gash on her foot," she continued. "I remember it even now, so much blood seeping out of her shoe. My father said it was very serious. He told my mother he thought she might die. But he treated it and dressed it, and it healed. And that's when we learned what a talented seamstress she was. She made our clothes. And she showed me a sketch of this very wedding gown."

Tori shook her head, astonished. She'd never known anyone whose life had been memorialized in a museum. "I can't believe you knew this woman," she said.

"I didn't just know her—I adored her," Marilene responded. "I was twelve, and she was about to turn eighteen, and she was like the most wonderful older sister to me. And she was so beautiful. She had this beautiful hair, honey gold, with the prettiest waves. And big eyes, and such a warm smile. And she made me the nicest dresses I'd ever had. She said her older sister was bringing the wedding gown—this very wedding dress—to America. She had two sisters—one older, one younger—and she hoped they'd all get married in it one day, one by one. They all planned to meet up in New York.

"Oh, that was just a lovely time," she added, taking off her glasses. Her eyes turned watery. "With my family and Giulia, and my teacher and this sweet couple that helped take care of the house—my goodness, I don't even remember their names anymore. And there was this young man, the son of a friend of my father's. Luca, his name was. I had such a crush on him! He was so handsome and so much fun, always teasing my brothers and horsing around with them in the yard..."

Tori held her grandmother's hand, moved by the depth of Marilene's memories. She'd always wondered how Marilene had dealt with growing up on a remote island. She wouldn't have gone to school; she wouldn't have had any friends. She must have been so lonely. No wonder she adored Giulia and the others, the staff and this young man, Luca. No wonder reading about her now would affect her so greatly. "How long did you know her?" she asked.

"She stayed with us for about a year," Marilene answered. "And then she left. She'd told me that if she ever left, she'd always come back, and I had no reason to doubt her. She never would have lied to me. At least that's what I thought."

"So... she didn't return?" Tori asked.

Marilene shook her head. "We thought she must have died. The war was still going on, and Rome was so dangerous. Why else would she leave and never come back?"

"Oh, Mar," Tori said, feeling sympathy for her grandmother. It had to have come as a shock, to learn that this person, who'd been like a sister to her, had actually been alive for decades.

"She's been right there in Rome," Marilene said. "She could be there still—"

"No, she died in the nineties." Tori pointed to the screen. "It says so here—"

"But that's not correct—look!" Marilene reached out to scroll down the page to the section where people could post comments. There was just one comment posted, the author listed as "Anonymous." Tori leaned in to read it:

Your information is wrong. Giulia didn't die in the 1990s. I met her not too long ago, when she designed my granddaughter's wedding gown. I wonder if she knows about this exhibit. I wish someone could find her and bring her to see it.

"So... so she may still be alive?" Tori said. "Is that what you're thinking?"

"Yes, that's what it means," Marilene said, clasping her

hands together, interlacing and then releasing her fingers over and over. "What do I do? What do I do?"

Tori wanted to offer an idea that would calm Marilene down. "Are you saying you want to find her? We... we could reach out to the museum," she suggested. "Maybe they could help us locate this woman who wrote the comment, who saw her recently..."

Marilene didn't respond, and Tori didn't know what else to add. Yes, it had to be shocking to learn that this woman could be alive. But Marilene was nearly panicked, and Tori didn't understand that reaction. She could only think that life had been so awful and incomprehensible during the war. The idea of living in an occupied country where Jews were being ripped from their homes and sent to concentration camps and where killing and brutality and evil were all around—it made sense that Marilene had never wanted to talk about it. Now she had uncovered this news, and it seemed that all of the emotions—the fear, the sadness, the sense of danger—she'd tamped down for decades were coming to the fore. Tori thought the best thing she could do was simply *be* here and try to comfort her.

"Mar, I'm sorry that this is so upsetting to you," she said. "Can I get you something? More tea, maybe?"

Marilene shook her head. She breathed in deeply and leaned on the arm of the sofa to pull herself up. Favoring her bad hip, she limped to the window and looked outside through the floor-length sheer curtain panels. The moon was just about full, and the street glowed an eerie yellow.

Looking a little more composed, she turned to Tori. "I didn't even ask you how your dinner was," she said.

Tori shrugged. "It was fine. We don't need to talk about it now."

"Just fine?"

Tori looked down at her hands.

"He asked you to marry him, didn't he?"

Tori nodded.

"And you turned him down?"

She nodded again.

"I knew he was going to ask you," Marilene said. "It was written all over his face these last few weeks." She paused, then walked back toward the sofa. "He's a good man, sweetheart. You won't find another like him. And he loves you so much."

"I know," Tori said, her voice quivering. "I love him, too. But I can't bring a man into this family now. What if it doesn't work out? I can't put Molly through that... I can't risk changing her life and then maybe having it all upended—"

"But why would it be upended? Honey, he loves Molly. She could use a father, you know. She's going to be a teenager soon, and it would be good for her to have a mother and a dad."

Tori blinked, feeling a need to protect herself. "Mar, of all people, why would you say that? You never married. You raised Mom alone."

"And I struggled, and your poor mom did, too—"

"You can't blame what happened on your being a single mother. Having a man in the house doesn't automatically make things perfect. Do you really think that if you'd married some guy when Mom was eleven, that she wouldn't have grown up to—"

Marilene limped back to the window, and Tori felt horrible for having raised her voice. This was the last thing Marilene needed right now. "I'm sorry," she said.

Her grandmother seemed not to have heard the apology. She stayed where she was, facing the night sky.

"There's something else you need to know," she finally said. "Giulia was married when she arrived on the island. And she was pregnant. She had her baby, and then she left."

Tori looked at the back of Marilene's head, puzzled. "What

does that mean? She left her baby with your family?" Marilene nodded. "So what happened to it?" she asked.

Marilene turned back around. "It was a little girl," she said. "And she grew up to have a daughter named Tori. Giulia, the woman who sewed the wedding dress? She's your real grandmother."

SIX

MAY 2019

Tuesday

"What are you talking about?" Tori demanded. She was certain she must have misunderstood. Or that something was seriously wrong. Was Marilene confused? Was this an early sign of dementia? Was she mixing up something she'd read about the dress with her own life? Was she having a stroke? Should they call an ambulance?

Tori went to the window and then took Marilene's hand. Her grandmother had always been thin, and at this moment she felt quite fragile.

"Come sit," she said, gently drawing her back to the sofa. Feeling her heart start to race, she willed herself to take a deep breath as she helped Marilene sit. She needed to get control of herself. And the situation.

"Mar, are you okay?" she said, her hand still on Marilene's shoulder, as if she needed steadying. "Maybe we should get you to a doctor—"

"I know what I'm saying," Marilene said, shrugging Tori's hand away. "I never in a million years thought I'd be having this conversation with you. But this dress—as innocent as it seems to you now, it holds the key to your entire life."

Tori studied her. She didn't seem deluded or confused. She was firm and clear. Marilene had always maintained that she'd married the son of a family friend when she was seventeen, and that her husband had been killed in a boating accident. And that she'd headed to America with her child shortly after that. And although there'd been no reason not to believe her, Tori had often wondered about the story. Marilene's details had seemed too sketchy. But she'd never expected anything like this.

She sat down on the sofa next to Marilene. A part of her wanted to snuggle in close like a little girl, and let Marilene tell her it would all be okay, the way she always did. Marilene was so good at making her believe that she was strong and smart and could handle anything. But now she felt a chasm forming between them.

"I'm listening," Tori said, hoping that this would stop the chasm from widening.

"Giulia named the baby Olive," Marilene said. "Your mother. Oh, she was a sweet little thing, a beautiful little girl with light hair and green eyes. And when she was only a few months old, that's when Giulia left. She sailed on the same small fishing boat that had brought her to us. She'd gotten word that her sisters and her husband had all died in the war, so we thought maybe she'd gone to try to find her husband's family. His name was Vincenzo, she'd told us. His family owned a dry goods market on the mainland, and he would ferry supplies out to Parissi Island—that's how they'd met. We were hoping she'd find his relatives. We thought that would make her grief a little easier to bear."

"And she never came back?"

Marilene shook her head. "The war ended, and life was moving on," she said. "But Giulia never returned. Five years passed, and no sign of her. My father was preparing to go back to Rome and resume his career, and to send my brothers to school. And then my mother got sick, and she needed more medical care than my father could provide. They couldn't raise Olive—my mother was too ill, and my father needed to take care of her. They decided to bring her to the authorities."

"But that didn't happen," Tori said. "You kept her—my mother."

"I couldn't give up Giulia's little girl," Marilene said. "I knew where my father kept his money, and I took what I could find and snuck off the island. And brought your mother to America. I had some contacts here, people who'd stayed with us on the island years ago, who helped me get settled. I told everyone that Olive was my baby, that my husband had died and I'd left Italy behind because I couldn't handle the memories. I put our old life behind me and never spoke with my parents or my brothers or anyone back home. I didn't want to risk revealing our whereabouts and losing your mother."

"So you're not my grandmother?" Tori asked. Now that she had all the facts, this incredible conclusion was unavoidable. "You've been lying all these years? How can that be?"

Marilene shook her head. "I'm sorry, my Tori. I thought it was for the best. I wanted to put all the tragedy behind me. You have no idea what those years were like—worrying about Giulia, waiting for her to return, and then worrying about how Olive would adjust to the big move here. It was a terrifying decision, when I left. I didn't want to ever have to think about it again."

Tori looked down at her hands. Then she looked again at Marilene. "Did my mother know? She had to have known, didn't she? She was five years old when you brought her here."

"She knew something was wrong when we snuck off the island that evening," Marilene said. "I told her to start calling me Mama, even though we'd told her for so long that she had a mother who'd be coming back for her. I didn't know what else to do. I didn't want anyone to suspect she wasn't mine, because I thought I'd be accused of kidnapping her—which I suppose, in a way, I did. Eventually, we put that whole trip behind us, and I was sure she'd forgotten. Or thought those early memories were just a dream. Although there's a part of me that thinks she never recovered from the trauma of that night. Those nightmares she had. Who could blame her?"

She pressed her lips together. "I was doing the best thing," she said. "I didn't want your mother to be sent to an orphanage or adopted by someone who didn't even know her. I couldn't bear that."

Tori tried to speak, but she didn't know what to say. "Her mother was alive," she stammered. "Giulia was alive."

"But she didn't come back. What else was I to think, but that she had died? What else was I to do at that point?" Tori watched her clench her fists again, her cheeks reddening. "And the more I think about it, the angrier it makes me. I gave up everything for her baby, don't you see? I gave up my family, my home, everything I had. My parents had no idea where I went. They had no idea I'd left the country. I left no trail.

"Oh Tori, I don't regret it," she said firmly. "I loved your mother as my own. Even in her wildest days, even when she was testing me to my very limits, I loved her. As I love you and Molly. You are my family, you always have been."

"Of course we are," Tori said, because she couldn't bear to see Marilene hurting like this. And because it was true, even though she couldn't help but be angry. Marilene had wronged both her and her mother by keeping all of this to herself. She glanced back at the computer. The shocking comment, that Giulia was still alive, was still on the screen. What were they to do with this information?

When she looked up, she saw that Marilene was studying it, too. "If this is true, if Giulia is alive, I want to know why she never came back," Marilene told her. "I want an explanation. I deserve one. And so do you. Why did she make a life for herself in Rome instead of coming for her daughter?

"If she is alive, I need to talk to her," Marilene added, a measure of anger in her voice that Tori had never heard before. "So I can know once and for all why she never came back."

SEVEN

MAY 2019

Wednesday

"Why isn't Mar taking me to school today?" Molly asked the next morning as she tossed her backpack into the back and then climbed into the front passenger seat.

"She was up late last night," Tori answered, putting the car into gear and backing out of the driveway. "She wanted to sleep in this morning."

"Why did she stay up late?" Molly asked, taking a sip of coffee from her stainless-steel travel mug. Tori knew it probably wasn't a good idea for someone as young as Molly to be drinking coffee. But she didn't have that much, only a few sips in the morning, and it was more like coffee-flavored milk. That was just the way Molly had grown up. Surrounded by two women who were big coffee drinkers, she'd become one of the gang. They were a team, the three of them. Without a father or a normal childhood, she'd grown up more quickly, in some ways, than a lot of her friends.

Tori took a gulp of coffee from her matching mug. "I guess to wait for me to come home last night."

"Did she ask you about Jeremy?"

"What about Jeremy?"

"About whether he asked you to marry him? We both knew he was going to. That's probably why she stayed up late. She wanted to be the first to know."

"You talked about it?"

Molly took another sip, and as they rounded the curve, some coffee sloshed upward from the cup and splashed onto her navy-blue sweatshirt. "Damn!" she exclaimed, as she wiped it with her fingertips.

"Molly!" Tori scolded. "Don't talk like that."

"I'm just saying it sucks that I splashed. I poured too much into the cup this morning. Damn winding road! Good thing it's a dark sweatshirt, so it won't show when it dries."

Tori looked at her, then turned back toward the road. Molly was a great kid, smart and funny. She did well in school and had a lot of friends. But she was a bit of a loose cannon, using words she shouldn't be using and often acting more like sixteen than eleven. Tori loved being a mother, she loved raising her daughter, but sometimes she worried that their life was a little too unconventional. Molly often behaved more like a pal, a roommate, than a daughter. Tori wondered if she was doing something wrong. She wasn't like the other moms of Molly's classmates. In a way, she was younger than her age—what with dating Jeremy all these years and living with her grandmother—or, at least, the woman she'd believed was her grandmother. How funny, that she was immature for her age and Molly was so precocious. How had that happened?

And yet they were kindred spirits. Tori also would have been angry about sloshing coffee onto her clothes. She would have blamed herself, too, for pouring too much coffee into her cup. She would have also said, "Damn winding road!"

"So did he?" Molly asked.

"Did who what?"

"Did Jeremy propose? Are you engaged? Or did you say no? I'm your daughter, this affects me, too. I have a right to know. I have a right to know about my life."

Tori had to concede that Molly had a point. "Okay, then. No. I'm not engaged."

"Why not?"

She bit her bottom lip and concentrated on the road, not knowing how to answer. Molly wasn't a girlfriend, and she wasn't someone who should be speaking like this. She was a child, and she shouldn't have an intimate knowledge of her mother's romantic entanglements. Should she?

"When I am ready to discuss my personal relationships with you, I will do so," she said. "And for now, there's nothing you need to know. When there is, rest assured I will tell you."

"Fine," Molly said with a shrug. "No skin off my nose."

Tori looked at her, shocked and a little amused. Where had she picked up that expression? Where had she learned to be that rude? "Please be respectful," she said.

"I'm perfectly respectful. That was respectful. You said it was none of my business, so fine. I'm okay with that. None of my business."

"Good," Tori said. They kept driving. The thing was, her daughter wasn't being respectful. But maybe she had a point. Maybe she was entitled to know the details of what had happened last night. It had to be a very big deal to her, her mother's reasons for turning Jeremy down. Maybe this passive-aggressive stance was simply a way to assert herself and gain some control over her life.

"Okay, I'll tell you if you want to know," she said. "Jeremy... Jeremy did ask me to marry him last night."

"And what did you say?"

"I said no. Because I'm... comfortable with the way things are. I don't see a reason to make any changes." She gritted her teeth and continued to drive, her eyes glued to the road. She felt even stronger about her decision today than she had last night when he'd proposed. Way too much had happened last night to throw her world into chaos. The news that Marilene wasn't her actual grandmother, that her real grandmother was a dressmaker who had apparently been living quite contentedly in Rome despite the heartache and trauma she'd caused by abandoning her child—it was shocking and made Tori feel unsettled, as though the ground under her feet had sunk several inches, or the atmosphere had taken on a different hue. And armed with this news, Marilene seemed bound and determined to confront the woman who had uprooted her life, the woman she'd decided was dead because there was no other explanation for her disappearance.

From the corner of her eye, Tori could see Molly studying her as though she were a complicated puzzle piece.

"Mom, did you and Jeremy break up?" she finally said.

Tori hesitated then nodded. "I... yes, that seems to be what we did."

"Damn," Molly said.

Tori didn't have the inclination to scold her again.

"Yeah," she murmured. "Can't argue with that."

They reached the traffic circle in front of the school building and waited in line until she could pull up to the front walkway. "Have a good day, honey," she said, but before she could get the whole sentence out, Molly had scrambled out of the car and was rushing after some friends. "Kate! Sophie! Wait up!" The girls stopped and waited for her.

There was a sudden loud blast as the driver behind her leaned on the horn to get her to move. Startled, she put the car into gear. She hadn't realized she'd been sitting there. She didn't even know how long it had been.

Leaving the school drop-off point, Tori drove downtown and parked in the merchant parking lot, then made her way to the store. It was only nine o'clock, and South Main was quiet, as only the diner on the corner and the bakery down the block were open. Inside, she started up the coffeemaker, then sat down on the stool by the front counter and powered up the computer. The garment bag with the wedding dress she intended to change up was still draped over an armchair. It seemed like a million years ago that she'd decided on the asymmetrical hem.

There was still almost an hour before the store would open to customers. She supposed she could get started on the change to the gown right now. But she couldn't bring herself to begin the work. She didn't feel as inspired as she had yesterday.

Because sitting here by herself, all she could think about was Giulia. Her grandmother, her *real* grandmother. The beautiful woman with the wavy, honey-colored hair. The woman who'd sewn a remarkable wedding gown that ended up on display in a museum.

The woman who'd abandoned her daughter. Her baby.

Could there be any excuse for Giulia not coming back? Knowing her husband was dead, had she decided that she didn't want to raise a baby on her own?

Tori knew she was getting carried away, letting her thoughts take off like this. And yet the more she thought about it, the more she believed that Marilene had a right to be angry. And after giving up her family and her home, she had a right to answers. Even after all these decades, she had a right.

She put her elbow on the counter and rested her forehead on the heel of her hand. Could Giulia possibly know how much damage she'd done? Because Olive hadn't been the only daughter abandoned by her mother; Tori had faced that outcome, too. She thought now about her mother, the mother she barely knew. Marilene had often said that Olive had been a nervous, anxious child, and Tori remembered her that way as well. Scattered as a parent, someone who barely remembered to brush her hair before taking Tori to school each day. Someone who would refill her square, wide-mouthed glass three or four times each evening with clear liquid from the fat bottle with the yellow label that she kept in the refrigerator. Growing up, Tori had known that her mother was suffering, was tortured by something, but she had no idea what it was. And maybe her mother hadn't known what it was either. But what Marilene had said last night—how very awful, that Olive had been ripped from the only home she'd known and instructed as a five-year-old to start calling Marilene "Mama."

Tori remembered her father as sweet and helpless, someone who tried hard but couldn't calm her mother down when she was in one of her moods. They'd both had trouble with alcohol, Marilene had told Tori in later years. In fact, her father had been drunk when he crashed his car into the side of a bridge one winter night when Tori was ten. He'd been going to the mall that evening to buy Olive a Christmas present. Tori's mother had never recovered from the loss of her husband.

Tori rarely thought about her mother. But now she recalled that beautiful face, those long eyelashes and silky blonde hair, and she felt hot tears in her eyes. Was it possible that Olive became such a troubled child because she knew she'd been abandoned? Because she'd waited with Marilene's family for a mother who never came back? Might Olive have been a different person, a happier person, if Giulia had returned to her?

It was jarring, too, to think that Giulia designed wedding gowns. What else did Tori have in common with this woman? She had always thought she got her independence, her spirit, from Marilene; but did she? If she ever were to meet Giulia, would she recognize her own dark eyes? Or Molly's dazzling green ones? Would she spot her small ears or her bottom lip, relatively thick compared to her thinner upper one? Or her oval-shaped face, which she used to hate when she was growing up, wishing it was heart-shaped like her mother's? How could she know who she was anymore, when the biological thread she shared with Marilene had turned out to be nonexistent?

Suddenly she felt as angry as Marilene was. She, too, wanted to know why Giulia never returned for her child. How could she choose to settle in Rome, knowing she left a daughter behind? Did she know that Marilene had given up everything to raise her daughter? And what would she say if she knew what a troubled life Olive had led? And how that troubled life had impacted Tori even all these years later?

Like Marilene, she wanted answers.

Like Marilene, she believed she deserved them.

But how? How could she find a woman now in her nineties who was thought to have died more than two decades ago? How could she track down the person who had left the comment on the museum's website about meeting Giulia? The specifics about Giulia were buried deep on a tiny island in Italy, tucked behind olive groves, lost in the long-forgotten history of Marilene's family as they hid from the horrors of the Second World War. Even if she wanted to, could she find out the truth?

She booted up the laptop on the counter and navigated to the English version of the Parissi Island Museum website, which Marilene had found last night. She scrolled through a few pages until she found the picture of the wedding dress. Once again, she was blown away by its design. She longed to touch the fabrics, run her fingers along the seams, trace the scallops along the neckline, and feel the column of tiny pebbles that served as buttons. She yearned to know what had inspired her grandmother to create such a masterpiece. And what her grandmother would think, would say, if they could ever meet. Would Giulia even want to meet her granddaughter and great-granddaughter? Would she be heartbroken to know how her daughter's life had ended? Would she want to know all about the family she'd turned her back on?

Tori went back to the home page and clicked on the link

that brought her to the "About Us" section. Then she scrolled down to the email address for the museum's director, which seemed the best contact for her query. She felt it would be best not to reveal that Giulia was her grandmother because she thought that sounded so outlandish, and she didn't want the man to think she was some kind of a kook who should be ignored. So she clicked on the address and carefully crafted her request:

Dear Signor Mansirio,

I hope you can help me. I came across your website and saw the museum exhibit with the wedding dress designed in the 1940s by a woman named Giulia Sancino. I know someone who was part of Giulia's life for a period after Giulia left Parissi Island. She believed for a long time that Giulia had died, but we came across the comment below the exhibit description, which seems to indicate that Giulia may still be alive. Would it be possible to put me in touch with the person who commented, so I can try to find out how to locate Giulia?

Thank you very much for your help.

Sincerely,

Tori Coleman

She reread the email over. It seemed a big ask, especially since the person who'd posted the comment hadn't given a name. If the person who'd seen Giulia had opted to be anonymous, why would the museum director have access to the poster's identity? And even if he did, why would he give it to Tori? Under these circumstances, would Signor Mansirio even bother to respond? Was it even reasonable to assume that he spoke English and would understand her note?

Tori breathed out heavily. Whatever the case, it was very late right now in Rome—what were they, six hours ahead? There was nothing more to do than wait and see if she received an answer.

For good measure, she wrote a response to the comment on the website page, saying that she was looking for information about Giulia and asking the commenter to reach out to her and to please provide an email address. Then she translated both her email to the director and her comment on Google Translate and resubmitted both through the website's Italian version. She hated not knowing what would happen, if she'd ever hear back from either person. This was the kind of situation she avoided. But there was nothing more to do now. If luck was with her, tomorrow she'd have some kind of answer. Some kind of clarity.

Some route to meeting her grandmother.

EIGHT

SEPTEMBER 1943

Marilene left to help her mother with dinner, and Giulia was alone in the bedroom once more. Pushing away the quilt, she sat up in bed and lowered her feet toward the floor. The bandage on her bad foot was indeed huge. It looked like a boulder soldered to her leg just beneath her ankle. Gingerly, she rose onto her good leg, holding onto the edge of the nightstand for balance. Bracing for the kind of throbbing she'd felt down at the shore, she tested putting some weight onto her bad foot. It was awkward to walk, but surprisingly there was no pain. Luca was right: Marilene's father was a very good doctor.

She limped over to the wall to pick up the cane Luca had left her, thinking of what he'd said when he put it there—that Marilene's father sewed people up and sent them back out. What did that mean? Why would people come here if they were injured? Just to see Marilene's father—was he so well-known? And what Luca had said about sending them back: Back where?

Along the same wall as the cane was a doorway that she now saw opened into a bathroom. She limped closer and looked in. It was clean and bright, with marble fixtures and a large white tub. She vaguely remembered being in here earlier today, when she'd bathed and then changed into the nightdress she was wearing now. That lovely woman who'd helped her—Marilene's mother, most likely—had run the bath and left her with fresh towels and beautifully scented soap. She remembered how the bathwater turned gray from the dirt and sand caked on her skin. The towels she'd used and left on the brass hook behind the door were nowhere to be seen. Nor was the dress she'd been wearing. Instead, there was a fresh set of fluffy white towels on a white wooden shelf.

She splashed some water onto her face and used one of the clean hand towels to dry off. She folded it and placed it on the marble counter alongside the sink. On the other side of the sink, she noticed a small hairbrush with a comb stuck into the bristles and a ceramic dish with hair barrettes of various sizes. This family, she marveled. They'd thought of everything. They were evidently accustomed to having guests and wanted them to feel at home. And yet, she knew that nothing could replace her own family. Looking in the mirror over the sink, she pulled her hair, now clean and dry, into a low bun and brushed her unruly bangs toward the side. What a change from a few days ago. How attentive she'd been then to her shoulder-length waves, which Annalisa would help her set at night after braiding Emilia's long hair. When she undid the rollers in the morning in front of the ornate, gold-trimmed mirror and gently brushed out the curls, she looked just like Rita Hayworth or Gene Tierney, those beautiful Hollywood starlets from the American movie magazines. But now, Marilene's compliments notwithstanding, her reflection was grim. She stroked her fingers along her once-round and dewy cheek. Her skin looked gray and felt rough, gritty. Her eyes were sunken.

Putting her appearance out of mind, she limped back to the bedroom. A fresh yellow blouse and a pair of cotton pants with buttons on the side, similar to the ones Marilene had been wearing, were neatly folded on an upholstered stool near the foot of the bed. She assumed those had been left for her to change into and slipped them on. The pants were a little snug but not too bad. There was also a pair of blue, silky slippers.

It was all so odd, she thought as she returned to the bed to put one of the slippers onto her good foot. It was as if this family had anticipated her very arrival. But their home was so remote. How could they have anticipated and gathered what she would need? And if all this preparation wasn't for her, then who was it for? Who were these people—this girl, this family? Why were they here, in what seemed to be the sole house on this little island? How did they survive? Growing up, Giulia had lived in a small but bustling town with neighbors and markets and cars and a library and a post office and even a movie theater and plenty of restaurants. How did this family get by?

She turned toward the window, where the sun was lowering. She had no idea if she was facing Parissi Island or not. She didn't know what direction her boat had ultimately turned toward. She thought that possibly she could see the mainland in the distance, but she wasn't at all sure—maybe it was Parissi Island or even another island in the region. She'd never been a strong student, certainly not in geography. Back when she was in school, she'd avoided textbooks whenever she could, preferring glossy magazines and romance novels. The ladies who'd come to their father's shop to drop off clothes for mending or hemming or resizing always complimented her looks, as she gathered the clothes they'd placed on the counter. They'd say she resembled her mother, whom they remembered as a beauty, inside and out. Giulia believed that her mother was all that, even though she knew her mainly through stories and the photos their father kept upstairs by his bed. She'd died when Giulia was five.

But in time, the compliments hadn't seemed enough. Giulia had been sure she was destined for big things. Maybe even a life in America and a Hollywood career. She had the face and figure for it, that's what everyone said. And the sparkling personality, too. She'd reveled in the fact that nearly all the boys at school had crushes on her, which made her sister Annalisa call her shallow. But she didn't take the insult seriously. She knew Annalisa loved her, and she loved Annalisa in return. That's why she'd been so excited when Annalisa suggested they secretly light out for Parissi Island. They were both ready for something new, something bigger than their small town, their small life. Annalisa dreamed of being a scientist and finding a cure for the heart ailment that plagued their father. She'd learned that Patricio, their estranged uncle and the owner of the island, was inventing a medical device that could cure heart disease. Once they'd decided to go, and to bring Emilia along as well, Annalisa had crafted a note to send to their father, assuring him that they were safe and would be returning before long.

And so they'd taken off. Annalisa, who was one year older than Giulia and far more mature than her eighteen years. Sensible and smart, a leader. Emilia, a little bit spoiled and babyish but affectionate and eager to please, even funny when you gave her a chance. And her, the middle sister. Yearning for dreams so big, she almost couldn't articulate them.

How exciting it had been to leave their village for such a big adventure. How sure they'd been that they'd return home to their papa within a few short weeks, with stories to tell and a cure for his sick heart. Although they'd been scared, as they'd never traveled away from home before, they'd been confident, too. Because they were together. Yes, they bickered—all the time before they left home. They bickered about who worked faster, who had harder chores, who was being lazy. But they stuck together. With no mother around as they were growing up, they needed one another.

How she wished she could speak to them now.

Dressed and with her cane to help her, Giulia made her way out of the bedroom. She knew the family was expecting her, and she wanted to see them, too, to ask them to help her find her way to the mainland and ultimately onto the boat that would take her to New York.

Tightly grasping the wooden banister, she went down the curved staircase, taking the steps slowly. Reaching the landing, she surveyed the first floor, as she had barely been conscious when she'd arrived. Just like her bedroom, the rest of the house looked welcoming, clean and pleasant. The evening sun streamed in through the windows. There was a rug by the front door, the color a deep muted blue like the sky at twilight, and inviting sofas in the living room. The ceilings were high, and the rooms were spacious.

From deeper in the house, she could hear two men's voices, one that sounded older and one younger, arguing. Moving closer, she saw them and realized who they were. The older man was Marilene's father, and the younger one was Luca. And quickly she realized they were talking about her.

"She must have been followed," the older man said. "Why didn't they catch her?"

"Perhaps they didn't notice her. Or maybe they didn't care. One little rickety boat—"

"But she's a Parissi—"

"But they wouldn't have known that. And besides, they probably expected her to capsize and drown. It's quite a feat. Others wouldn't have made it."

"Sounds like she's made an impression on you."

"I'm only saying that she defied the odds to arrive here."

"Yes, and now she's our problem. Her presence can be helpful, but it also puts us at great risk."

"You can't blame her for that. She didn't intend to be here. She wanted to get to the mainland—"

"Luca, be careful. You can't allow yourself to feel for... well,

well, well, see who's joined us," the doctor said as he looked her way.

"I'm sorry," she said. "I didn't mean to interrupt..." She hadn't realized that by coming here, she would put these people at some kind of risk—although the conversation suggested she'd done exactly that.

"No, no. We're glad to see you up and about," the doctor said. "You look much better. Doesn't she look better?"

"She looks remarkable," Luca said. Giulia felt herself blush.

Just then Marilene walked in from the kitchen alongside the woman who had drawn Giulia's bath and helped her change out of her wet, dirty clothes. The woman had long limbs and a strong bearing, with sharp cheekbones and a firm jaw. Her hair was short and straight, tucked behind her ears, and she was carrying a platter with what looked like a dish Giulia remembered from home, pollo alla Romana, which their next-door neighbor used to make for them every few weeks. It consisted of braised chicken pieces with tomatoes, peppers and spices, and it smelled just as heavenly here as it had when her father had dished it out for them. Behind her, Marilene carried a serving bowl with cooked potatoes and a loaf of golden-brown bread.

"She does indeed," the woman said. "Hello, Giulia. We are very glad to have you as our guest. I'm Cellina and this is Pietro, my husband, in case you didn't quite hear us introduce ourselves earlier today. I know you've already met Luca and our daughter, Marilene. Are you ready for something to eat? I hope so, you are looking still so weak."

"I'm better," Giulia said, feeling comfortable with this warm woman even though the circumstances were so strange. "Thank you for all your hospitality."

"Our pleasure. Now let's get this meal started. Boys!" she called. "It's dinner time! Please, Pietro, please help me serve."

The little boys came running in. "Luca! Luca! Didn't you bring us any candy?" one of the boys asked.

"Candy?" Luca exclaimed, putting on a dramatically confused expression. "You must have me mixed up with someone else!"

"No! No! It's you!" the other boy shouted, grabbing and shaking Luca's arm. Luca scooped him up and turned him upside down, holding him around the waist.

"Me too, me too!" the first boy sang out, and Luca lifted him with his other arm and turned him upside down, too, holding both boys like sacks of laundry.

"Oh, Luca!" Cellina cried. "Be careful, they are not playground toys!"

"No? I think they are!" Luca said and shook them again. Watching him, Giulia unexpectedly felt her eyes tear up. With all that had happened over the past few days, it was good to see some sign of normalcy. Joy, even. It made her think of her father, her sisters, her home. She missed her life back at the tailor shop so much. More than she'd ever expected to when she and her sisters had left home. How were these people able to laugh and tease, considering what she and her sisters had learned—that Italy had surrendered to the Allied forces in Sicily and the Nazis had invaded the country in response? Rome was now occupied, and if what had happened on Parissi Island last night was any indication, the world was falling apart all around them.

"Luca, please. It's time to eat," Cellina said.

"Okay, okay." Luca righted the boys and put them down. "I have candies for you, but after you eat your dinner—"

"No! Now!" the first boy shouted.

"Later," Cellina said. "Giulia, I believe you've met our boys. This is Massimo and Matteo." She pointed first to the stouter one, who had short, dark hair parted neatly on the side, and then to the smaller one, whose hair was lighter and finer, his elbows and knees protruding from gangly limbs.

"Yes. They're adorable," Giulia said.

"They're *monsters!*" Marilene exclaimed.

"Marilene!" Cellina scolded. "And boys, please sit down."

The boys both found their seats, and Luca reached behind the breakfront. "And here's some special candy for your parents," he said. He displayed a brown wine bottle and handed it to Cellina. "The best of the year. You will love it."

"Oh, Luca! Aglianico! My favorite!" She studied the label, then put it on the table. "Thank you. Now sit, everyone. Let's eat."

Giulia remained standing, not sure where to go. Noticing her, Luca pulled out the chair next to him and offered her his hand. "Please?" he asked.

She limped forward and he took her cane and hooked it over the back of the chair. She grasped his hand. It was strong and steady. She leaned on it as she sat down.

"Thank you," she murmured. She wasn't used to interacting with a stranger in this way, and it unnerved her. In the past, charming young men had offered her a chair because they wanted to please her, not because she needed their help.

He sat down beside her, with the children on the opposite side of the table, Marilene in between her brothers, and the parents on the ends. He uncorked the wine and poured some for the adults, then looked at her and lifted the bottle. She shook her head. She'd had so little to eat today, and her stomach was still unsettled. Though she adored wine and had tasted some of the most delicious varieties at Parissi Castle, it didn't seem a good idea to indulge tonight.

Meanwhile, Pietro picked up the serving spoons and portioned the chicken onto plates stacked next to him. Cellina added on potatoes and passed around the bread. They behaved as though it were the most normal thing in the world, to have a scared, injured stranger at the dinner table. Giulia reminded herself that Marilene had said the family often hosted strangers. "Thank you," she said and accepted her plate, wondering who those strangers were and what they all had in common.

"Let's eat!" Pietro said, and Giulia picked up her knife and fork. The food tasted fresh and well cooked, the chicken flavorful, the potatoes soft and well-seasoned, the bread fragrant and crusty. She'd gotten so used to multicourse, lavish meals at the castle, she'd forgotten how good a simpler dinner could be.

Pietro cut into his dinner, and Giulia could feel his eyes on her as he brought his fork to his mouth. It was as though she were some new gadget or tool, something recently delivered that he didn't know what to do with. She replayed in her head what she'd overheard him say to Luca as she walked toward the dining room: "She must have been followed... she's a Parissi..."

"So, Papa, Giulia *did* come from Parissi Island!" Marilene exclaimed. Giulia was grateful that the silence around the table had been broken. She only wished Marilene had brought up another topic. She didn't want to be the center of attention among these people, who evidently had concerns about her. But the possibility of Marilene raising any other subject was remote. The girl was obviously in awe of her for having lived at the castle, a place that had so clearly captured her imagination.

"So we've gleaned," Pietro said in a measured tone.

"She danced in that ballroom! The big one you can see from my window! With the ladies in their gowns and the men so beautiful in their tuxedos, and the music, and the hairdos, the jewelry..." She rested her chin on her palm. Then she lifted her head and looked at Giulia again.

"Oh, tell us more!" she pleaded. "What did the dresses look like? Did they shimmer? Did they float on air when the men spun them around? Did they wear tiaras on their head? And shoes with jewels on the backs of the heels? That sparkled as they turned and twirled? Diamonds, or—"

"Enough!" Pietro said. "Cellina, where does she get this nonsense?"

"From the magazines, of course," his wife answered, as she nudged Massimo and then handed him his fork. "The ones they deliver with the newspapers."

"And how do you have time for this? What about your studies?"

"Papa, stop! I only read the magazines when I'm done with my assignments. Signorina Ottavia said I'm the best student she ever had. Ever, ever, *ever!*"

"Is that so?" he said, with a wink toward his wife.

"Of course it's so! You know it's so. You were there when she said it. Don't tease me, it's not nice!"

"Not nice! Not nice! Na-na-na-na-not!" Massimo said, and his brother giggled, causing a small piece of chewed chicken to burst from his mouth onto his plate.

Pietro took the boy's napkin from his lap and handed it to him. "So tell us, Marilene. "What did you learn today? When you weren't filling your head with thoughts of tiaras and beads?"

"I learned about the American Revolution," she said. "And the Declaration of Independence."

"*Liberté, Égalité, Fraternité!*" Massimo shouted, punching the air with each word. Matteo giggled, his hand over his mouth.

"No, that's the French Revolution!" Marilene groaned. She rolled her eyes and looked at Giulia. "Ignore them. They are so ignorant."

"They're only five," Cellina said. "They are good students, too."

"I knew that was French when I was five." Marilene rolled her eyes.

"I'm not sure that's true," her father said.

Giulia took in the banter, trying to make sense of this family's household. Signorina Ottavia, she figured, was a tutor. But why were these children living here and learning privately in their home? That seemed straight out of the nineteenth century, when wealthy families had governesses and such—or so she'd thought, from the novels she liked to read. Why weren't these three in a real school, meeting other kids and being normal children?

"Let's move on. What are you reading?" Pietro asked.

"*Don Quixote,*" Marilene answered.

"And for what reason did Signorina Ottavia choose that?"

"Signorina says it set the stage for the evolution of the modern novel," Marilene explained.

"I see. Then it's a good choice," Pietro said. "We learn who we are by studying where we've come from. That's a lesson you will need to remember, children. We planted the seeds of today long ago—the seeds that brought us to where we are as a country. We are here because the seeds were allowed to go bad. You must plant better seeds so that when you are adults, Italy will be different."

"Signorina Ottavia said the same thing," Marilene said. "She was talking about Mussolini and the way the church leaders bent to his will, which helped him amass all the power, which led to where we are now..."

Giulia continued to listen, fascinated by the conversation. She was sure this teacher, Signorina Ottavia, was right, and Marilene was an excellent student. And the whole family seemed smart, too, even the little boys, as silly as they were. She hadn't grown up in a family that discussed politics and literature, as this family did. Her father was clearly less educated than Pietro. He knew one thing: how to sew. Or maybe, two. He also knew a lot about being Jewish. He'd taught her and her sisters about that. But it wasn't book learning, his Jewish knowledge. It was stories. He knew many Jewish stories that he loved to tell. Sometimes they reduced him to tears because they meant so much to him.

"Pietro, can we change the subject?" Cellina said. "We have two guests tonight. Let us talk about something lovely. Luca, tell us about the wine you've brought us. Tell us where it comes from and where you found it, how you chose it. Tell us about your childhood in the vineyard. Such beautiful memories..."

The meal continued, and Giulia listened as attentively as she could, but Luca's calm, harmonious voice allowed her mind to wander. As he spoke about being a young boy running barefoot through his father's vast vineyard, seeing the red grapes growing in bunches, each one covered in protective netting, in fields that seemed to stretch to the horizon, she thought again about her own childhood. Though they'd been raised without a mother and in a modest home—only two bedrooms, which meant that Emilia slept on the sofa in the living room—she and her sisters had grown up comfortable and happy. They were loved by their ever-present father and cared for, too, by the many neighborhood women who checked on them and brought food and cakes, who gave them clothing their children had outgrown, which Papa would transform into fresh and well-fitting garments.

As Giulia grew older, she was the only one of the three who fell in love with Papa's craft, who learned to adore dressmaking and considered it an art as wonderful as painting or sculpture. By the time she was Marilene's age, she was studying the fashions in her movie magazines and teaching herself how to make similarly beautiful dresses, blouses, and skirts for herself and her sisters.

Giulia turned her head toward the far window, in what she thought was the direction of the cove where she'd arrived earlier today. This was all well and good—feeling warm and clean, eating nice food, listening to pleasant conversation. But she had no intention of staying. Hopefully by tomorrow her foot would be healed enough for her to proceed to the mainland. If she needed more treatment, surely she would be able to find a doctor there. Or maybe she'd consult one on the ship to America. Her ticket was paid for. All she had to do was find the ticket office where it was waiting for her. She just needed help getting there.

"Hmmm-mmm," she heard—the sound of Cellina clearing her throat. She turned to see husband and wife exchange telling looks.

"Giulia looks tired," Cellina said. "We're keeping her up, and she needs her rest. Did you have enough to eat, dear?"

"Oh, yes," Giulia said, nodding. She felt full, even though her plate was far from empty. "Plenty. It was all delicious. I can't even begin to thank you for all you've done for me today."

"Cellina, why don't you take the children into the kitchen for some dessert?" Pietro said. "Maybe a taste of the treats Luca brought?

"And Giulia..." he added firmly. "I know you are tired, but would you join me in my study for a little chat before you retire? I went down to the shore to take a look at that conveyance that brought you here. Maybe you can tell me a little more about it? I have a keen interest in small craft construction."

She looked at him, knowing that his words were more of a demand than a request or invitation. And somehow she was sure they weren't going to talk about her boat.

"Of course," she said as he handed her cane to her.

She took one last glance out the window.

She wondered when she'd be aboard her little boat again.

NINE

MAY 2019

Wednesday

Dinner was quiet that night. The only noises were the clink of silverware against plates, the muted sound of meatloaf being chewed, and the dull thwack of water glasses being set down on the table after having been lifted for a sip. Tori looked first at Marilene and then at Molly. Marilene's gaze was directed down toward her plate. Molly was glancing around the kitchen, first at the backyard-facing window, then at the ceiling, and then at the chunk of meatloaf on her fork. Her eyes met Tori's and she shrugged and turned back to the window. Tori continued eating, feeling the heaviness of the atmosphere with each bite.

She didn't exactly know what was wrong, but she supposed some of this was the aftermath of her turning down Jeremy's proposal. Although she hadn't discussed it further with either Molly or Marilene today, she knew they'd felt a seismic shift in the dynamics of the household. They were aware that Jeremy wasn't coming over tonight, that he wasn't planning any more ice cream outings for all of them, that there was no need to ask Tori if she'd be home for dinner this Tuesday or if she'd be having dinner at the club where Jeremy was playing. Even to Tori, the house felt too big for the three of them, and the table felt strangely empty. She knew that if Jeremy was gone for good, in time they'd all get over it. They were resilient adults, she and Marilene. And Molly was a busy sixth grader, with activities and friends and homework to complete, tests to study for, ballet classes and rehearsals to attend. This mood wasn't going to last.

"So... how was everyone's day?" she asked.

"Just fine, dear," Marilene said. Molly looked up, using her tongue to swipe some food out from between her back teeth and the inside of her cheek.

"Anything new?" Tori persisted.

"Mmm-mmm." Marilene shook her head.

"Any homework tonight?" she asked Molly.

"A little," Molly muttered.

"Need any help?"

"No. I can do it."

"Any decisions about the ballet casting?"

"She said she'd have the list next week," Molly said, sounding as though she didn't have the energy to say her teacher's name. As though there were simply too many syllables in Mademoiselle Diana.

Tori put down her fork, but neither Marilene nor Molly seemed to notice. She supposed she would have expected more of an effort, at least from Marilene, to make the mood around the table more cheerful. After all, Tori was on the verge of losing the man she loved, the man who had been a huge, steady part of her life for the last five years. She wondered if maybe Molly and Marilene were mad at her for saying no to Jeremy and refusing to move forward with something they both thought was right for her. And for them, too, for that matter. Or maybe they believed she was managing the situation well. She knew they both thought she was as strong as they came. She handled stress well, and without a lot of drama. Maybe they didn't want to drag her down when she was probably fine. That she had done what she wanted to do.

And yet, watching her grandmother and her daughter eat their dinner, Tori came to the conclusion that there was something wrong with the three of them. With the way they dealt with change. The way they didn't speak about things that affected them, things that mattered. And the more important the event, the more necessary it became to stay quiet. She had never seen Marilene as upset as she was last night. But here she was today, going about her normal routines as though last night's revelation had never taken place.

It was as though they didn't have it in them to confront and express emotions—anger, disappointment, frustration, sadness—in the way other people typically did. They let loose only when they were pushed beyond their ability to hold back. She'd seen Marilene get a bit teary, as she'd done last night, but she'd never seen her break down and cry. And she didn't think Marilene or Molly had ever seen her cry. She hadn't cried when her mother died, and she didn't remember Marilene crying either. She'd come close to breaking down when Jeremy had left her at the door after dinner last night; and her eyes had welled up earlier today when she'd thought about her mother. But in the end, she'd held herself together.

The question Jeremy had asked suddenly came back to haunt her: What was she scared of? More importantly, what were they all scared of? Was this the lesson that she and Marilene were teaching Molly—that when things got rough, when you couldn't exert control, you pulled back? Where had that lesson come from? And why did they cling to it so desperately, like a buoy in a turbulent ocean?

Did her mother's life have something to do with it? Or her still-inexplicable death?

When dinner was over, the three of them cleared the table and Marilene loaded the dishwasher, the only sound the water rushing from the faucet to rinse the plates and silverware. Molly went upstairs to finish her homework, and Marilene went to the living room to watch a little TV before bed.

"I'll come up in a little while to say goodnight, okay?" Tori called up to her daughter from the landing.

"Okay. Whatever," Molly said, her back to Tori as she climbed the last few steps.

"Is something wrong?"

Molly paused and turned around. "He asked you to marry him and you said no. And now he's gone, right?"

"I told you that's what happened."

"And I still don't get it. Why won't you just marry him?" Molly's tone was indifferent, but Tori could hear a slight edge of emotion coming through. She was glad Molly was speaking up and tried to answer in a way that wouldn't alienate her daughter.

"You don't just marry somebody, honey," she said. "It has to be right. And it's not now. It's not the right time. You're going to be a teenager soon, and I want to focus all my attention on you, instead of on starting a new married life—"

"Oh, no," Molly said. "Don't blame me, it's not my fault—"

"I'm not saying it's your fault. I'm explaining—"

"Explaining why you keep doing the completely wrong thing," Molly said. "I like Jeremy. He was normal. Jeez, I wanted to have a normal family for once."

Tori stiffened. She didn't care so much for herself, but she worried that if Marilene were to hear Molly say such a thing, she would be quite hurt. Since last night, Tori's anger toward Marilene had softened a bit. She still felt she should have known the truth years ago; but she also recognized that Marilene had made a huge sacrifice, leaving her home and family to keep Olive with her.

"Honey, stop," she said. "You don't understand what you're saying—"

"I know exactly what I'm saying," Molly told her. "I'm saying that this would be nice, you know? Something new. My friends all change. Their families change. They get new babies or new jobs or new houses. But we just keep going and going and going. You live in the house you grew up in. Isn't that... weird? I can't wait to get out of here, graduate high school and go to college and finally do *something*.

"I don't get it, Mom," she said as she turned her back on Tori. "I really don't."

Tori sighed. "I'm sorry you feel that way, Mol. Families are complicated..." But Molly was already upstairs. "I'll come up in a few minutes to say goodnight," she said again. Molly didn't respond.

Tori went to the hallway closet and pulled out Sheree's wedding gown, which she'd brought home from the store that afternoon. Taking it to the kitchen, she spread a cloth over the table to protect it and then pulled it out of the garment bag. Laying the bodice on the table, she sat down and adjusted the skirt so it draped onto her lap. Then she lifted the bottom part of the skirt and ran the existing hem between her thumb and the pads of her other fingers, trying to ascertain the intricacies of its weave, characteristics that were helpful to feel as well as see: texture, fluidity, weight. It was funny, she'd taken a few sewing classes when she was growing up and a few art and design classes in college, and she kept up with style columns on wedding blogs and social media. But she had never formally studied fashion. She'd just always had a knack for seeing the best combination of style and function when it came to fabrics. Most of her clients found her through word of mouth, and they were always surprised to learn she'd never had any formal training or apprenticeships. They often wondered where on earth her talent and skill had come from.

And now, it seemed she had an answer. *Giulia.* Her grandmother. Her biological grandmother. The one who had sewn a wedding dress now on display in an Italian museum. She likely hadn't had any kind of formal training either.

Did that kind of talent get handed down through the generations? Molly's teachers always said she was a fine artist. "You must get your talent from your mom," her art teacher, Mr. Rosen, had told her—and she'd repeated it to Tori and Marilene —a few weeks ago when she'd handed in a mixed-media collage. And other teachers had noted her strong hand-eye coordination, which made her good at sports. Her physical education teacher had mused during last year's teacher appreciation lunch that maybe the same hand-eye coordination that made Tori so good at fashioning garments was behind Molly's strong serve and wicked cross-court shots during the recent tennis unit. He suggested that she continue to play and then try out for the middle school tennis team when she started sixth grade in the fall.

Tori wondered what else could Giulia have handed down. A fierce need for control? An unwillingness to give in, even if that meant giving up the most wonderful man you'd ever met? Rock-solid stoicism?

Or were those things not passed along in one's DNA? Might they be passed down through example and through trauma? She thought now of one afternoon when she was eight and had gotten lost for a time in Bloomingdale's in the mall. The thing was, she hadn't thought she was lost at all. She and her mother had been standing in line for a table at the store's café, and she'd wandered off a few steps to look at a display of stuffed animals in the nearby toy department. She'd heard a commotion and come back to find her mother hysterical, her face red and her eyes open wide, the whites enormous. "No!" she screamed. "No! Where is she?" When she'd spied Tori, she'd stormed over and screamed, "Don't you ever, ever, *ever* do that again! Don't leave me, do you understand? Don't leave me!"

Tori hadn't understood what she'd done, but she'd been hugely embarrassed at the crowd that assembled to watch the scene play out. Her mom grabbed her hand and dragged her toward the elevator, as some soft laughter started to erupt among the onlookers. "My God, the way she was carrying on, I thought she'd lost a toddler or something," one said. "That was a big kid! And she was right over there!"

Her mom had sent her to her room for the rest of the day and threatened to ground her for even longer if she ever "pulled a stunt like that" again. Tori tried to explain that she hadn't meant to upset her mother, that she hadn't thought she was doing anything wrong; she'd simply been looking at the toys. She'd known exactly where her mother was the whole time. But her explanation made her mother even more unhinged. At home that night, she heard her mother carrying on to her father: "She just left! She just left! She never came back!"

Tori wanted to open the door and scream out, "I didn't leave! I didn't go anywhere! And of course, I came back! I was right there!" But she knew she'd anger her mother even more if she got involved in the conversation. She opened the door a crack and looked down the staircase, watching her parents on the living room sofa, her sweet father cradling her distraught mother in his arms as he kissed her head. She loved her mother so much. She was sweet and fun, the kind of mom who had pillow fights and made shadow puppets on the wall and told deliciously scary stories in the dark every Halloween, after taking Tori and her friends trick-or-treating around the neighborhood and then snuggling with Tori in bed, giving her a cup of seltzer to try to settle her stomach after eating too much candy. Seeing her mother so worked up that night, Tori made a promise to herself that she wouldn't scare her mother ever again. That she'd always stay right by her mother's side and do exactly what her mother wanted. That she'd never again give her mother cause to worry.

Thinking back now, Tori knew that was a hard task that would have become impossible. How could Tori have stayed in her mother's sight or been constantly in touch with her mother as a teenager, especially in those long-ago days before cell phones? Wouldn't she have rebelled? Wouldn't she have wanted to stay out with her friends, go to parties, go on dates? Would her mother have let her take the train to New York City with her friends, as all the high school kids did and all the middle school kids dreamed of doing? Would she even have allowed Tori to learn to drive? What kinds of fights would have been in store for the two of them? What lengths would Tori have gone to, wanting only to get her mother off her back and fit in with the other, "normal" kids who had "normal" parents?

In the end, Tori never had to face those questions. Her father had died when she was ten, and Marilene had given up her apartment and moved in with Tori and her mother. The next summer, her mother died, too—a freak accident that Tori couldn't bear to think about. In later years, she'd come to think her mother's death had been a blessing. Her poor mother had been so tortured, so frightened in a way Tori never understood. It often seemed that she couldn't live in her own skin, except when she was drinking. The fits and the tantrums were constant. In the days after the funeral, Marilene had assured Tori that her mother was finally at peace. That was a comfort.

"*She just left!*" her mother had shouted that night they came back from Bloomingdale's. Tori stayed in her room with nothing to eat until her father brought her a sandwich after dark. "*She never came back!*"

I did come back! Tori had wanted to shout. *I never left!*

But now she wondered if her mother hadn't been talking about her at all. Maybe Tori's momentary disappearance had triggered memories that were never more than barely beneath the surface. Maybe that night she'd been talking about her mother. The woman who left her behind. The woman who never came back. Giulia.

Was it possible that her mother had been so traumatized as a little girl by her mother's abandonment that she never could recover? Had Giulia ruined her daughter's life, and had her actions ultimately left Tori motherless, too? Had she rendered both Olive and Tori unable to fully embrace the wonderful feelings that made life worth living? Joy? Ease of spirit? Trust? And, in Tori's case, love? How could Giulia have made that her legacy?

Tori asked herself the question again as she studied the hem on Sheree's dress. Because it still didn't make sense, what Giulia had done. If she'd settled comfortably in Rome after the war, as the museum's website stated, that meant she was alive and well all those years that Marilene and Olive waited for her on the family's island, and all those years after they'd left for New York. How could she have stayed in Rome?

Exhausted and spent, Tori returned the gown to the garment bag, then hung it in the hall closet. It was after nine thirty now. She'd been sitting in the kitchen for an hour and hadn't even made a cut or sewn a stitch. She realized that the TV wasn't playing anymore, and the living room was empty. Evidently, Marilene had gone upstairs to sleep. Tori went to Molly's room and gave a quick knock on the door, then stepped inside. Molly was in bed, the covers tucked around her chin, as she gave Albie, who was stretched out beside her, a belly rub. Her table lamp was on and her school tablet was next to her.

"Honey, time to go to sleep," Tori said.

Molly nodded. "I will. I'm almost done." She gave Albie a kiss on his head.

"Onto your bed, Albie," Tori said, and he gathered himself up and jumped off Molly's bed, then scampered to his dog bed on the other side of the room.

Tori sat next to her daughter and stroked her long hair.

"Mom, why don't you marry him?" Molly said. "I don't understand. We're all sad without him. What's the big deal? I'm okay with it. Why aren't you?"

Tori shook her head. "I don't know," she said. "I don't understand either." She kissed Molly's cheek, then rose and went to the door. "I really don't, honey," she said as she left the room. "I don't understand myself at all anymore."

The next morning when she awoke, her phone screen signaled that she'd received an email overnight. Opening the mail app, she saw that it was from the director of the Italian museum.

Dear Ms. Coleman,

Unfortunately, I have no way to know who the commenter is or how to find that individual. We were surprised, as you were, to learn that Giulia Sancino may still be alive. We've tried often to locate her with no luck. The best I could suggest for you is to come here and search through our archives. We allow access to members of the public with serious research interests. We have much material from the war years that was donated by the owners of the surrounding islands, but sadly we do not have enough staff to identify and catalog all the items. Perhaps you might find some clues and enlighten us as well. I am sure you would enjoy our beautiful museum.

Cordially,

Francesco Mansirio

Direttore, Museo del Castello di Parissi

Pushing away her phone, Tori sighed, disappointed. His

note wasn't helpful. Was she really supposed to leave her family and her work and travel to a remote island off the coast of Italy to pore through some old documents in the faint hope that she'd uncover some random information that could lead her to Giulia?

And she hadn't heard anything from the commenter. Maybe she never would.

It wasn't practical to go, she told herself. How could she drop everything to take on this fool's errand? But on the other hand, knowing she might possibly get the answer she sought directly from Giulia—the answer that would explain what had happened, the answer that might provide the level of clarity that she, Marilene, and Molly so badly needed to navigate their future... how could she not?

TEN

MAY 2019

Thursday

"You're going to Italy?" Molly asked. "I want to go to Italy!"

Despite the seriousness of the conversation, Tori smiled sympathetically at Molly, who was sitting on the living room rug, petting Albie's belly. She had told Marilene her plans earlier that day, and in anticipation of her trip, Marilene had suggested the three of them have dinner at their favorite Italian restaurant. Tori also suspected Marilene wanted to do something different for dinner, since Jeremy normally would come to the house to eat with them on Thursday evenings.

They'd shared an array of family-style pasta dishes along with a Margherita pizza. And now that they were home, Tori had told Molly that she was heading to Italy. She'd decided it was best not to tell Molly the whole truth right now. She would tell her the complete story at some point; but it didn't make sense to spring everything on her today and then head out for Europe, disappearing just as Molly would likely be coming up with more and more questions. Her daughter was going to be shocked to learn that Marilene was not her biological great-grandmother. It seemed better to save that news for after she'd returned.

"Of course, you want to go to Italy," she said. "And you will. But not this time."

"Why not?"

"You have school. And besides, it's only a quick trip. There won't be time for sightseeing."

"You're just going to look at a dress?"

From the living room sofa, Tori glanced across the room at Marilene, who rested her elbow on her armchair, her chin lowered and her eyes focused downward. Tori could tell that she didn't approve of this trip. She suspected that having had a couple of days to think about it, Marilene now wished they'd never seen the postcard with the wedding dress. Maybe she'd decided no good could come from dredging up her past. But for Tori, dredging up the past was exactly what was needed— because Marilene's past had become Tori's present. And Molly's future. Tori couldn't stay home and will herself to forget about Giulia's existence. No, she had to try to find Giulia. If Giulia was still alive.

She turned to Molly, who glared at her, her chin jutting forward. "You're just going to look at a dress?" she repeated. "No one goes all that way just to look at a dress. You already saw it on the website."

"I also want to meet the designer, if I can find her," Tori said. "The dress is in a museum that recently opened, and there may be some documents there that can help me find out where she lives now."

"Just google her!" Molly said.

"That doesn't always work." She had tried repeatedly to find a Giulia Sancino in Rome last night, browsing search engines and pulling up links to both Italian and English websites. It turned out there were many Giulia Sancinos in the world, including an apparently very important economist based in Minnesota who had written at least a dozen academic books. But she could find no listing for a dressmaker living in Rome. Given Giulia's past and her age, it was entirely possible that she would have no internet presence.

The only information Tori could find about the island where Marilene had grown up and where Giulia had landed was that it had changed hands numerous times and was now known as Mauricio Island. It was owned by Carlo Mauricio, the head of a family of bankers with no ties to the Ciani family at all.

"The museum director said they tried to find her, but they haven't been able to," Tori told Molly. She didn't mention that even if she did find the right Giulia somewhere online, it was doubtful she'd get the woman to answer an email. Not everyone her age was as comfortable on the internet as Marilene was. More to the point, this woman had left her baby decades ago and, from all appearances, never tried to find her. Why would she willingly respond to an inquisitive email now?

"And you can't wait until summer to go?" Molly said. "So I could come, too?"

"I can't, because of the store," Tori said. It was true. Brianna had finals coming up and was starting a summer internship program in fashion design in New York next month. She was happy to take care of the store for the short term, and Marilene had offered to step in and help if necessary—she did the books, after all, so she was familiar with the vendors and the merchandise.

Of course, the other reason Tori had to go right away was Giulia's age. If she was alive, who knew what kind of health she was in? Tori needed to track her down as soon as possible.

"I'll take you another time," Tori said. "When we can do the things you'd want to do."

"How long will you be gone?"

"Ten days," she said.

Molly sighed dramatically. "I guess it's okay." She paused a moment, then continued. "I guess I have to stay here anyway. Because of the ballet show, I mean. I don't want Mademoiselle Diana to think that I'm not interested in being Alice or I'm not serious about the recital, which she might think if I just went away. I should be here to keep up with everything."

"You really think that?" Tori said, her heart aching a bit for her daughter, who feared she'd be penalized for taking a family trip.

"She might think someone else cared more. Whatever, it doesn't matter now. When are you leaving?"

"Sunday evening," Tori answered.

"Fine, okay." Molly gave Albie a final rub and then went over to sit next to Tori. "But you better bring me back a lot of whatever they have in Italy. Like chocolate or really good pizza sauce or something, okay?"

"Of course." Tori wrapped her arms around her daughter, hoping to bring back something even better. News of a great-grandmother who wanted to meet her. Who had a valid reason for never coming back to reunite with the baby she'd left behind. Who had plenty of answers that made good sense.

She kissed Molly's head, feeling uncomfortable that remembering the ballet cast was what had changed Molly's mind about wanting to go on the trip. Molly's need to "keep up with everything," as she'd said, was so characteristic of her—and a little troubling. It was as though she didn't believe she could trust what would happen with the casting unless she maintained the status quo. And strangely, Tori knew just how she felt. It was so similar to what she'd told Jeremy about why she didn't want to get married. *I have order. Why make a change?*

They both equated ceding control with unbearable risk. That wasn't good. But she didn't know how to change that. For herself or her daughter.

ELEVEN

MAY 2019

Sunday

Tori was busy through the weekend, packing her suitcase and purchasing last-minute supplies for her trip. She made sure to call Sheree to let her know about the new asymmetrical hemline and promised it would be ready for a fitting soon after she returned. And before she knew it, she had arrived at JFK for her Sunday evening flight.

Marilene, Molly, and Brianna had all wanted to come and say goodbye at the airport, so they'd parked in the short-term lot and walked together to the terminal. Tori checked her suitcase and then found the signs for security.

At the entranceway to the checkpoint, she turned to face the three of them. "Okay, you guys," she said. "Take care of each other. Stay in touch and I will, too." She stood for a moment surveying each one. They were her life. Even Brianna, whom they'd only known since she'd hired her two years ago, was like one of the family. And suddenly, Tori felt anxious about saying goodbye. She was safe with this little group, this bubble. It was the three of them and their love and predictability, she now saw, that had kept her together since her break with Jeremy. And it made her nervous now, to be separating from them. Who knew what she'd learn and how it would affect her while she was away?

But she had to go. She'd been feeling so lost ever since she found out about this grandmother she'd never known. Almost as if she no longer knew who she was. She hoped that if she could meet Giulia, she would be at home in her own skin again.

She hugged Brianna first. She knew Brianna was nervous about running the store alone. "You'll be fine," she told her. "I know you can handle it. Marilene can be there right away if you run into any problems. And you can also text me anytime—even if it's the middle of the night in Italy."

Brianna nodded, breathing in as she did. It seemed that Tori's sudden departure had unsettled her. Tori hadn't told Brianna the whole truth about Giulia, and now she felt guilty. Brianna had to be sensing there was more to the story than a dress in a museum exhibit. But she hadn't wanted to burden Brianna with all this drama. And maybe there was a lesson here that Brianna was still too young to understand. Life got complicated the older you got. You made a decision to leave your baby, or look after a baby, or say no to the man you loved, or leave for Europe to discover what had happened all those years ago— whatever the decision, the ramifications reverberated for weeks, for years, for lifetimes. It didn't matter if you made the choice as an impulse or if you put a lot of thought into it. A choice was something that could change lives. And the hard part was, you often couldn't know what the effect would be until the choice was long in the past. There was no way to know the outcome in advance, so that you could change your mind and pick an alternative.

Funny, she thought. She was learning this lesson only now. No wonder she was agitated, too.

She reached out and hugged Molly. "I love you," she said. "Call me anytime you want, okay?"

"Mom, it's only ten days," Molly said. "And actually, I think this is cool, what you're doing. Finally, we have something new going on."

"I'm glad you're happy," Tori said. At least someone saw this as a wonderful adventure.

She turned to hug Marilene, who felt so small in her arms. And when she pulled away, she saw fear in Marilene's eyes. "We'll be okay," Tori murmured, as she adjusted her stance so Brianna and Molly wouldn't hear her. "If I can, I will find her. And we'll both finally have the answers we need."

"I want a good reason for why she didn't come back," Marilene whispered. "And I'm scared there won't be one. I loved her and... I want to forgive her but after everything with your mother..." She stopped, as if she had so many feelings, she didn't know how to organize them in the few moments she had. Then she reached into her pocket and pulled out something that she tucked into the tote bag Tori was carrying. "Something to look at later," she said.

Tori went to reach for it, but Marilene grabbed her hand before she could. "Not now," she said. "I found it in my drawer last night. I don't think I could bear to see you look at it now. You'll see it on the plane. Go on," she said, gesturing toward the security line, which had nearly doubled in size since they'd reached it.

Tori nodded. "Okay," she said. "Oh, and... if Jeremy calls the house, just tell him..." She hesitated. "Never mind. It's not going to happen."

She stepped backward and gave a final wave. She hadn't been on a plane to Europe in years. The last time was when she tagged along with Jeremy to Paris for a cousin's wedding. She didn't think she'd ever gone on a flight alone. It was strange to realize that, as she'd always thought she was a sophisticated woman. But maybe she wasn't as sophisticated as she thought.

"Bye," she said softly. Then she turned, and with her back to the three of them, showed her ticket to the agent.

On the plane, Tori asked for red wine with dinner, and as she took a sip, she felt herself start to relax. She enjoyed traveling. Every couple of years, she'd taken a few days off to attend Fashion Week in New York City, an hour's drive from home, to help her stay current with wedding gown trends. And then there was the weekend with Jeremy in Paris a few years ago. Before that, she'd spent two weeks after her junior year at college touring Venice and Florence with a group of girlfriends. But this was different. She wasn't a student soaking in the culture with her pals over summer break. And this wasn't like the trip to New York, with those dash-in, dash-out visits to showrooms, armed only with a notebook for writing down impressions or sketching ideas. This was a search, a fact-finding mission, and she had no real sense of how to proceed. That wasn't her comfort zone.

Although it could be, she thought. And when she let herself entertain the idea, she knew there was something fun, even exhilarating, about the next ten days. Maybe Molly was right, she thought; maybe she had been in a rut for a long, long time: working at the shop, designing for wedding clients, being a good mother to Molly and a good granddaughter to Marilene; paying the household bills, keeping up with car payments and grocery shopping and everyone's doctor and dentist appointments. It was a nice, steady life. But was it enough? She didn't know what was behind her sudden tinge of excitement, but the idea of leaving for a short time, meeting new people, and making discoveries was lighting her up.

Wanting to know even more about where she was going, she

opened her computer and navigated to the "History of the Castle" page on the museum's website. She learned that the museum had opened only six months ago. It was housed within a sixteenth-century castle, which was once privately owned by a wealthy Italian family. Part of the building was still under renovation and slated to become a five-star resort in the coming year.

She read on:

The sole structure on Parissi Island, Parissi Castle, gets its name from the wealthy Parissi family, who were the original owners more than five hundred years ago. In the years leading up to the Second World War, ownership had been passed down to Patricio Parissi. Born in 1900, Patricio was an inventor and scholar, as well as a patron of the arts. Under his watch, the castle was a magnet for some of the most famous artists, inventors, architects, philosophers, and writers of the early to mid-twentieth century, who were happy to accept his invitation to stay at the castle, sometimes for years, to work on their masterpieces. The castle was reportedly a place of high-minded conversation, lavish parties, and luxurious accommodations. A staff of upwards of two dozen, many of whom were young people hoping to apprentice with the guests, ensured that the castle was spotless, the artists had ample supplies, and the meals were plentiful and sumptuous. Among the guests were Patricio's three nieces—Annalisa, Giulia, and Emilia.

Tori froze after taking in that last sentence. Could this be true? That her grandmother, Giulia Sancino, wasn't simply any dressmaker living on the island; no, she was a member of this wealthy, aristocratic family?

Oh my, Tori thought. That means I am, too.

She continued reading:

This lively and creative existence came to a crashing halt in
September of 1943, when the Nazis, who'd invaded from the
North following Italy's surrender to the Allied forces, stormed
the castle. It was rumored that among the guests and staff was
a ring of anti-Fascist activists who brought messages to the
Allied forces via supply boats to the mainland. There was a
warning that the Nazis were approaching, but it came too late
for many. Out for retribution, the Nazi invaders killed Patricio
and all of the guests who hadn't fled the castle in time.

Tori breathed out and shut her computer, suddenly aware
that being in a rut had saved her from facing horrible truths as
well.

When the meal service had ended and the cabin lights
dimmed, she put her earphones into her ears, chose a peaceful
playlist on her iPhone, and closed her eyes. Soon, she felt herself
drifting off. When she awoke, the plane quiet except for the hum
of the engines, she suddenly felt she was about to cry. It was the
strangest thing. She took the napkin from under her cup of wine
and pressed it to her mouth, trying hard not to make any noise.
Lowering her head, she took a deep breath, then held it as long as
she could before letting it out with a trembling exhale. Fortunately
her seatmates, a young couple in the middle and window seats,
were huddled together and fast asleep, both wearing eye masks.
She pressed her lips together and tried to calm herself down.

She realized that she'd been having a dream, one of those
terrible dreams where she had to be somewhere but couldn't get
there. Slowly the details came to mind. She'd been in an unfamiliar building, and she knew that Molly was on her way home
and would be wondering where she was. Tori walked down a
hallway searching for an exit, and then suddenly she was
rushing into a classroom to take a test that she wasn't prepared
for. She looked through the test questions helplessly, and then

she was back in the hall, and Molly was facing her, screaming: "You never do anything, you always get it wrong, you left too soon, and now Marilene is dead!"

Then the scene switched, and Albie was lost, and Tori was running through the neighborhood to try to find him, furious with herself because she'd allowed him to leave the house on his own. She ran all the way downtown, and then she spotted Molly through the window of the store, reconstructing the hem of Sheree's wedding dress by hand. "You don't have to do that," she said as she tore into the store. "Go to school and be with your friends!" But Molly kept pushing the needle through the fabric that was spread onto her lap, saying she didn't mind, it was okay, it was all okay...

Tori rubbed her forehead with her fingertips, hoping that recalling the dream would help her settle down. But it had seemed so real—Marilene's death, Albie's disappearance, Molly's willingness to do her mother's work. And she'd felt so guilty about all of it.

She remembered that when Molly was little and had bad dreams, she would sit alongside her on the bed and urge her to imagine the end of the dream with a happy ending—where Molly tamed the tigers or scared the bad guys away from the house or turned off the faucet in the bathtub before it could overflow and cause a disastrous flood. She thought about trying to do that herself now. But there seemed no way to end her dream happily. She'd always prided herself on managing things at home well, but suddenly she regarded her life as forever on the brink of unraveling, with Marilene and Molly and herself one step away from catastrophe. It felt at this moment as though she was hanging onto everything she'd created by a thread, like the one Molly had been using in the dream to sew Sheree's hem.

What had brought this all up? Was it Jeremy's proposal?

This impromptu trip to Italy, which had no clear agenda or goal?

Or was it the revelation about a grandmother she'd never known and distant relatives murdered by the Nazis that was messing with her head?

A flight attendant came by and handed her a packet of tissues and a cup of cold water. Embarrassed, she smiled and thanked him. She took a few sips, then remembered that Marilene had slipped something into her tote bag at the airport. She leaned forward to reach inside, then pulled out a square cut from an old newspaper. It had a black-and-white photo of three young women in ball gowns with their arms around each other —and when she looked closely at it, she realized they had to be Giulia and her sisters. Sure enough, the caption identified them: Annalisa, who looked to be the oldest, tall and thin with dark, wavy hair; Emilia, the baby, with her hair in braids, her face full, her smile wide; and Giulia, there in the middle. She was the most beautiful of the three. Her hair was lighter than her sisters', shiny and combed under just above her shoulders, with her bangs parted on the side and rolled away from her forehead. She looked like she could have been a model, with her big eyes and delicate, heart-shaped face.

These women were her family, she told herself. Her grandmother and her great-aunts. And yet she didn't know them. Theirs was not a story she'd grown up with, but they were part of her. And her story was an extension of theirs.

She shook her head and took another sip of water. What if, after all this, she actually was able to find Giulia? What would it be like to meet her? Would there be something in her eyes, her mannerisms, her smile that she would recognize as familiar, as *family*? Or would Giulia be a stranger?

And what if, after she'd tracked Giulia down, her grandmother had no desire to meet her? What if she had no good reason for abandoning her baby, other than that she simply didn't want one in the first place? What if she didn't even care about the sacrifices Marilene had made, the sad life Tori's mother had led, or the beautiful little person that was Molly, her great-granddaughter?

It was too much to worry about.

The only way to proceed was to treat this whole trip as a dress pattern.

One step at a time.

TWELVE

SEPTEMBER 1943

Pietro's study was adjacent to the living room, up three wide steps with decorative black iron balustrades at either side. Giulia followed him up the stairs, grasping the handrail and leaning heavily on her cane. On the second step, Pietro paused and turned back to support her by lightly grasping her elbow. It was the doctor in him, the healer, she thought, that compelled him to do that. And while it was a generous gesture, she didn't sense generosity in his manner. Mostly he made her feel nervous and under suspicion. Though she had met Luca only a few hours ago, she wished he were here, too. He was charming and friendly. He made her feel safe and at ease. As though he were merely a guest in this home in the middle of the Mediterranean, looking for a peaceful interlude on his way to wherever he was headed next.

Although the intensity of Pietro's eyes, as he'd looked at her during dinner, told her this wasn't some happy waystation for carefree travelers.

The study was dark, even when Pietro switched on the lamps that sat atop two end tables on either side of a sand-colored upholstered sofa. There were two brown leather armchairs across the room from the sofa, both facing a large black desk with a high-backed chair. Behind the desk was a window, the shutters closed. On a tall, square table sat a radio, brown with big black dials, the same kind that her father had kept in the kitchen. There'd been no radios at the castle; her uncle, Patricio, felt that news reports were intrusive and disruptive to the creative process. He allowed only Rome's main daily newspaper to be delivered to the island along with food and other provisions that the supply boats brought over.

Pietro gestured for his guest to sit in an armchair, as he took his seat at the desk. Giulia maneuvered to the chair and sat down, then placed the cane on the floor next to her.

"Are you comfortable?" Pietro asked her. "Any pain?"

"No, *Dottore*," she said. "Not at all. I'm very grateful. I was in so much pain when I got here."

"Call me Pietro. Please," he said. "It was quite an injury. The cut was deep. How did you injure yourself so badly?"

"It happened as I was getting onto the boat. I tripped on a loose board."

"I see," he said. "Well, the seawater made it worse. It could have been catastrophic if an infection had been allowed to spread. You could have lost your leg, or your life. We will check it every day and change the dressing. But I think you're out of danger."

"Again, I... I don't know how to thank you." Giulia watched him, hoping for some sign that his distrust was easing. But he still looked guarded. Almost hostile.

"So... Marilene seems quite taken with the stories you told her about Parissi Island," he said.

"I didn't tell her much, really." Giulia felt defensive. Judging from dinner, she recognized that this man liked to know what information others were feeding his daughter. "She knew a lot already—about the guests and the castle. She told me about seeing the dancing from her window. But it was a wonderful place. So many artists and writers and musicians having the time to devote to the creation of the most beautiful art. My uncle built something truly unique there."

"Yes, I know. I have quite a lot of admiration for your uncle. I never met him, but I appreciated all he did. It was horrendous, what happened. We were shocked and horrified. It must have been terrifying to you."

She looked down at her hands. "We knew that the Nazis had invaded, and there was word that they planned to overtake the island. Everyone was getting ready to leave. People were being ferried to the mainland as fast as the supply boats could go and then come back. We all had plans for where to go once we arrived on the mainland. But the Nazi soldiers came sooner than we expected. And there was panic."

"And you were able to escape on that rickety little boat? How did you manage that? We heard that no one still on the island was able to leave once the Nazis came ashore."

She thought back on that awful morning, how things had been orderly and then, without warning, they weren't. Her sisters were already gone, as was Vincenzo. Giulia had been able to secure passage to Argentina with the painter she'd been apprenticed to at the castle, and he'd told her that from there, she could easily travel to New York. She'd packed her suitcase and was ready to say a final goodbye to her luxurious bedroom, the gorgeous ballroom, and the welcoming kitchen. To the beautiful castle that she'd foolishly believed she'd someday return to. Then came the screaming, and then gunshots and the sound of marching boots and ugly German commands. The grand staircase was jammed, the people forced together, too many for anyone to make it down. She didn't remember the sequence of events after that, because she'd felt a sudden, overpowering urge. For what, she didn't know. Maybe self-preservation? She'd never known that she had such a deep desire to live. Maybe everyone did.

"There were too many people on the grand staircase, and the Nazis were shoving them back," she said. "But I knew... I'd been shown... there was a hidden staircase at the other end of the castle that led through the kitchen pantry and alongside the dining room, then down to a small boathouse. I grabbed some food and water on my way out. That boathouse—that was where they stored the *pattino.*"

She held back tears, thinking of the day Vincenzo had shown her that little staircase, the dock, the funny-looking boat. She'd met him there as often as she could, sometimes three or four days a week, so they could paddle around the adjacent inlet. She remembered how fast he could make the boat go, how she wanted to be able to do that, too. Taking the oars, she felt the mist that rose as the boat gathered speed, then threw her head back and shook her hair, the cool droplets bathing her shoulders. Oh, the fun she'd had that afternoon with her friend, competing for who could row fastest. On that endless day, the world seemed to have been created with her in mind.

"And so you are... the middle niece, right?" Pietro said, his firm tone pulling her out of her reveries. "The daughter of Patricio's sister and the Jewish tailor she married?"

She caught her breath and stared at him. How could he know that? She remembered that Marilene had said her father liked to know about the visitors who came to their island. She wanted to be honest. But she felt defensive and slightly ashamed, as though she were a lab specimen being examined and proving not up to standards.

Pietro smiled gently. "Please don't be alarmed. We recognized you from your picture. It was in the newspaper. We get the Anzalea newspaper here with our weekly supplies. The Rome paper, too, for that matter."

"I was in the newspaper?" she asked.

"Both papers. They carried your pictures," he answered. "It was important news when Francisco Parissi disowned his daughter for marrying a Jewish tailor years ago. That was your mother, Olivia, yes? So it was news again when you and your sisters reunited with your uncle Patricio. Especially since he became the head of the Parissi family after Francisco died..."

He reached to the side of his desk and picked up a newspaper, which had been opened to an inside page and folded back. He leaned over to hand it to her, and she studied the large, grainy photograph. There she was, Giulia with her sisters in the splendid ballroom of the castle, dressed in gowns, with jewels around their necks and in their hair. She didn't remember anyone taking a photo. But she did remember what a glorious night it was. The last concert performed at the castle before the news of the Nazis' imminent arrival broke. She'd felt so joyous that night. Surrounded by such beauty and luxury. How naïve, to think it would always be that way for her.

She turned her head. It was absurd, and she might even have laughed wryly if the mood here wasn't so tense. How many times had she admired her reflection in the mirror when she was growing up, after she'd styled her hair into perfect curls that framed her face and hugged her shoulders, wishing for the attention of a photographer? But it had never occurred to her that as the niece of Patricio Parissi, she might end up as a person worthy of such coverage. Parissi Island had felt so private.

And yet, perhaps she shouldn't be surprised. Her older sister, Annalisa, had frequently gone to the library to read about their uncle in newspapers and magazines. That was how she'd learned he was inventing medical devices. As head of the Parissi dynasty, he'd always been big news.

"Where are your sisters now?" Pietro asked softly.

Giulia handed back the newspaper. "I'm not entirely sure," she told him. "My older sister, Annalisa, had passage to New York. She intended to go with Aldo, the boy she planned to marry. My younger sister, Emilia, had gone back to our village to take care of our father. Although we got word that he died just before the Nazis arrived."

"I'm very sorry," he said.

"Thank you," she murmured, her gaze downward. How she wished they'd had a chance to tell their father goodbye. She and Annalisa had hoped to come back with a cure for his heart. They never meant to leave him forever. To never see him again.

"We heard Emilia went into hiding because the Nazis were planning to round up Jews in and around Rome," she continued. "Which is where our town is. My uncle, Patricio, was going to find her. And my..." her voice caught in her throat as she thought of Vincenzo, "...our friend was going to try to find her, too. We were all going to meet in New York."

"And you don't know where any of them are right now?"

She shook her head. "I only know where they intended to go."

He nodded slowly, making her feel uncomfortable anew. Like a chess piece he was contemplating, trying to decide where to move it. But even though he was in control of his family, she decided, he wasn't in control of her. She'd told him what her plan was, and while he very likely had saved her life, that didn't give him the right to determine what she did next.

"Anyway," she said. "My foot is feeling much better, so I will be happy to take my leave tomorrow and continue on my way to reunite with my family. One of the artists on the island arranged passage for me to Argentina. He said my ticket would be waiting for me in Anzalea if we got separated."

Pietro seemed not to have heard the last part of what she said. "You left the castle on your own, then?"

She nodded. She wasn't proud of it. So many people had been trying to get down the front staircase. It hadn't occurred to her to bring anyone else along with her as she was running. She was thinking only of survival.

"With no one else?"

"No, sir."

"And no one would have been waiting for you somewhere in the castle? No one would have taken another *pattino* to try to follow you?"

"There was only the one."

"And no one would be following you on another boat? No sister, no..." he paused. "Not even this... friend you mentioned?"

"I told you, they all left before me. None of them would have known how I got out." She felt herself starting to get angry with his interrogation. She wasn't the type of person to confront or challenge those in authority, especially men. Her experience with men was limited mainly to younger men, and her strategy had always been to win them over with her charm and appearance. But so much had changed, and she had to change, too. Annalisa would never let a man get away with intimidating her like this. It was time she took a page from her older sister's book.

"So as I said, I will be leaving tomorrow," she said.

His face remained impassive. When he spoke again, it was as though he hadn't heard her.

"It's a nice house we have here, don't you think?" he said. "Not the best construction, not the fanciest furniture. But you see, it was never meant to be lived in as a permanent home. It was designed as a summer place. We came here to escape the heat of Rome when I was a little boy, and when I inherited the island, I thought I would use it the same way my father did.

"But now everything's different," he said. "My childhood friend was a newspaper editor in Salina and he wrote a column criticizing Mussolini's racial laws. The day after it was published, he was found dead in the street."

He let out a small "Mmmm," as if he was reliving that moment now. Giulia knew about the racial laws. They had started to be enacted when she was twelve. She remembered, because that was the year when some of her father's customers stopped coming to his store. Not many; their village was small,

and people liked her father very much. But it was the beginning. A trickle. His Jewishness—not his skills as a tailor or his
kindness when people couldn't afford to pay—suddenly was
becoming his most relevant characteristic.

"I don't want to subject my children to a government I
cannot believe in," Pietro continued. "A government that hires
assassins to kill people who speak out. A government that unites
with vile animals who round people up and send them to camps
to murder them. I brought my family here. It is my intention to
protect them until the war is over and Italy's sovereignty—its
sanity—is restored."

She nodded because she didn't know what more to say or
why he was telling her this. She wasn't very knowledgeable
about the Fascists or politics, other than the changes she'd experienced at her father's shop. Their father had tried to protect
her and her sisters from the hatred he'd started to feel. And after
they'd left their village, the castle had been quite isolated, too.
Then, suddenly, the Nazis were invading Italy, occupying
Rome, and storming Parissi Island among other places. These
were events nobody in the castle ever thought about. Everyone
had been too busy creating art and music, writing glorious
poems and novels, living in a world that was far more fragile
than they ever imagined.

She waited, but he said nothing. She wondered if he was
thinking of his murdered friend. Finally she felt she had to
break the ice. She was sorry for him, but she had friends and
relatives of her own to worry about.

"*Dottore*... Pietro... is there something you want from me?"
she asked.

He sighed and took off his glasses, then massaged his forehead with one hand before looking back at her. Without his
glasses, he looked softer to her. His eyes were sunken, the skin
underneath them like small, delicate pouches. But his gray hair
was neatly combed back, his beard neatly trimmed. He seemed

the kind of man who took command of what was under his power and didn't waste time on things he had no chance of controlling.

"My dear," Pietro said. "I know you want to leave. But you've come here and now you are to stay. At least for a while. That foot is in bad shape. I didn't dress your wounds to have you lose a foot—"

"But it's healing, you said. And I'll have it taken care of. I'm sure there are doctors on the mainland I can contact before I board the ship to America.

"I'm not your responsibility," she added. "I can take care of myself from here."

"But it's not just your wounds," Pietro said. "It's who you are. You are well-known. If we recognized you from the papers, others will, too. They will find you and arrest you."

"Me?"

"Of course, you. They came after your uncle, didn't they? They came after all his guests. They thought he was harboring spies. They would love to capture his family, too.

"And don't minimize the fact that you're the daughter of a Jew," he said, his voice cold. "That, too, would put you in great danger, now that the Nazis occupy northern Italy."

"I can change my appearance. I'll cut off my hair. I'll wear boys' clothing—I can sew some up very easily from whatever fabric or old garments you can spare. All I have to do is get to the mainland, and there's a ticket waiting for me."

"A ticket with your name on it?"

"Well, yes, of course, and..." She paused, realizing what he was getting at. It wouldn't matter that she'd changed her appearance if she had to use her real name once she reached the port. "I'll figure it out," she said. "My uncle gave us all some cash, I can bribe the ticket agent if necessary."

"It's not that simple—"

"But it's my problem, isn't it? What does it matter to you? I promise I won't tell anyone where I've been if that's what's concerning you. I won't tell anyone that you helped me or took care of my foot.

"They'll be expecting me in New York," she added, her voice low and firm. No matter how nice they'd been, nobody was going to keep her against her will.

She watched him looking at her, as though he were deciding how to proceed. And it bothered her, this manipulative, controlling way of his. At that moment, she remembered the conversation she'd overheard between him and Luca just before dinner, and what Pietro had said: *Her presence can be helpful, but it also puts us at great risk.* What was that all about? What was going on?

"*Dottore*, is there something you want from me?" she repeated.

He stood and put his hands in his pockets. "Giulia," he said. "You are here, and you are alone, and you can help us do something very important. This string of little islands south of Parissi —we are not just landowners. We are part of an organization that's working to undermine the Nazis. The more we can disrupt their operations and take out their leaders, the easier it will be for the Allied forces to succeed.

"You know every inch of Parissi Island, where senior Nazi officers are now stationed," he said. "You can help us infiltrate that castle."

THIRTEEN

MAY 2019

Monday

The plane landed at Da Vinci Airport at seven a.m. Rome time. Although she was exhausted, having barely slept on the flight, Tori felt exhilarated as she left the plane. There was something so profound, so stirring, about being an American arriving in Europe. She recognized that feeling, that awareness of the vast trail of history that lay beneath her every step.

Swept along with the tide of people in the crowded terminal, she made her way to the tram that led to Passport Control, then retrieved her bags. She continued on through Customs, following the steps she had written out yesterday to get herself from the airport down to Anzalea, the port city from which ferries left for Parissi Island. The signage at the airport was in multiple languages, so she easily found her way to the ticket machines for the Leonardo Express, the train line that all of the tourist websites she'd consulted had suggested for the trip to Roma Termini, Rome's main train station.

Inside the train, she relaxed in the surprisingly roomy seat and looked out the window. For a while, all she saw were intersecting train tracks bordered by modest apartment buildings. But then she spotted the Porta Maggiore—the massive white travertine gate that was part of Rome's ancient walls. She shivered at all this country had been through in its history, and at how tightly bound to that history she, Molly, and Marilene were.

The trip was quick—about forty-five minutes, and she arrived at the station with plenty of time before her ten-thirty train down the coast to Anzalea. Spotting a coffee bar on the central concourse, she decided to treat herself to an espresso. At first she was amused at how small her serving was, but the coffee was so strong that she could only take in a tiny sip at a time. Still, she loved it. The taste felt explosive on her tongue, the bitterness smooth and not at all unpleasant. She smiled to herself, thinking, I could get used to this. But then she wondered: Had her grandmother loved coffee? Did she love it still?

She emptied her cup and went to the food market to purchase a panini and a bottle of water to have on the train, then found the platform listed on the departures board. She'd booked a stay in Anzalea at a small family-owned guesthouse that earned good ratings online. It was a quick walk from the center of town where the train would leave her, according to the website, and the rooms were considered small but clean and comfortable.

Shortly before ten thirty, the train to Anzalea arrived, and she stepped on and stashed her suitcase in the luggage compartment near her seat. Then she sat down and tried to relax for the trip. As the train rolled out of the station and through the city, she waited for the gorgeous views of the Mediterranean. Gazing out at the landscape, she thought back to the two weeks she'd spent in Venice and Florence with friends from school. One of her friends' mothers had arranged for them to have a private tour guide. She was on the board of the Art Institute of Chicago and wanted her daughter to see and understand the importance of Italy's most iconic works of art.

Tori remembered the tour guide, an Englishwoman in her late twenties named Ava, who had come to Italy as a twenty-year-old on the first leg of her planned solo tour all over Europe. She'd explained to the girls that she'd started her adventure in Rome, intending to stay at a cousin's apartment for a week at the most. But as luck would have it, on her first night in Rome, she was introduced to a handsome Italian that she fell in love with on the spot and married six weeks later—so her first stop on her adventure became her last. She'd joked when she first introduced herself to the girls that she'd insisted to everyone and anyone who would listen, "No! I have to leave! I have to go on to Spain and Portugal and Greece and Turkey! I'm on an adventure!"—all the while somehow knowing she wasn't going anywhere.

Tori and her friends had talked about the tour guide at the youth hostel where they were staying in Florence. "So romantic!" her friend Harriet sighed. "To meet your true love and have that change all your plans and everything you thought you wanted to do."

The others had nodded, and Tori did, too, but she also felt confused. It didn't make sense to her that Ava had given in that quickly. She believed that if you had a plan, you should stick with it or you'd regret it all your life. She'd thought often of her mother on that trip. She had the sense that if her mother had been more organized and centered, if she'd seen herself as capable of sticking to plans and reaching goals, maybe she wouldn't have died so young. Olive had always behaved as though life was no more reliable than a house of cards. Small problems—a clogged bathroom sink, a car that failed to start one morning—paralyzed her. She was ruled by emotions like fear and insecurity, which caused her to feel lost or unglued so easily. Tori was never going to make that mistake.

A week later on that long-ago trip, they'd arrived in Venice, and Ava brought them for a trip down the Grand Canal. At the dock, a crowd was waiting, and port employees were organizing the people and loading them onto the boats. Suddenly there was a change, possibly because so many tourists had arrived, and people started to be diverted to smaller vessels that would travel along an alternate canal. At that point Ava snapped into action, holding the girls back and letting others who didn't know better file past them. She even pretended at one point to lose her wallet on the ground, so no one would suspect that her true motive was to get her girls onto the Grand Canal.

Soon, an official figured out what she was doing, and began yelling at her harshly in Italian. Tori and her friends watched, terrified by the man's anger. But Ava stood her ground and remained silent as the man carried on. Evidently she didn't care how rude and threatening the man was. Because by the time he had finished his tirade, the boats headed for the secondary canal had all left. She winked at the girls as they stepped onto a larger boat.

She'd done them a huge favor, the girls agreed as they traveled toward Venice. They saw historic palaces, churches, and bridges that they would have missed had they followed the official's directions. Tori had new respect for Ava, who had known what she wanted to do and had found a way to make sure she'd done it. Earlier she'd thought Ava weak for canceling all her plans for a man, but now she felt that Ava was far smarter than she'd given her credit for. Maybe finding her future husband was exactly what she'd wanted to do when she left England. Maybe she had gotten her way all along. There was something so cool about a woman staying calm in the face of change and disruption, and keeping her eye on the ball. If the canal official had wanted to teach Ava and the girls a lesson about subverting power, he had failed. It was Ava who had the power; she was the one who had reached her goal, and all the girls had benefited from her sly calculations.

It was a lesson Tori thought about often during that trip and many times after. Power was elusive and hidden and flexible. Sometimes it took a long time to figure out who had it or how to get it. But it could deliver something amazing. It could deliver both a husband and the Grand Canal.

At one o'clock, Tori arrived in Anzalea. The weather was perfect, warm but not hot, the cloudless sky a rich cerulean blue. As she rolled her suitcase away from the train station, she was surprised by the charm of the little town. She hadn't thought it would be as lively and pretty as this. The train station opened on to a vast piazza, with pastel-colored stone buildings along one side, many sporting yellow- or orange-striped awnings that shaded outdoor restaurants, cafés, bakeries, flower shops. On the near side of the piazza, there was a long, rectangular park with stone benches and lush trees with thick bark and overflowing foliage. The town was quite cosmopolitan, as people seemed to represent a range of ethnicities and were speaking a variety of languages—English, Italian, Spanish, and others that she didn't recognize. Young couples strolled hand in hand, some eating vibrantly colored scoops of gelato in massive waffle cones, and a mix of adults of all ages sat at tables under the awnings, eating tiramisu from wide goblets, or cannoli and other pastries, or sipping deep-red or bright amber liquids from short, slim glasses. Looking beyond the park and toward the Mediterranean, she could see a smattering of ferries heading out from a landing on the shore.

And in the distance, there it was—Parissi Island, which she recognized from images on the museum's website. The vast castle was perched at the top of a steep hill saturated with trees and shrubbery and set against that singular blue sky. It was a gray medieval-looking structure, with domes on either end and a narrow tower positioned toward the back. Tall windows lined the main part of the building as well as the tower. Tori had seen many old buildings—churches, museums, palaces—when she'd traveled in Europe with her college friends the summer she traversed the Grand Canal. But they had always seemed like relics or sets designed for movies, so removed were they from her life. And yet this castle, the storied Castello di Parissi, was different. Yes, it was impossible to think of someone other than a member of a long-ago dynasty or a fairy-tale princess living in a place so remote and imposing; and yet, her actual grandmother had once called that place home. The thought gave her chills.

Turning away from the water, she surveyed the piazza. Her muscles were a little like jelly from the flight and time change, and she didn't know how much longer she could stay on her feet. She decided the best thing to do would be to check into the hotel she'd booked, find someplace to get an early dinner, and then go to bed so she could make her way to the museum in the castle first thing in the morning.

With some help from the map app on her phone and a shopkeeper who pointed the way, she headed to a corner not far from the piazza. There she climbed a stairway, thankful that the steps were short as she pulled her suitcase up off the ground, and turned onto a narrow sun-bleached brick road, the bricks a pink-tinged shade of gold. To her right was a stone wall with shallow urns holding small plants, the leaves pale green and the petals dusty red. Beyond the wall, she could see the Mediterranean shimmering in the sunshine.

The road was bumpy and uneven, and her suitcase rumbled as she dragged it along. She proceeded under a pair of orange archways and then down a small, pebbled street with pink-and-yellow-tinted buildings with yellow shutters on either side. Finally she spotted a sign for her hotel, the Albergo Marza. It looked lovely, with bright pink and white flowers in planters on each side of the entrance. Relieved that the place seemed at this point to live up to its reviews, she opened the blue wooden door and stepped inside.

The lobby was small and welcoming, with sheer white curtains letting in the breeze from tall, narrow windows on either side of the door. There was a round moss-green rug on the ceramic tile floor. Ahead of her was a chest-high wooden countertop, with old-fashioned mail cubbies affixed to the wall behind it and a doorway that appeared to lead into an office. To the right of the desk was a door with a sign that read "*Ufficio.*"

She rolled her suitcase forward as a man appeared in the doorway. "*Buon giorno,*" he said, his tone warm and welcoming.

"*Buon giorno. Sono* Tori Coleman," she replied, using one of the phrases that she'd learned online the night before she left. The others were *Dov'è l'isola di Parissi?* and *Dov'è l'abito da sposa?*—two questions that she'd hoped would get her to Parissi Island and over to Giulia's wedding dress in the museum, no matter what else she encountered. Other than that, she would be lost in trying to communicate. She'd hoped that what she remembered about Italy still held true, and that most people dealing with the public spoke English.

Fortunately, the man behind the desk did. "Ah, our American visitor!" he said, with only a trace of an accent. "We've been expecting you. *Benvenuta.* Welcome."

"*Grazie.* Thank you," she answered. She liked him immediately. He was a heavyset man of about seventy or so, with tousled white hair, a wide face, and a nose with a roundish tip that looked like it could have been crafted by a child out of modeling clay. His smile was boyish, thanks to his small, even teeth, and his eyes were a clear, pale blue. Although she was far away from home, he somehow made her feel comfortable.

"I'm Emilio Fucilla, and my family and I are happy to have you. How were your travels? Did you fly into Rome?"

She nodded. "It was pretty easy, but still a lot of traveling since last night. I'm so tired."

"Of course, you are," he said. "I assume you are here to visit the castle?"

"Well... yes," she said, surprised that he knew that. "What gave me away?"

"That's the only reason people come here," he said. "It's pretty new for us locals, all the tourists showing up."

"It hasn't always been that way?"

"No, no," he said, shaking his head. "Anzalea was a sleepy port town for many years. But everything changed once they started renovating the castle and opened the museum last fall. We get a lot of historians now, people writing books, students. Or people just looking to see Italy as they imagine it. Big castles in the middle of a beautiful sea."

"It is a beautiful sight," Tori said.

"It changed everything for our little town, when the new owners bought the island and the castle two years ago. Lots of new shops, cafés. And many of us locals work in the museum over on Parissi Island. I am there as a security officer three days and two nights each week.

"And where are you traveling from?" he asked.

"New York."

"New York City?"

"Close, about an hour's drive."

"Ah, that's someplace I would love to visit sometime," he said. "I've always wanted to go to America."

"You've never been there?" she said. "I was sure you had. You speak English so beautifully."

"Ah, but you see, I spent most of my childhood in England," he said. "My father moved there a long time ago. I think he had bad memories of being a young man here during the war. But at some point, he was ready to come home to Italy. He's in his nineties now, still going strong. You'll meet him while you're here. And my daughter and son-in-law, and my granddaughter and her girlfriend, too. We all work together. A true family business.

"So I see you'll be with us for nine nights?" he said, looking at the computer screen on a small desk to his side. "I'll need your credit card and passport to check you in, and then I can take you to your room."

She nodded and handed over what he'd asked for. She signed the guest slip, and he gave her a key with a tag numbered "8." Then he came around the desk and picked up her suitcase. "It's a bit of a climb, I hope you don't mind," he said. "But I've put you on the fourth floor. It has the best view. You can see the castle right outside your window."

He motioned to her to go ahead toward the stairway, and when she started up the stairs, he followed behind. She felt bad for him, carrying her suitcase on this narrow stairway. He wasn't a young man, and he didn't appear to be especially fit. The light-blue sweater he was wearing over his shirt was working hard to stay buttoned. But when she looked back, she saw that he was quite strong and appeared to be handling the climb with less difficulty than she was. She supposed that he probably climbed these stairs at least a few times a day, showing guests to their rooms or coming upstairs to fix whatever problems arose. There were two guest rooms on each floor positioned opposite one another, and she could hear noises coming from some of the rooms. The stairway grew narrower the higher they went, so that on the third floor, a young couple had to wait until she and Emilio reached the landing before heading down. Tori had the sense that the building was pretty old, judging from the uneven floorboards.

Finally they reached the top floor and Emilio unlocked the door to her room. She went inside and held it open for him. He rolled her suitcase past her, then lifted it onto a luggage rack.

"Now, please get settled and feel at home," he said. "If you need anything, call downstairs and one of us will be happy to help you. And keep in mind that to get to the castle, you need to buy your ticket here on the mainland. We sell tickets at the front desk, or you can buy them at most of the cafés and shops on the piazza. The first ferry is scheduled to leave for Parissi at ten in the morning, and the last one back leaves the island at five in the afternoon. Make sure not to miss that last ferry. Otherwise you're stuck there until the next morning."

"Got it," she said. "Thank you for the information."

"If you're hungry, there are plenty of places to get a meal," he added. "Many close in the middle of the afternoon, but then they reopen. We serve a small breakfast here from seven to eight each morning. And if you have any questions about the island, please ask. My grandparents grew up in this town, and we've owned this building continuously since then, even when we were living in England. My father especially has a wealth of information, so don't be shy."

She reached for her bag to draw out some money to tip him, but then changed her mind. He was the owner, and she thought he'd probably be insulted by the gesture. He certainly didn't seem to be expecting anything, as he headed right to the door after he'd finished talking.

"Have a pleasant stay," he said and left the room.

The door closed with a slam behind him, and she listened to the echo. When it finished there was silence. She looked around. The room was small but nicely furnished, with a full-sized bed and pretty blue floral linens. There was an uphol-stered armchair and a glass-topped round coffee table in front of it. A writing desk was positioned in the corner. Across the room was a door that opened out to a tiny balcony. She stepped outside and grasped the railing. Ahead of her, Parissi Castle rose from the sea, looking like a massive mural and not an actual building.

She walked back into her room. Even though Emilio had

been nice and the hotel was very comfortable, she started to feel homesick. Pulling her phone from her shoulder bag, she called Marilene's cell phone. She knew it was eight thirty in the morning back home, almost time for Molly to leave for school. But she hoped they could talk for even a few short minutes.

"Hello?" Marilene said, sounding surprised. Tori knew she probably didn't get many calls at this hour.

"Hi, Mar," Tori said. "You must be about to get into the car, but it's afternoon here and I wanted to say hello."

"No, it's fine. I'm glad you called. How was your trip? How's the hotel?"

"Is that Mom? Is that Mom?" she heard Molly call out. A moment later, Molly was on the phone. "Mom! Are you in Italy?"

"I am."

"What's it like?"

"It's lovely," she said. "How are you? Heading off to school?"

"Yeah. In a minute. What did you do today?"

"Well, I arrived in Rome and then took a train down to this little town where I'm staying, and I met a very nice man who owns the hotel. And tomorrow I'll be going to the island where that dress is. So tell me about you—how was your night last night after I left?"

"Fine. Regular."

"Did you finish your homework?"

"Yeah."

"What did you have for breakfast?"

"Marilene made pancakes."

"Oh, lucky you." Tori paused. She didn't know what else to ask. It wasn't like at home, when conversation was so easy. She wanted to say more because she didn't want to get off the phone. She missed Molly, even though she'd only left a day ago.

But she knew she should let her go. Molly didn't like being late to school.

"I guess it's time to leave for school. Does Marilene want to say anything else?"

"No—I think she's in the car. I better get going."

"Yes, go ahead. Kiss Albie for me. We'll talk later. I love you."

"Okay. Bye Mom."

Tori waited until Molly hung up and then put her phone down, thinking of her dream on the plane, how Molly had been doing all that sewing and not complaining at all. The image of Molly's sweet face from the dream was haunting. She'd been sewing as though that was something she had to do. But it wasn't her job; it was her mom's job.

Tori looked out the glass door toward the castle, thinking about what the dream might have been telling her. And suddenly she realized that she'd been so angry at Giulia for leaving her baby and causing so much sadness—and yet here she was, doing the same thing.

Oh, that's ridiculous, she told herself. Giulia left forever. She would be gone for less than two weeks. And Molly knew exactly where she was and when she'd be back.

Still, she thought, if she found Giulia and was able to talk to her, it was possible that she'd hear things she didn't want to know. Maybe she'd learn things that would make her see her whole life differently. Things that might change her in ways she couldn't even imagine. Would she later wish she'd never come? Might it be true, that old saying that ignorance was bliss?

Tori looked at the massive castle.

She chose to come here, and for better or worse, here she was.

There was no turning back now.

FOURTEEN

MAY 2019

Monday

Too tired to function any longer, Tori allowed herself a half-hour catnap, which stretched to two hours when she slept right through her phone alarm. Determined to stay organized, she rose and began taking her clothes out of her suitcase and giving them a good shake before hanging them in the tiny wardrobe or placing them in the shallow chest of drawers by the bed. She hoped that unpacking would calm her. Despite the nap, she was unnerved by how alone and claustrophobic she'd felt after speaking with Molly. She was far from home, and the fourth-floor room was so small and narrow. She needed to go outside and be among people again. And she also should eat something. Maybe a good Italian meal would settle her nerves as well as fill her stomach.

Anticipating that the weather would grow cooler as the evening approached, she took a shower and put on a pair of jeans and a short-sleeved top, then found the light jacket she'd packed. Grabbing her shoulder bag, she made her way down the three flights of stairs. As Emilio had mentioned, his daughter was now at the front desk—Tori recognized her immediately, since she had the same small mouth and clear blue eyes as her father. She looked to be in her mid-forties, and was wearing a sleeveless yellow button-down dress. Her thick, dark hair was pulled into a low bun, some gray tendrils hugging her temples.

"*Buona sera*," the woman said. "*Posso aiutarla?*"

"Um... *mangiare*... food?" Tori stammered.

"Oh, you must be the American guest my father told me about," the woman said. Her accent was pretty and much thicker than her father's. "Hello, I'm Donata. You are wanting... something to eat?"

Tori nodded.

"It will be best to walk back to the piazza near the ferries," she said. "There are many good places there, and you can eat outside and watch the sun lowering over the water. You shouldn't have any difficulty, as everyone speaks English. Do you remember how to walk back there?"

"Yes, thank you. *Grazie*," Tori said. Another pang of homesickness made her stomach sink. She envied this family, being together right now. She missed Molly and Marilene.

She went outside and retraced her steps along the sun-bleached brick street. Slowly, she felt refreshed by the sea breeze, which was cool on her arms, and the scent of green shrubbery mixed with a touch of citrus. The neighborhood was more crowded now than when she'd arrived, with people walking and riding bikes all around her. She reached the piazza, where restaurants were coming back to life, the waiters rolling back the awnings and setting votive candles on round bistro tables in anticipation of the coming darkness. Lines were forming alongside many of the eateries, and hosts were efficiently seating the parties and offering menus. Tori tried to make sense of the posted menus on the walkway outside of each restaurant, but many did not have English translations.

Deciding to take a different tack, she looked around to see

what was coming out of the restaurants' kitchens. At the closest one, she watched as a mustached waiter placed a huge bowl of pasta in the center of a group of diners seated on the patio. Though she couldn't tell what type it was, the rich red sauce looked delicious, and when the smell of tomatoes and herbs reached her, she knew she'd found the perfect place. She hoped there wouldn't be a problem asking for a table for just one.

That's when she noticed that the pasta had been served to Emilio and a couple—a man and a woman about the same age as he was. Evidently noticing her at about the same moment, Emilio waved and gestured to an empty chair beside him.

"Signorina Coleman," he called. "Join us for dinner!"

She hesitated. She wasn't sure she could carry on a whole conversation over dinner with people she didn't know, especially if the others at the table didn't speak English. Yet she also knew that it would be difficult to order a meal by herself, given that she hadn't been able to make sense of most of the menus she'd seen. Plus, Emilio was warm and friendly, and she could use a little company this evening.

She nodded. "*Grazie.*"

He stood and pulled out the empty chair for her, then introduced her to the others. "This is Tori, our guest visiting from New York," he said, then turned to Tori. "And this is Gabriella and her brother Dante. They are good friends who own the bookshop at the near end of the piazza."

"How nice to meet you," Tori said as she shook each one's hand.

"*Molto piacere,*" the woman responded. She was wearing sunglasses and a pink-and-black geometric scarf around her gray ponytail. "The pleasure is ours." Her brother, a slender man with long, thinning gray hair, wearing a pressed white polo shirt, nodded.

The waiter returned with four wide-mouthed bowls, setting one before each of them. He also placed a wine glass before her and filled it from the bottle in the middle of the table. Then, manipulating two forks expertly in one hand, he divided the pasta among the four of them.

Emilio lifted his glass. "*Salute*," he said, and Tori and the others followed suit. The wine was the color of rubies, and tasted rich and fruity, though not overly sweet, with a subtle spicy kick. Then he tucked his napkin into the top of his button-down shirt. "*Buon appetito!*" he said, and everyone nodded and picked up their forks.

He leaned toward Tori and added, "Bucatini all'Amatriciana. The best dish Anzalea offers. I guarantee it."

"And Emilio is a pasta expert—as you can tell by how tight his shirt is!" Dante joked.

Emilio wagged a finger good-naturedly at Dante, then went on to list the ingredients—pomodoro tomatoes, pecorino cheese, chili peppers, white wine and something called *guanciale*, which he translated as salted pork jowl. While that didn't sound particularly appetizing to her, the dish looked wonderful, and so she speared one of the narrow tubed-shaped noodles on her plate. She closed her eyes and chewed, releasing a satisfied sigh. Then she opened her eyes and nodded at Emilio. He was right —it was heavenly, and quite likely the most delicious pasta dish she'd ever eaten. The pasta was firm and the sauce clung fast to it, full of flavor—slightly sweet, slightly tart, a little sharp, and lusciously rich.

"So, Tori, is this your first time in Italy?" Gabriella said after they'd all savored their first bite. Tori loved how she pronounced her name, placing the emphasis on the second syllable and elongating the "ee" sound.

"No, I was here many years ago, when I was a student traveling through Europe," Tori answered. "But I've never been to this particular area before."

"Not many people have," Dante said. "It was a hidden gem. Now it's become quite overrun, with the island and the castle opening up after so many years. It's almost like New York City... what is that called? Times Way? Times Place?"

"Times Square, *fratellino*," Gabriella said, teasingly patting her brother's shoulder. "How ignorant you are! Times Square— the crossroads of the world, yes?"

"That's what they call it," Tori said. "And it's not quite as busy here. But it is more crowded than I'd expected."

"I envy you," Gabriella said. "It's lovely being here for the first time. I grew up in *Roma* and have lived in many cities around Europe. But there's nothing quite as wonderful as your first sight of this castle rising out of the Mediterranean. I'm afraid I've gotten used to it. That's why I love being surrounded by visitors. Even the loud ones are silenced when they first take in this view."

"It is stunning," Tori agreed, looking out over the blue water, shining with the reflection of the lowering sun, the gold seeming to stretch across the horizon. The castle somehow looked closer than it had earlier in the day, and the color now appeared more charcoal than slate. The tower and domes cast shuddering shadows on the water.

"And what brings you to the castle?" Gabriella said. "If that's where you're headed during your stay."

"Yes, the castle," Tori said. She hesitated before continuing. Somehow her story seemed too private to share. Too fraught. But then again, she had nothing to be embarrassed about. Many people went searching for family these days. And besides, these people all lived here, in the shadow of Parissi Island and Parissi Castle. Maybe one of them had information that could help her find her grandmother. "I recently learned that my grandmother stayed there for a while."

"Is that right?" Dante said. "How interesting. When was that?"

"She was there when the Nazis attacked the island. It's a complicated story. I never met her, and actually, I only recently learned that she was my grandmother. But the museum may have some information about her, I think. And there's something there on display that she made. A wedding gown."

The three of them froze. "Yes?" Gabriella said, lowering her fork. "The wedding gown in the center gallery? Your grandmother is Giulia Sancino?"

Tori nodded, surprised that Giulia was so well-known. "Although as I said, I only just learned of this. I'm hoping to meet her, and I'm hoping the people at the museum can help me find her."

"She is still alive?" Gabriella said. "I thought she had died long ago."

"I read that, too, on the museum's website. But there was a comment under the photo of the dress from someone who said they knew her. The person said she was still alive and making dresses, at least until recently. I wrote to the museum director but he couldn't tell me anything about the person who commented. I'm hoping there is some information at the museum that can lead me either to my grandmother or to the person who saw her. Maybe there's something in the archives, they said I could search there. You see, she... well, I have a lot of questions for her," she added quietly.

"Of course, you do," Gabriella said. "Wouldn't we all like to reunite with a grandparent from long ago?"

"And she has a great-granddaughter, too. My daughter, Molly. She's eleven."

"How lovely," Gabriella said. "Is she traveling with you?"

"No. She's home. Staying with my... with a close family friend," Tori said, correcting herself. But while it may have been accurate, identifying Marilene this way left a bitter taste in her mouth.

"She has school," she added. "Now wasn't a good time for her to come with me."

"Well, then you must find Giulia. For your daughter's sake

as well as yours," Gabriella said firmly. "Unfortunately grand-parents leave us much too soon, don't they? Way before we ever really know them as people. Way before they can know how their own story continues."

"*Amen per questo*," Emilio said. "No truer words were ever spoken." He lifted his wine glass and smiled at Gabriella—holding his gaze a little longer than Tori would have expected. His eyes sparkled from the sun before he looked at his glass and then took a sip and returned to his meal, his cheeks reddening. In that moment, Tori had the distinct impression that he might be in love with her.

"That island was the scene of quite a tragedy," Dante said, as the conversation continued. "So many talented artists died when the Nazis came and destroyed all that Patricio Parissi had built. Did you know that he created a glorious retreat there, and that artists and writers and inventors came from all over the world to do their best work? Such a loss for the families they left behind. Such a loss for humanity, too. Who knows what works of art and literature, what brilliant inventions never saw the light of day?"

"But apparently Giulia Sancino may be alive," Gabriella said. "Oh, for your sake, Tori, I hope she is. And I hope you find her."

"Thank you," Tori said. "If she is alive, I have to find her. I don't think I could go home without knowing for sure where she is."

They finished eating, and Tori felt the time change catching up with her again. Emilio paid the bill—"my treat," he insisted when the others tried to contribute, and then Dante suggested they go down the street for an after-dinner *digestivo*.

"Grappa, or maybe Limoncello?" he said to Tori. "That would complete your first evening here in Anzalea to perfection."

"I think I need to get some sleep—I'm fading fast," Tori said.

"But thank you for dinner, Emilio, and thank you all for the wonderful conversation. It was a beautiful beginning to my trip."

"I'm working at the castle all day tomorrow, so perhaps I will see you," Emilio said. "And please remember to be on time to the dock for your return."

"Good luck on your search, Tori," Gabriella said. "What a wonderful story it would make if you do indeed find your talented grandmother. For you and her. And for your daughter, too."

They all started to rise, and Tori saw Emilio reach for Gabriella's chair to pull it out. Then he took her shawl from the back of her chair and held it out. Gabriella looked at him, her smile amused but warm, before turning around so he could drape it over her shoulders. As she grasped the ends and crossed them over her chest, Tori found herself thinking about Jeremy. How she missed looking at Jeremy the way Gabriella was looking at Emilio. How she missed the feeling so neatly captured in Gabriella's and Emilio's eyes as they looked at one another. Would they ever look at each other that way again? Or had she closed that door for good?

FIFTEEN

MAY 2019

Tuesday

The next morning, Tori had a quick breakfast of coffee, fruit, and *cornetti*—the Italian version of a croissant—in the small dining room off the hotel lobby, then went to purchase a ticket to the castle from Emilio's daughter, who was again at the front desk. She left the hotel for the piazza and arrived at the dock in time for the first ferry of the morning. Dressed in a blue sundress and comfortable tan loafers, she found a seat on a bench on the top deck. With her hair in a high ponytail, she enjoyed feeling the cool breeze on her neck and shoulders. The sun was strong, and the air smelled sweet with the scent of lavender, and as the shore grew distant, she could make out fields of poppies and sunflowers on either side of the piazza. Around her on the boat were families and groups of adults exclaiming over the vistas and pointing with excitement toward the nearing castle. She was excited, too—although she envied all these people whose trip seemed entirely for pleasure.

As the boat gained speed, she thought back to when she had

traveled to Venice and Florence that summer after her junior year. She didn't remember such a view, although she was sure she must have seen the beautiful waters of the Mediterranean. But this was so different. Or maybe she was different. She was older now. She saw more. She looked ahead at the colors, the blue-green of the sea, the way the droplets sparkled and glistened as the boat caused them to spring up from the surface of the water. She saw the colors of the island in the distance, the blended tones of orange and bronze along the walls of the steep hills. The ferry veered left as it approached the island, with Parissi Castle high atop a rocky hill. It looked like it belonged in a fairy tale, and she felt transported back in time.

She reached into her shoulder bag to get her phone to take a picture, but then took out her sketchbook and a pen instead. She usually felt inclined to sketch when she was in the city, the skyscape with tall buildings suggesting angles and lines and shapes for necklines or hems or sleeves. Or she'd sketch at the beach at twilight, looking for shimmering water or glistening waves or translucent cloud formations that she could translate into trims or bows or fabric or knots. She'd never considered herself a person who loved earth tones. She wasn't much of a hiker. She worked with whites all the time, sometimes with hints of gold or pink.

But this scene triggered a different region of her brain. As the boat approached the island, she noticed something profound in the colors of the medieval-style castle and the surrounding earth. Something timeless and universal. She didn't often think about what came before or what would last after she was gone. Life moved quickly at home, as she lived in a town where shops were always changing hands or new places were opening up, capitalizing on trends in fashion, dining, or whatever. But now she was heading toward something that had been around for centuries. It made her wonder how she had come to live her very everyday life. Getting through the day to get to the next day, finishing one dress so she could get to the next—that was the rhythm of her existence. When Christmas was over, she was already thinking about spring. Was she missing something by letting life flow so quickly by?

Twenty minutes after departing, the boat reached the shore of Parissi Island, and she disembarked with the rest of the passengers. Even though the resort wasn't open to overnight guests yet, the museum had apparently received a lot of good coverage and was becoming very popular. Most of the visitors were speaking English and appeared to be American, she noticed. She left the boat and made her way over to where a small group was beginning the climb uphill. She'd read online that there was an outdoor elevator around the back, but it was very small and intended only for those who couldn't use the steps. She didn't mind though—she was glad to walk up with the other visitors. She wanted to see everything close up—the stone steps, the iron railings, the way the side of the castle would change in scope and color as the sun hit it from different directions while she ascended.

The climb was tougher than she'd expected, and soon she was out of breath. She tried to distract herself by looking at the stone stairs, which glistened in the sun like crystals. The sparkling parts had a kind of three-dimensional look, an appearance that was eye-catching and beautiful. She yearned to render it in her notebook. Keeping up with the crowd, she finally approached the top set of stairs. It opened up to a courtyard with wide square slates and several groupings of deep-green shrubs. It was charming and pretty and symmetrical. She followed the others through the huge doorway.

The lobby was airy and pleasant, the chairs and sofas sporting cool gray tones, the plate glass windows stretching from floor to ceiling. There was a strong security presence, with many guards wearing navy-blue vests with the logo of the museum imprinted where a breast pocket would be. The guards made Tori feel uncomfortable, as though she didn't belong there. And the truth was, she wasn't there merely as a sightseer, as the others were; she was searching to find someone who, by all appearances, didn't want to be found. She felt like an intruder.

She went through a metal detector and then to the information desk. There were several stations with different languages posted, and she found the one for English. She decided it made sense first to see the wedding dress before asking for the archives. She was dying to see it.

She reached the front of the line and told the woman she was looking for Giulia Sancino's wedding dress. The woman pointed to the grand circular staircase to the right. She murmured *"Grazie,"* and followed her instructions. At the base of the staircase she began climbing once again. The top of the stairs led to a long corridor, and she walked among the crowds, passing rooms with open doors. Inside each one, as far as she could glean, there was a display of artifacts related to a particular era in the castle's history. Ahead of her was a sign on the wall with a diagram of a gown and an arrow pointing forward and then to the left. At the corner, she made the indicated turn. A few steps ahead, she looked inside a doorway that opened into a large space that could have once been a concert hall or a ballroom, she thought. A sign hanging from the ceiling indicated that the wedding gown was straight ahead.

There were two guards standing watch near the dress, and many people gathered around it. Suddenly feeling cold and trembling, she wove her way through the crowd and toward the center display.

I'm going to see the dress my grandmother made, she thought. *My grandmother who made wedding gowns like me.*

But even as she thought that, even as she knew that she must have inherited her passion for fabric and closures and shape from this woman, she couldn't believe it was true. Deep inside, who was this woman, this Giulia? She was even more curious than ever to know.

SIXTEEN

SEPTEMBER 1943

When Giulia awoke the next morning, fog blanketed the air outside, tinting the bedroom gray. There was a small alarm clock on the nightstand that said it was eight a.m.—the latest she'd slept since she'd left her father's home. She'd had trouble sleeping last night and kept replaying in her head all that the doctor had said after he'd told her that he needed her help: that having high-level Nazi officers a boat ride away was both an opportunity and a danger; that the landowners along this string of islands were determined to take advantage of the opportunity instead of waiting for the Nazis to come for them as they'd come for Parissi and everyone staying in the castle; that their mission all along had been to garner information about the enemy's plans and intercept messages to forward to the Allied forces coming north from Sicily.

"Many of your uncle's staff were members of the Resistance," he'd told her. "The head housekeeper, Signora Russo? Did you know her?"

"Of course," Giulia had answered. Signora Russo had been in charge of all the kitchen and household workers. She was a beautiful, impeccably dressed woman, with blonde hair she styled in rolls away from her forehead, the rest gathered in a ponytail and tied with a red ribbon. She'd been the most wonderful baker—Giulia and her sisters, and everyone in the castle, had craved her tarts and chocolate pastries. She'd been generous and welcoming when the sisters had arrived on the island looking for work, before it was revealed that they were Parissi's nieces, and Parissi insisted they be treated like royalty. "She was lovely and kind," she told Pietro.

"And dead, no doubt," Pietro had said, his voice a mix of anger and cynicism. "She was the leader of the spy network on Parissi Island. We think that's why the Nazis were so brutal when they stormed the island. They wanted to make an example of you all."

Giulia's lungs seemed to twist in her chest at his words. She felt the ache deep inside, as she raised a hand to her temple, suddenly feeling light-headed and dizzy. "I don't think I can take much more tonight..." she'd murmured.

But he hadn't let her off the hook. "I'm sorry to make you face this now. But there's no turning away. You've come to us at a pivotal time. And though the situation in Europe may get worse, we have the means to make a difference. Because now we have something we haven't had before, at least not in the work I've been doing. We have an inside track into a building that now houses some of the most important Nazi officers in Italy."

She withstood the weight of his attention, as he studied her. Her usually sharp brain felt muddled. Still, she grasped what he meant.

"And that's me," she said, finishing his thought. "I'm the... inside track."

"You've been there, you know it," he said, his firm voice tinged with the excitement of recognizing a stroke of luck in an otherwise hopeless situation. "You know where the stairways are, the doorways, the private entrances. Where the closets are, the pantries, the storage areas. You know how the kitchen is arranged, where the knives are, the meat shears, the tools we can use. You know how to find Patricio's private tower, where we're sure the most senior officers have their desks and living quarters."

"But... what does that—"

"With your help, I can create a map of the castle that will guide the Resistance fighters now masquerading as mechanics, boatmen, and guards," he said. "We want to level the castle—or as much as possible. And take down as many officers as we can."

"Level it? You mean to destroy it?"

His eyes fixed on hers.

"But... but this is my family's home..."

"Giulia," he said. "This is war. And we need your involvement. Do you understand me? There's no other choice. This is going to be our project, starting first thing tomorrow. You're going to tell me every aspect of the castle, from the tiniest nooks to the biggest ballrooms. You're going to tell me, and I'm going to draft the map, and you're going to make sure I get it right."

She'd tried to leave at that moment, looking around for her cane and then grasping the arms of her chair. "Please, *Dottore*," she said. "I have to lie down—"

"Of course," he said, although he made no effort to rise. "But just a few more things you must know. Rules, if you will, that are necessary for the smooth running of this household. First, there is to be no discussion of the Resistance outside of this study. My children are to be shielded from any mention of it. Cellina and I are determined to protect our children. We don't want them to grow up knowing how close the threat of war is. For now, it's more of a game to them, especially the boys, who see the Nazis as little more than evil characters in a story-book. I will not have my children growing up terrorized. Their childhood will not be taken away from them. Is that understood?"

She nodded.

"That's the rule for the entire household," he told her. "Because it's not merely us. Signor and Signora Brambilla ostensibly help with the upkeep of the house, but they are fighters, too. As is the children's tutor, Signorina Ottavia. And you should know that the house often serves as a waystation for members of the Resistance who are injured and require medical care, or who need to hide out between operations. To the children, they are merely guests."

"I see," she said, when she recognized that he was waiting for a response.

"Luca, too," he added after she'd spoken. "He tells the children stories about the vineyard to explain why he comes and goes so often. He is our liaison with Rome. He travels there for meetings and reports back when he returns. As far as the children are concerned, he is a family friend who is helping with research for a medical book they think I am writing. That's how we explain why he and I are in my office so much. They think we just use that"—he pointed to the radio—"for news. But we use it for communications. Now, we will have to assign you a job, to explain why you are staying after your foot heals sufficiently for you to leave. You will convince the children that you are glad to be working and living here. Is that clear?"

Is that clear? Even now she heard his threatening tone, as she sat up in bed, shivering from the dank chill of the foggy morning. Didn't he understand that she was a child, too? Only seventeen, at least until her birthday in a few weeks. Only a few years older than Marilene. But he didn't see her that way. And she supposed he was right.

She felt so much older than her years, after what she'd been through at the castle on that horrible morning. Word of the Italian surrender to the American forces in Sicily had spread, and it was rumored that the Nazis, who had invaded Italy from the north, planned to set up an operation on Parissi Island. The guests and workers began packing up, wanting to make sure they left before the Nazis arrived. How foolish they'd all been, to think they could outsmart the Nazis and circumvent the war. They were no different from Pietro's children, the little boys who saw the Nazis as merely storybook villains. But Marilene and her brothers were children, and their father was intentionally shielding them from the truth. She and Annalisa and all the others at the castle had no such protector. No, they'd all been too wrapped up in their lives, their vision too clouded by their beautiful work and their gorgeous surroundings, to see what should have been obvious. That they had waited too long. That they'd been shielded by their own naïveté.

Stepping out of bed, Giulia limped to the closet and saw that someone had left more trousers and tops for her. She also noticed some bolts of fabric in the closet—mostly cotton and linen, but also wool and silk in a range of colors. She wondered who had ordered them and for what purpose. At another time, in another situation, she'd have loved to pore through these fabrics. To feel their texture, to drink in their colors. To create something beautiful out of them.

She dressed and combed her hair before clipping it back with a barrette. Then she stopped at the small writing desk by the wall and looked inside the single drawer. As she'd hoped, there were some blank pads of paper inside, along with a few pencils.

She took out one pad and a pencil and brought them to the bed. Wanting to forget the doctor's harsh voice and sobering directives, she sat and began to sketch a sundress for the beach. Drawing fashions always made her feel good. Alive and creative. At the castle, surrounded by people who were attending to their art and pursuing the most wonderful and ambitious of dreams, she'd begun to think of becoming a fashion designer. She was meticulous in her work and had an observant eye, her mentor, Savio, was always telling her. Big cities had large, thriving fashion houses that would be thrilled to take on someone with her talent, he said. Especially New York, he'd said. Having been trained at Parissi Castle, she'd be in high demand.

She paused as she considered the sundress she was sketching, then tore the page off the pad. With a fresh sheet before her, she found herself drawing the wedding dress she'd sewn at the castle. She'd always loved garments with intricate constructions, and this wedding dress, which she'd made for Savio to study as he sought to enhance the realism of his paintings, was the most intricate garment she could ever have dreamed up: with hard materials like buttons and stays and beads alongside soft materials like silk and tulle; and with a stiff, form-fitting bodice above a romantic, drapey skirt. She'd worked so many hours on it that the construction was seared into her brain, and she reproduced it now on paper—the scalloped neckline and gleaming closure made of dozens of tiny opalescent pink pebbles from the shoreline of Parissi Island; the expansive skirt, the silk reflecting the light as it flowed.

She continued to draw, but it was hard to focus with the uneven light coming in from the windows. Still determined not to think about her meeting with Pietro last night, she decided to go downstairs and outside to sketch, where natural light could bathe the page.

She pushed herself up off the bed, then limped out of the room and downstairs, the pad and pencil in one hand and her cane in the other. The house was still. She walked slowly, placing her bad foot gingerly on the steps and using the banister to keep her balance. Remarkably, she didn't feel much pain at all. Yesterday, she would have hardly imagined she could feel this good, but now she felt stronger and refreshed. A hot meal, a comfortable bed, and the doctor's ministrations had already had a good effect.

She thought back to what Pietro had said. He wanted to help end the war and save lives. And save his homeland. And that was noble. But his family was here, and they were safe. Not so her sisters, Giulia thought with a pang of dread. They were out in the world, two Jewish girls trying to make their way to America and likely venturing into Nazi-occupied areas, their faces as recognizable as hers. After hearing all that Pietro had told her last night, she was certain she understood the danger more than they did. She had to make sure they were safe.

She reached the kitchen. It seemed she was the only one awake. By now the fog had started to burn off, and sunshine was streaming through the windows. The kitchen was beautiful, with big windows, a large wooden table, and chairs sporting yellow floral cushions. In another life, she might have been happy to stay in this house, with this family, for weeks or even months. But this was the life she had, the life where she wouldn't feel herself again until she was reunited with her family.

She looked out through one of the windows. The outdoor space behind the house was pretty, with a patio featuring stone benches and a trellis that led to a woodsy area with thick bushes and greenery. Finding the door, she stepped outside and paused, feeling the cool morning breeze on her arm. It had been on a day like this, she remembered, when Vincenzo had brought her down to the dock at the rear of the castle to show her the *pattino*. It had seemed such a silly conveyance to her. Whimsical, with its sides painted in blue and white stripes. Big enough for just one person, or maybe two if you squeezed together tightly on the narrow bench.

Just try it, he'd said. She knew her older sister, Annalisa, would scold her if she knew what was going on. Annalisa always complained that nothing but boys filled Giulia's head, and she needed to learn not to fall in love with every fellow who smiled at her. But she couldn't help it. She was good at flirting. She liked falling in love. Not staying in love but falling in love. She'd loved being around men who found her beautiful and irresistible. She liked when boys smiled at her. She'd kept her hair brushed and shiny and always painted her lips and then waited for smiles—from students at school, from boys she passed on the streets of their town, from customers at her father's tailor shop. She knew that plenty of boys came there not because they needed their pants hemmed or repaired, but because they wanted to see her.

And Vincenzo, the young boatman who had taken the three sisters from Anzalea to Parissi Island—he was cute, with long, golden hair and thick, soft-looking lips, and she liked sneaking off with him. What was the harm? She was seventeen and every day was an adventure. And besides, she'd thought, Annalisa wasn't the be-all and end-all. Sure, she was the older sister, but only by a year. And even more important, they were both Parissis. And Parissis were rich and invincible. The world was full of possibilities now that they knew just who they were.

"It's easy. It's fun," Vincenzo had said the first time he'd brought her out to sail. And so she'd giggled and stepped onto the rocking and rolling raft-like boat, and he climbed on and sat down alongside her. He'd used an oar to push them off away from the shoreline, and then he'd placed her hands on the oars, putting one arm around her shoulders. She'd loved the feel of his hands, strong and rough. She'd loved the way his arm felt so warm and exciting along her upper back. Together, they'd paddled out a bit into the small lagoon, and then she'd turned her head. His lips were right there, and impulsively she kissed him. A delicious kiss that said *we are young, we are free, we are amazing!* All she wanted to do was fill her days with such pleasure. With frivolous rides on a colorful boat with a lovely boy.

How she would have scoffed if someone had told her that one day soon, she'd be using the *pattino* to escape Parissi Island. That what Vincenzo had taught her about the rear dock and the way to paddle the flimsy boat would save her life. That the life she had on Parissi Island would dissolve like this morning's fog.

That Nazi officers would be taking over her uncle's beloved castle with his private, cherished tower. That so many of the people who'd shown her kindness and given her such encouragement—including her dear mentor, Savio—were very likely dead.

And that she would be asked to participate in the destruction of her uncle's castle. That the knowledge she had gleaned in those storied walls was now seen as a valuable tool of the Resistance.

She sat on one of the stone benches and began to sketch more of the wedding dress, remembering the way the folds of the fabric encircled the skirt. The sketch drew her closer to her memories of her family. Where were they—Vincenzo, Emilia, Annalisa and Uncle Patricio? She begged them in her head to be safe. To believe they would all be together again, just as they'd planned. *Please keep trying*, she thought. *Please keep trying, and I will, too...*

"That is lovely," a voice said from behind her. She was startled and turned to see a figure standing behind the bench, holding two steaming cups on saucers. "May I offer you coffee? Are you a coffee drinker?"

It was Luca.

SEVENTEEN

MAY 2019

Tuesday

Tori approached the display in the center of the room. The pedestal was hip height, the dress suspended, held up with wires with the skirt outstretched, the hem just grazing the surface of the pedestal. Facing the front of the dress, she stopped a few yards away from it, so she could take in the whole thing. Somehow the crowd around her seemed to fade away.

It was spectacular. Not merely beautiful, as Kelly, the bride who'd sent the postcard, had said. It was a work of art, complex and layered. The bodice was covered in beading, the neckline a blend of laces, the sleeves sheer and filmy but somehow full of body and shape. How Tori longed to touch it, to turn it over and examine all that couldn't be seen, to explore the way the parts had been put together. She knew there had to be sophisticated boning in place to keep the shape so precise, and yet the dress didn't look stiff or inflexible. Or heavy, or overdone. No, it looked light and airy and, in an ingenious way, organic—as though all the parts had emerged from a single piece of fabric directed to behave in a certain way by the dressmaker's skill and imagination. It was a perfect synthesis of textures and colors and shapes and mood.

Visionary, Tori thought. It was thrilling to think she was the descendant of an artist this brilliant. And yet, it was unsettling, too. How could Giulia—an artist who had poured so much love into the creation of this gown—how could this same person have abandoned her child? And how could she and this woman share DNA? In a million years, Tori could never come up with a reason why she'd decide to abandon Molly. If they were somehow separated, she'd search to the ends of the earth to find her.

She circled the dress a few times and, obeying the signs on the wall in English and other languages to refrain from using a flash, took a handful of photos from different angles on her phone. But she knew the photos wouldn't do the gown justice, just as the photo on the postcard and the image on the website hadn't. They could never capture the movement and sparkle and drama of the dress; they could never approximate the way the design made her imagination sing. And she wasn't the only one; she realized now that the space around her was still, the other visitors also mesmerized. People stayed as silent as if they were in a church sanctuary, moving wordlessly out of the room when they were ready to leave.

But Tori didn't think she'd ever be ready to leave. Facing the dress again, she felt her eyes sting. She knew that many people would find it silly that a dress could cause so much emotion, especially when Tori had never been one to cry. But that's what was happening.

And it was a dress, Tori now recognized, that accomplished something that her own creations never did. While her gowns were fashionable and skillful, this garment was on a whole different level. You had to believe in love for the long term to make a dress like this. A dress that was so delicate and intricate. A dress whose memory would last forever.

Tori's thoughts turned again to Molly. Though she knew it was still before dawn back home, she wished she could call her. She wanted to tell her that she loved her and would do anything for her, and that even with Jeremy out of their lives, they would be okay. Molly, in particular, would be okay—she would grow up to make good choices for herself, to do work that was fulfilling, to feel at home in the world, and to give her heart to the right person. Tori would make sure of that. She wanted Molly to feel confident about the future, to trust that she would be a happy adult with a life filled with love. And yet, how could she convince Molly of that, when her own actions were so at odds with what she wanted Molly to believe? When she'd refused to make a promise of forever to the man she loved? When she'd sooner walk away from him than move their relationship forward? How could she expect Molly to do otherwise when this was the model in front of her?

Brushing aside those thoughts, she took one last look at the exhibit. At the base, she found the short bio of Giulia that she'd seen on the website. But now she noticed a sentence in small print: "*A gift to the museum by an anonymous donor.*" Who could that anonymous donor be—and how had they gotten their hands on the dress? And why didn't that person or those people want to go public with the gift? Through whose hands had this dress passed? She thought that if the comment on the website turned out to be a dead end or there was no way to trace the comment back to an actual person, maybe she'd be able to learn who had donated this dress—and maybe that could be another route to finding Giulia.

She returned to the lobby to inquire about the archives. It was still morning, and she'd noticed a café on the other side of the lobby, so she could work for a couple of hours, stop for a break and a bite, and then return for a few hours more before making her way back to the ferry for the final boat. Of course, she didn't know if she would find anything in the archives. She didn't even know what items or documents could be there or how old they might be. But she had no other options at this point. Maybe if there was some information about where Giulia had been at other times of her life or about a husband or any other children she might have had, that could lead her on a path to where Giulia was now.

She joined the line for the English station at the information desk, and when it was her turn, she stepped up to the employee. "Hello, *buon giorno*," she said to the woman. "I was in touch with the director of the museum, Signor Mansirio, last week, and he told me that there are archives that are open to the public. I'm here to do some research into Giulia Sancino. Can you tell me where the archives are located?"

"I see," the woman said. She had delicate features and a soft tone, but there was something in her voice that told Tori that entry to the archives wasn't all that simple. "Yes, the archives are open to members of the public with serious research interests," she said. "Historians, writers working on books, students, and so on. Can you tell me what the nature of your research is?"

"I'm looking into some family research. Genealogy," she said. She didn't feel comfortable going into more detail. It would be such an odd thing to say—that the woman she thought was her grandmother up until a few days ago had unexpectedly revealed that her actual grandmother was the designer of the famous wedding gown upstairs. Even to her own ears, it sounded far-fetched.

"Genealogy?" the woman asked, a skeptical frown on her face.

"You see, I'm trying to trace her history, her lineage..."

"Is this for an academic study? Can you show me some credentials?"

"I'm not with a university," Tori said. "This is for personal research. Didn't you say the archives were open to the public?"

"To members of the public with serious research interests."

"But this is a serious research interest. Look," she said and pulled out her phone, then opened the mail app and scrolled down until she came to the email from the museum's director. "See?" she said. "I was invited here by Signor Mansirio. I wrote to him, and he said I could examine the archives."

The woman read the email. "Yes, I see. That does make a difference. Let me bring up the calendar..." She clicked on her keyboard, then looked up at the screen. "I can give you an appointment for August sixteenth..."

Tori was sure she must have heard wrong. "August? That's three months away."

"We have a lot of research requests since the museum is quite new, and a very small staff that oversees that department. We are booked several weeks in advance through the summer. Most researchers call ahead to book an appointment—"

"But I didn't know I had to. He didn't say that—see? He didn't say anywhere in the email that I had to wait three months—"

"He must have thought you'd understand that. There's been much media coverage of the museum. People are aware of the constrictions—"

"But I wasn't. *Please*," Tori said, her voice panicky. She had to get into the archives while she was here. She couldn't return in August. She couldn't afford another flight and another stay. Not to mention that the longer she waited, the more likely it was that Giulia might not be alive.

"The thing is, it's very important that I see the archived materials," Tori said, deciding to lay it all on the table. She had no other choice. "Giulia Sancino... I think she may be my grandmother. In fact, I know she is. And I've come from New York to try to find her and meet her. I don't know if she's in good health or how much longer she'll be alive."

"No, this is not correct. All the people who were at the castle when the Nazis arrived perished—"

"But she escaped to another island nearby. Ciani Island—at least it was Ciani Island when she lived there. And then someone met her not too long ago—she sewed a wedding dress for this person's granddaughter. The person posted about it... see?" She opened the museum website on her phone and found the comment, her fingers awkward and clumsy but still thankfully functioning. She started to show the screen, but the woman waved her off.

"I don't know what more to tell you, madam," she said. "These comments that people write—we have no way to tell if they are accurate or not. And even so, the fact remains I cannot let you into the archives until August sixteenth. You are welcome to make an appointment and return then."

"But I came from New York. Please, can you tell me where I can find Signor Mansirio? I'm sure he'll want to help me."

"He won't be able to. The archives are part of the research division. He's not in charge of that department—"

"Then who is in charge?"

Please, madam..."

"Or can you help me find the person who wrote this comment? Is there anyone who can track this person down and let them know I need to speak to them?"

"We have no way to do that. Perhaps if you responded on the website to the comment..."

"I tried. The person didn't get back to me."

"Then madam, please?" The woman pointed past Tori's shoulder toward the lobby. The line for the English information station was at least a dozen people long—way longer than any of the other lines.

"Oh, okay. Of course. Thank you," Tori said and stepped to the side so the next person could approach.

She pressed her forehead into her hand. This couldn't be happening. This whole thing couldn't be ending before it had even begun. How could she go home and tell Marilene she'd failed? How could she return with nothing to show for her efforts, for the money she'd paid to come here and the hopes she'd put into finding her grandmother? She tried to convince herself that if she had to go home this way, it wouldn't be the end of the world. She'd had a nice trip, met some interesting people, and perhaps most important, had seen Giulia's wedding gown in real life. She'd been close to it and had seen all the features including those opalescent pebbles that formed the line of buttons down the back. It would help Tori come up with new ideas for her own designs. Surely, that was a lot to have accomplished during an impromptu trip.

But no, she thought. That wasn't enough at all. She'd come with a purpose in mind, and she didn't want to go home without achieving it. She knew she was stubborn and a bit of a control freak, although she didn't like to admit it. Molly had similar tendencies. So maybe the best thing, she thought, would be to leave Italy and go home with a goal unreached. Maybe teaching Molly that some goals are simply unattainable, and some efforts don't produce the desired results, would be a good outcome of this trip. Maybe recognizing the limits of even a very control-oriented mind would be valuable for her daughter. And for herself, too.

She thought for another moment about this, then sighed and shook her head. This wasn't about control, about twisting and turning all the aspects of her life to assure there were no surprises. It wasn't about winning or reaching the finish line. Coming up with a way to locate Giulia when it seemed all but impossible—that wasn't the endgame. No, the endgame was very different. Because Tori couldn't shake the feeling that her life was unraveling. Jeremy was gone, Marilene was getting older, Brianna would leave soon for her internship, Molly was fast growing up, and as far as opening her own shop went, it seemed pretty likely that the landlord would rent the place out before she had enough money to feel comfortable approaching him about the lease. Something was going on in her life, some-thing she couldn't understand but that needed to be addressed. She knew it was illogical, but she truly believed that meeting Giulia could help her figure out where her life was meant to lead.

Yes, she was mad at Giulia for leaving her mother behind and causing so much anguish. She was mad at her for leaving Olive with Marilene's family, and putting Marilene in an impossible situation. And she was mad at Giulia, too, for how Giulia's selfishness had affected her life. And Molly's. She deserved an explanation. She deserved the chance to confront Giulia and make her understand all the sorrow she had caused.

There was something inside Tori that demanded to be heard. By the person who should be there for her. Tori didn't need control; she needed connection.

She sighed and went to a wooden bench near the wall to get away from the crowd. What would she do now? She supposed the most sensible thing would be to view airline schedules to see how much it would cost to change her flight back to New York. If she wasn't going to get any further with Giulia, she might as well cut her losses and go home.

That's when she noticed Emilio walking through the front entrance, zipping up his official sweater vest with the museum's logo.

He had said she should ask him if she needed any help. She supposed it couldn't hurt to seek him out now.

She rose from the bench and wove among the people heading toward the information desk and grand stairway until she reached him. "Emilio?" she said.

He looked startled for a moment, then grinned. "Tori! What are you doing out here in the lobby? I was sure that by now, you'd be hidden away in the back, elbow-deep in old documents."

She scowled. "I intended to be. But you have to make an

appointment to get into the archives. And the soonest appointment I could get is in August."

"August?" he said. "That's three months away!"

"The woman said they have a lot of people coming to do research, and their staff is small."

"Who would have known?" he said. "I never imagined this would be a problem for you."

"Me either," she said. "I hate to ask but... is there any way at all you can help me?"

He looked around, then rubbed the side of his eye with his index finger. "I don't know... I don't know how that department works. I'm not very important here at all, my friend. I just walk around and try to look intimidating so people don't touch the artwork or carry drinks from the café up to the exhibit halls..."

She watched him for another moment, then shook her head. "I'm sorry. I didn't mean to put you on the spot. I didn't know what else to do. I can't go home and come back in August. This was my only shot." She looked up at the ceiling. "I'm such a fool. Why didn't I think this out? Why didn't I..."

"No, wait," he said. "I do have an idea. Can you stay here for the rest of the day, find a way to occupy yourself?"

"Stay? Of course! This is the story of my family."

"Then meet me here, right here, at four fifty. On the dot. Okay?"

"But you said I needed to catch the last ferry at five. I won't be able to get back to the dock that quickly."

"I have an idea. And I think it will work. I'll see you then. Don't be late."

With that, he walked past her and toward a door marked *Ufficio di Sicurezza.*

She watched him go through the doorway. She didn't like depending on others, especially strangers. And she certainly didn't like asking strangers to break the rules, which seemed to be what she'd done. The way he'd sounded, she was pretty sure his idea involved doing something prohibited.

But at this point, her only choices were to give up or put herself in his hands.

So it wasn't a choice at all.

EIGHTEEN

MAY 2019

Tuesday

With nearly five hours to go before she would meet Emilio, Tori set out to discover more about the Parissis, her ancestors. She went back up the grand staircase and proceeded through the long hallway, past the room with the wedding dress and toward the other galleries on that floor. One was devoted to the origins of the castle in the late 1600s, when the then patriarch of the family, Gustavo Parissi, purchased the island and commissioned a Florentine architect to design the vast structure. And another gallery centered on Patricio Parissi, who headed the Parissi family when Giulia and her sisters lived in the castle. Known variously as an inventor, hermit, and benefactor, Patricio extended dozens of invitations to the greatest artists, scientists, and writers of his day. According to the display, he was also a generous employer, encouraging his guests to serve as mentors to members of his household staff who showed interest and promise.

Tori read all of the information in frames and on signs posted to walls, fascinated by the story of this unusual man. It seemed inconceivable to her that she was a descendant of such a wealthy family. She'd grown up modestly, in the small house where she still lived, her life nothing like the ones these relatives evidently had led. It was almost frightening, the disconnect between who she was and who her grandmother had been. While she recognized how much Marilene had given up to save Olive from a life with strangers, she nevertheless thought again how wrong Marilene had been to keep all this to herself. Yes, Marilene had her own reasons, her own awful memories, that led her to behave as she did. And the truth was, many people didn't find out about their heritage until later in life. There were so many television shows and articles these days about people— often celebrities—who studied their genealogy and discovered all kinds of surprising relatives from their past. Gangsters some- times, or heads of state, or other strange and unexpected characters.

But she wasn't a celebrity. She was a thirty-six-year-old single mother who suddenly was chasing ghosts and starting to feel that if she looked in the mirror, she wouldn't even recognize herself. A woman whose only friend at this moment was a seventy-something man who was about to break the rules as a favor.

And though it didn't make sense, she couldn't shake the feeling that her grandmother—the biological one, Giulia—was throwing obstacles in her path. Daring her to continue, hoping she'd be intimidated. So she wouldn't have to face Tori and explain herself.

It's not going to work, Giulia, she thought. *You're not going to scare me away.*

The last exhibit in the room was the saddest of all. It had framed posters that described how the Nazis had invaded Parissi Castle, and how those who weren't able to escape were either killed or arrested and sent to the mainland to eventually be deported to concentration camps. Along one wall, a row of tiny crystal vases along a wooden ledge commemorated guests and staff members believed never to have made it off the island.

Tori thought again of home and how much she missed Molly and Marilene. And Albie, too. She looked at her phone, and realizing that it was now about seven in the morning at home, decided to give them a call. She walked to the lobby and through a set of glass doors to a pretty sun-drenched patio.

"Hello?" Mar said sleepily.

"Hi, Mar. It's me. Sorry to wake you. I don't seem to call at the best times, do I?"

"Oh, it's fine. I'm getting up. How are you doing?"

"I'm okay. Just feeling a little lonely. I'm at the museum. There's a nice man here who's helping me. He's the innkeeper and he also works here. You wouldn't believe how many tourists there are. They say it's become more and more crowded each month, and—"

"Honey, can we talk another time? I'm still half asleep and I'm not even focusing."

"What? Oh, sure. That's fine. Molly's not up, is she?"

"No, and I think it's best to give her a little more time in bed. She had some trouble falling asleep last night."

"Why? Is something wrong?"

"No... well, the ballet cast was posted yesterday afternoon, and she didn't get the role she wanted."

"She didn't get Alice?"

"The teacher gave it to another girl. She made Molly the understudy and she's in all the other dances. But she's disappointed."

"Oh no. Oh, I feel horrible that I'm not there."

"She'll be okay. It was just a surprise. I could wake her if you want but I was going to let her sleep until seven thirty this morning. But I could..."

"No, you're right. I'll call later, okay? When she wakes up, just let her know that I called and I love her and I'll call again later."

"Of course, I will, honey. Take care and we'll talk later. Enjoy yourself. We're fine. Don't worry about a thing, okay?"

Tori agreed, but she hung up feeling terrible that she wasn't home for her daughter. She knew Molly must be crushed. Molly had worked out the whole cast list in her head and thought she knew exactly what Mademoiselle Diana would do. She was so strong and got her way so often. This was the first time Tori could remember that something hadn't gone according to her plan. And what was also strange was Mar's attitude. Enjoy yourself? It was almost as if Mar had forgotten, or no longer wanted to acknowledge, why Tori was even here.

It was exactly what happened all the time, now that Tori thought about it—her family pretending that certain disturbing events simply didn't exist. Like on that strange day she'd come home from school to hear the sound of someone crying. It was about a year after her mother had thought she was lost in Bloomingdale's—except this time, it was her father who was distraught. He worked as an accountant and never came home in the middle of the day, and she remembered feeling confused and terrified. She went upstairs to her parents' bedroom. The door was closed, and before she could completely open it, her mother came dashing out, her face red.

"Oh, Tori!" she'd said. "I didn't realize how late it was. Look at you, home from school already. You know something? I don't have much in the house for a snack, but I'm so in the mood for ice cream. What say you and I go get a couple of cones?"

For the life of her now, Tori had no idea why she didn't push her mother for answers about the sound of her father crying. She supposed she knew that her mother wouldn't want to talk about it and would try to avoid her questions. And she never liked upsetting her mother. She also remembered thinking that if she tried hard enough, she could convince herself that she hadn't heard the sound at all—that her father wasn't crying, that he wasn't even home. Which was exactly the situation when she and her mother arrived back from the ice cream shop: Dad wasn't around, and when he did come home at six, his normal time, he looked fine.

Tori never knew what had made her dad cry. She never asked about that day, and she was never told. But that was the day she realized that this was how they did things in her family —they ignored what they didn't want to face. Looking back now, she could see that life in her family had always been one big power grab. One ongoing effort by her parents to gain control of the narrative.

She looked again at her phone, hoping that Jeremy had called her and left a message, and maybe because of spotty reception it had only come through now. She wanted so much to talk to him. She felt as though she were losing herself, standing here on this patio surrounded by unfamiliar faces and foreign words floating in the air. Even now, all these years after that ice cream cone day, she had to admit that she still wanted control as much as her parents had. She'd come here to try to get answers, yes, but she'd also come here to try to know herself better. To learn about the parts she'd never known. The secrets she would refuse to ignore.

She couldn't help but believe that the opposite was happening: She was rapidly losing hold of the parts of her life that she'd thought would always be secure.

She went to the outdoor food stand to get a sandwich, and after eating, she returned to the museum, obsessively reading each plaque and leaflet as she explored the rest of the galleries. She thought of Marilene's family, her mother and father, and the way they tried to isolate their children from the atrocities of the war. Those people were her history, too. She wanted to learn more about them as well.

Before she knew it, it was four thirty. The museum galleries started to empty. In the lobby, the crowds were heading out the front door to make their way down the stone steps and over to the dock to catch the ferry back to the mainland. The workers at the information desk, including the English-speaking woman with whom she'd gotten nowhere, turned off the lamps at their stations. Tori arrived at the spot where she'd seen Emilio earlier and waited. At four fifty, he came down the grand stairway and over to her. He looked around stealthily, watching the people leave. When she and he were the only two in the lobby, he tilted his head, indicating that she should follow.

She followed him behind the information desk and down a long, dark corridor. At the end, there was a glass door that read *Dipartimento di Ricerca*, with "Research Department" printed underneath. He took out a large key ring and unlocked the door, then pulled it open.

"What the public doesn't know is that there's one more ferry that leaves at six o'clock to take the security officials back to the mainland," he was saying as Tori took in the scope of the room. "We spend the extra hour checking for lingerers and turning off lights, and then the night guard takes over. So, my friend, go ahead inside. Don't turn on any lights or you'll attract attention—there's still plenty of sunlight coming from the windows, and you can use your phone light if you need to. I'll be back for you in forty-five minutes. See what you can discover by then."

He turned and left, and she watched the door slowly glide shut. He'd been right—though the room was darkened, there was adequate sunlight streaming in from the high, narrow windows to guide her way. She went through the long room, past rows of tables and chairs with lamps and USB ports. Beyond the desks, she entered an area that looked like a warehouse, with aisles of metal shelving units that rose from the floor nearly up to the ceiling, all lined with cardboard boxes. There were rolling ladders affixed to the shelves.

She started at the left and walked down one aisle and up the next, not sure what she should be looking for. Signs were posted at various points along the shelving, and she assumed these identified what was in the nearby boxes, but the words were in Italian. She didn't know what she'd been expecting to see; she hadn't thought about it, as she'd been so fixated on getting inside. And she supposed she'd expected to be there during normal hours, when there'd be people to help her. The email she'd received from Signor Mansirio had been so friendly. She'd even assumed there'd be English-speaking staffers to help her find materials related to Giulia. How naïve she'd been, to think this would be easy.

She continued walking down one aisle and up another, trying to make sense of the signs. She supposed she could take out her phone and look up some of the Italian words to find their translation. But that would take time, and she didn't think it was the most efficient approach, at least not at first. Instead, she thought, she'd just keep looking, hoping she'd see Giulia's name on one of the signs.

That didn't happen—but soon there was a sign that caught her attention: "*Isola di Ciani.*" That was Marilene's family's island—the island where Giulia had shown up after she'd escaped from the Nazis. The sign had arrows along the bottom pointing in the direction of several large boxes beneath it. It seemed perhaps a little far-fetched to expect these boxes to reveal where Giulia now was, but having spent the whole day reading what had happened on this island, the entire collection of boxes had an even larger significance. The items they held told stories about the people who had once lived here in this castle and this region—their dreams, families, plans, hopes, work, and joy. The things that mattered to them, the things they loved. The people on Parissi Island had had so much to live for, and they had suffered horribly when the Nazis arrived as had so many others. Tori felt there was something right, something necessary even, in taking stock, as much as she could, of all that was lost.

She pulled one box off the shelf. It was tall and rectangular, the size of a moving carton in which you might pack linens and towels. Fortunately it wasn't heavy. She carried it away from the aisles, walking slowly since the box was so tall that she almost couldn't see where she was going. When she reached the open space where the tables were, she placed it on the floor. It was sealed with packing tape across the top, and she picked at an edge with her fingernail and then ripped the tape back carefully, knowing that she'd have to reseal the box as best she could before she left.

She pulled back the flaps and looked inside. There was a muddle of objects tossed haphazardly inside. It was hard to believe that this was the way the museum handled such precious artifacts. But then again, this was a new museum staffed mainly by local people who had personal ties to the area. When she thought about it that way, she realized that what had been collected and stored in this space, this assemblage of materials waiting to be investigated and cataloged, was pretty amazing.

At first, the box seemed to contain mostly junk. Tori thought that if she didn't know better, she'd have assumed the items were destined to be lined up on a folding table outside someone's garage, with handwritten prices on stickers. She would have sworn she'd seen similar items around town back home last June, the month when nearly everyone in town either held or thought about holding a tag sale. She pulled out old wall calendars from the 1940s; brass candlesticks; a ceramic serving platter covered in bubble wrap; a terra cotta garden pot; two small table lamps; a map of the world dating back to 1935; a wooden box with knobs that seemed to have once been a radio; a child's wooden toy train; a stack of white linen dinner napkins, faded in spots to yellow and brown.

She dug further, and then grasped a white envelope, about the size of a sheet of paper. It was sealed, and she peeled it open and looked inside. There were a handful of black-and-white photographs inside, and she pulled them out and started to go through them. The top one was a photograph of three children, including a girl about Molly's age. Tori studied the girl—her long chin, her thick eyebrows and hair, her wide mouth—and suddenly it hit her: This was Marilene! This was Marilene as a child—an image Tori had never seen before. She looked so young, so carefree—so different from the Marilene she knew, who always had a determined look on her face and a list of chores and responsibilities in hand to tend to. When had Marilene changed from someone who appeared so very relaxed? Was it when Giulia left? Or when she spirited Giulia's daughter out of Italy in the dark of night? It struck her again that Giulia had caused so much damage. But why? Was she selfish? Or was there more to the story?

She looked more closely at the picture. Marilene was wearing a one-piece outfit, with a button-down top, loose shorts, and a thin, ribbon-like belt. Next to her were two little boys, twins evidently, their hair cut short. These had to be the brothers Marilene never saw again after she left Italy. They looked cute and entertaining and mischievous. Taking in these sweet children, Tori realized anew how much Marilene had sacrificed when she left her home with Olive. How awful it must have been for her to sever all ties with the family she loved; and how sad, to never make contact with them because she wanted to keep her whereabouts hidden, so Olive could stay with her. Tori wondered how often Marilene thought of these two boys, who now would be... what, around eighty? Over the years, she must have tried to imagine what had happened to them: Were they happy? Had they married? Did they have families of their own? Were they still alive?

Tori put the picture aside, but her chest sank as she thought about the pain of such a loss. Taking a deep breath, she silently vowed to talk with Marilene about her family when she returned—and to help find out what had happened to them, if that's what Marilene wanted to do. Maybe Marilene felt as she did—that she wanted a resolution: if not a reunion then at least some closure.

She turned back to the group of photographs. The second one was of her grandmother, Giulia, when she was a teenager, eighteen or so. Tori recognized her immediately, since she was familiar with Giulia's appearance, having studied the newspaper photo Marilene had put in her bag while she was on the plane. Giulia was standing in some kind of airy, light-filled room. Again, Tori couldn't get over how very lovely she was. She was wearing a white sleeveless blouse and dark shorts, holding a basket that seemed to be filled with spools of thread. Her wavy hair was pulled back into a long ponytail. Beside her was a tall man, about Giulia's age, maybe a little older. He was very handsome, with dark hair that fell over his forehead, a straight nose and large, intense eyes. He was wearing a short-sleeved button-down shirt, dark slacks, and sandals, and Tori could see his very broad, very muscular physique. She wondered who this man could be. He was clearly too young to be Marilene's father; could he have been another relative there for a visit? Or... was he Giulia's boyfriend? Someone she was in love with? Maybe even the man who would become Tori's grandfather?

Putting the photos aside, she looked deeper into the box and pulled out a hard-backed notebook. There was only one page inside; the rest of the pages seemed to have been ripped out. The page that remained had several handwritten paragraphs, the penmanship cramped and dark, as though the writer had pressed heavily with the pen. Holding the notebook up to the light from the window, Tori thought that in several places, she could make out the word *Giulia*. It was repeated at least six times. Whoever had penned these words had been writing about her grandmother.

"Tori!" came a loud whisper from the front of the room. "Come now or we will miss the boat!"

"Coming!" she whispered back. She put all the photographs and larger objects back into the box, pressed the tape down, and returned it to the shelf. Then she tucked the notebook into her bag.

She needed Emilio to translate the words on the page.

She wanted to know what their author had written about her grandmother.

NINETEEN

SEPTEMBER 1943

Giulia nodded at Luca and thanked him, then took the cup and saucer he was offering. She breathed in, expecting the delicious aroma she remembered from the castle—strong and slightly floral, with a slight hint of chocolate. But this coffee smelled nothing like that. And it tasted thin and watery, not at all like the rich espresso Signora Russo used to serve. Giulia winced at the memory of that beautiful woman, and what Pietro said had happened to her.

"Not very good, is it?" Luca said, misinterpreting Giulia's expression.

"No, it's not that—"

"Because it's been impossible to get coffee beans during the war. Your Signora Russo must have been some kind of magician, if you had real coffee at the castle. Roasted barley is a sorry substitute, I know. But it's not so bad once you get used to it."

"No, you misunderstood," Giulia said, not wanting to appear rude. "It wasn't the coffee I was reacting to. It was... I was only thinking..."

"Sad thoughts?" he asked.

She smiled at his kindness. "I suppose."

"Unfortunately, there seem to be a lot of those these days," he said. "That's why I love coming here. The kids, they... they entertain me. They know so little, so they can be exactly what kids should be. I never grow tired of them."

She nodded, thinking of what Pietro had said last night, how he wanted to protect his children from any knowledge of the war and the danger. Luca was right, they were entertaining because they were so carefree. As children should be.

"May I join you?" He gestured toward the space next to her on the bench. She shifted over, then watched him as he came closer and sat down. He had lovely eyes, she thought. Such a stunning green. But serious eyes, too. Eyes that had seen a lot. He appeared older than Vincenzo and the boys in her class back home, but maybe that was an illusion. He might have been a young man, but he clearly had an old soul.

She noticed that he was gazing at her sketchpad, which was resting on her lap. "You are an artist," he said.

"I'm... I'm a dressmaker. I work with fabrics, not paints."

"That looks like a wedding dress."

"It is. It's from memory. Something I sewed. At Parissi Island."

"It must have been beautiful."

She moved the sketchpad to the bench and put her cup alongside it. "It was."

"Where is it now?" he asked.

"Hopefully on its way to New York. With my older sister. It was for our future, that I gave it to her. In America."

"I see," he said and took a sip of his coffee and then set his cup on the bench, too. "And how is your foot this morning?" he asked.

"Better," she said. "I'm anxious to get this bandage off."

"I don't blame you, it must feel very uncomfortable," he

said. "But listen to Pietro. He will tell you when it's safe to remove it. He's a brilliant doctor. He trained at the University of Bologna and practiced at some of the best hospitals in Italy. He's performed complex surgeries and published many papers. He was very well-known in medical circles before he left for here. Three years ago this December."

She felt her lips press together and turned her head, not sure if he noticed her discomfort at the mention of Pietro. She couldn't ask him about last night. That was one of the rules, that she could talk about what Pietro said to her only when she was in his study. Still, this news about the doctor surprised her. She'd thought he was a small-town doctor, like the one they had in her village when she was young. She couldn't help but think that it must have been a hard decision, to give up such an important career. But he did it for his family, his children. He loved them so much.

They were silent for a moment. Then Luca spoke. "Did he upset you when he spoke to you last night?" he asked. "I thought he should have waited a day or so. You'd been through so much. But he was worried you'd start asking questions and upset the children. Or leave before he had a chance to tell you everything."

She looked at him and scowled. "I'm under the impression we are not supposed to talk about what goes on in the study. He made that very clear. Along with everything else."

"I think perhaps his words were too strong," Luca said. "He's only trying to do the best for his family. And his children's future. I think one can understand that."

"I don't like being pressured to do something that feels..."

"Feels what?" he asked.

"If I do what he wants, I'm only digging myself further into this place and putting myself more in danger. And making it harder to leave. The more I help with all his plans, the more I'll be stuck here and unable to help my own family. He has his family, and I want mine. And you want yours, too, I imagine. It's what everyone wants."

"Sometimes there are things bigger than oneself," he said.

She looked down, thinking of Signora Russo. The poor woman who was among those brutally murdered, according to Pietro. Giulia remembered that she had had hopes for her future, too. She had told them often that she was going to work for a few more years, save up money, and then move in with her son's family in Switzerland. She was excited about that. Of course, some would say she was a hero for what she'd done, the messages she'd relayed about the Nazis. But was this the way she'd wanted to end up? Did she want to be a hero, if it meant dying like that? Was that what her son wanted to have happened?

"You have to understand, Giulia," Luca said. "Not everyone is clear-headed. The war has done damage. Everyone is in pain. In so many ways."

He leaned over to pick up a long blade of grass. He studied it between his fingers. "Pietro was my father's closest friend," he said. "They were boys together. They had big dreams. Pietro always wanted to be a doctor, and my father wanted to be a writer. He grew up to be an editor. Everyone read what he published. Then he began writing editorials against fascism. He thought he was safe, that newspapers were safe. He published three and was writing a fourth, but that one never made it into print. He left his office one night, and the next morning he was found shot dead on the street."

She raised her hand to her lips, startled. This was the story Pietro had told her last night. His friend who'd been killed. It was Luca's father. "I'm so sorry," she said.

"I was thirteen when it happened," he said. "And afterward, Pietro and Cellina made it their business to take care of the family he left behind—my mother, my sisters, and me. They were profoundly anti-Fascist, as my father was, and became even more so after that. Pietro had inherited this island, which his family had used as a place to stay in the summers, an escape from the city. But when Mussolini sided with Germany—that was all Pietro could take.

"Of course, he doesn't plan to stay indefinitely," he said. "Just until the end of the war. It was good news when Italy surrendered to the Allied forces. Now they are making progress from the South. For Pietro, it was a decision between leaving the country entirely or withdrawing to this place temporarily. He chose to come here."

"And you did, too? What about your family? You said you have a mother, sisters? Do they know where you are?"

"No. I don't want to put them in danger. My mother and her brothers are still running the vineyard in Tuscany. I will reunite with them all... when this nightmare is over."

"Vineyard? I thought that was just a story. That's what I understood from Pietro."

"No, that is true," he said. "It's been in my family for a long time. Although I'm no longer involved. We supplied Parissi Island with wine, by the way. We would send cartons on one of the supply boats a few times a month. My parents named different varieties after their children. Luca, that was the wine we sent to the castle for years. We were told that Patricio loved it. The label had an image of a house and a tree swing. Did you ever have any?"

She smiled. "I remember that wine. They served it at all the special events. It was delicious." She couldn't help but feel warmth for him now. How wonderful it had been, to see that deep-red color as the wine flowed into her glass, to take that first sip, the flavor bold but not overpowering. How sweet, that his was the tree swing on the label. She felt a new connection with him, deeper than his handsome eyes and strong build. They both were tied to Parissi Island. And now they were both here.

"I'm sorry about your father," she repeated. "I lost my mother when I was young. Not because of anything like that. She died giving birth to my youngest sister. Who died, too. I know what it's like, to grow up without a parent."

"You never recover," he said. "And I've always been aware that my father could have prevented his own death. He could have kept quiet like many people did. But that wasn't his nature. He hated the Fascists. He couldn't stand by idly while Italy lost its way. I'll never stop regretting that I didn't know him better. I was just a boy when he was killed."

She looked down. "So you know why I have to leave," she said. "For family. I'm not political. I'm just a sister looking for her sisters."

"Ah, but you have to be political these days," he said. "You have to care. How can you not care what happens to Italy? This is everything. You can't run away. This country is your home, the home of generations who will appreciate all we sacrificed."

"But this family ran away. Pietro ran away. You said so yourself."

"Well, in a sense. But in another sense, they're fighting even harder. They take in Resistance fighters who are injured. They transfer messages to the mainland to thwart the Nazi plans. It's brave work, and it's dangerous work, because it can't go on forever. Something will break. Either the Nazis will be defeated or they will find and kill us here. It's only a question of which and when."

"Then we should leave. We should all leave."

He dropped the blade of grass and turned to look at her directly. "They are quite brave, Pietro and Cellina. They put up a good front, but they know they are in danger and time is running out. That's why he sees you as so valuable. He needs you, now more than ever. The Nazis are so close, right there on Parissi Island. They could come here at any time. They could start to wonder what other activity is going on here in this string of little islands. They could suspect the work we are doing."

Giulia shook her head. "I don't even want to hear this," she said. "I told you, I'm not political. I'm just a person—"

"A Jewish person—"

"A person who needs to leave. I need to go. My family is expecting me."

"Giulia, don't be naïve. There's little chance you'd ever get to America. I'm sure Pietro went over this. Don't you see? You are Parissi's niece, and you are your father's daughter. The Nazis would be delighted to find you. You have a target on your back."

"Exactly," she said. She heard her voice rising in tone and growing shaky. She couldn't listen to any more of his words, even if they were true. "My whole family is in danger," she said. "I have to help them—"

"And there's something else you haven't taken into account," he told her, ignoring the growing panic in her voice. "If you leave and they find you, if they see how your foot was treated, they will know that you had help. They will track you back here. They will find this family, and that would be the end of them. And of the good work they're doing."

"What are you saying?" she asked. "That I have to stay here to save them? To save you? To save all of Italy? I'm just one person."

He was silent.

She started to protest further, to say that her concerns weren't small at all. But then she let out her breath. This was exactly what Annalisa always accused her of, thinking only of herself. And here the stakes were bigger. The lives of all the people on this island were at risk. Did she still have it in her to think only of herself? And her own family?

Just then the little boys came running out.

"Luca! Luca, more candy!" they cried.

"More candy?" he asked, feigning insult. "What about what I gave you last night after dinner?"

"It's gone!" they told him.

"It's gone? Well, maybe it's just lost. Here, let me see if I can find it!" He dashed after them and they ran away, circling the trees. She couldn't help but smile. So innocent, these children. They had no idea what was going on in the world. Her heart ached for them, growing up this way. Her heart ached for the whole family, having withdrawn here so the children wouldn't need to know about the war. Her heart ached for the people of Parissi Island who were arrested or killed. And for Italy, the Italy Pietro had known, the Italy Luca's father had tried to save by writing editorials against the Fascists.

Pietro was asking her to help keep his family and the others on this island safe. And, in a way, to keep others safe—all the others, all the Jews who were in peril now and would continue to be until the Nazis were defeated. And what he needed from her was information about the layout of the castle, to help the Resistance do its work. Was that so much to ask? If she left, she'd be putting these brave people in danger. And the children, too. Shouldn't she be brave as well? Wouldn't her family understand, if she took a little longer to come home? Wouldn't they agree that she did the only right thing?

Did she even have a choice?

Luca came back to the bench. "What is it?" he said.

"I'm thinking..." Looking up at him, she shrugged in resignation. "I'm thinking that my sisters are smart and capable, and they will be alright. And if I'm delayed, if I take a little longer to follow them to America, they will understand."

Standing before her, he reached out a hand and gently touched her shoulder. She felt herself blush and looked down, as he went back to playing with the boys. She would stay for now, she thought. She would think of bigger things—Italy, this family, the Jews of her country, the future of the world. She would give Pietro the information about the castle. And she would leave when it made sense to go.

She only hoped it wouldn't be too long. And that when she got to America, she would find that her family had arrived safely, too.

TWENTY

MAY 2019

Tuesday

Together, Tori and Emilio rushed out of the building and down the winding stone staircase. Tori was nervous as she watched Emilio make his way down the steps. He looked so unsteady. She'd discovered long ago on many hiking trips with her frisky pup Albie that going downhill could be harder than going uphill, requiring less stamina but a lot more balance. And as far as stamina went, Emilio's breath grew more labored every time they reached a landing and turned to go down the next flight. Even though the sun had dropped behind the castle and the stairway was heavily shaded, she could still see his forehead and cheeks gleaming with perspiration. She was glad he was guiding her by grasping her elbow—not because she needed assistance but because she hoped it would keep him upright.

Finally they reached the bottom of the staircase and made it to the dock as the final group of castle employees were being loaded onto the boat. They climbed to the upper deck and slid onto one of the benches.

Tori rested her arm on the ledge and looked out over the

water. The surface was unsettled, bouncing and swaying as the ferry maneuvered alongside the shore and took off for the mainland.

She turned to face Emilio, who was wiping his forehead with a handkerchief. He swiped it over the bottom half of his face and then tucked it into the back pocket of his pants. "I don't usually take those steps two at a time," he joked.

"I'm sorry," she said. "I didn't mean to hold you up. The time went so fast."

"No need for apologies," he said. "I could use a good workout once in a while. The important thing is, did you find what you were looking for?"

She gave him a sideways look. "I'm not entirely sure," she said. "I think I need some help." She paused, then took a deep, courage-building breath and reached into her shoulder bag. "I think there's something here, but I..." She pulled out the notebook.

His jaw dropped. "You took it?" he hissed. He pushed the notebook face down onto the bench. Then he chuckled and shook his head. "Surely you know that you're not supposed to take things from a museum. Or is that not true in America?"

"No, it's true," she said, matching his chuckle. "But it's in Italian. I couldn't read it, so I had to bring it to you. I'll put it back. I promise."

"Meaning you intend to go there again?"

"I have to," she said. "There are more boxes from Ciani Island. That's the island Giulia went to, the island where my grandmother—the grandmother I grew up with—lived." She went on to tell him about Marilene and all she'd learned when the postcard with the wedding dress arrived at the store.

"So those are the boxes that would have information about Giulia, if there's any information to be had," she concluded. "Let me show you." She started to lift the notebook, but Emilio pressed it down again and glanced around. Evidently satisfied that none of the other staff members on board were close enough to see it or hear their conversation, he removed his hand and nodded.

She opened the notebook. "It's strange, there's only one page," she said. "All the other pages seemed to be torn out. And see—I can make out the name Giulia in the handwriting at least six times. So I think it's about her."

She held it out to him. "Can you read it?"

He removed a pair of wire glasses from the pocket of his museum vest and put them on. Then he took the notebook in both hands, resting the bottom edge on his belly, and scanned the handwriting.

"Well?" she asked.

He squinted a bit, then eyed her, and she could tell he'd read something he thought, for some reason, she might not want to hear.

"It's okay," she told him. "Whatever it says."

He looked at the notebook again and started to translate, his voice gentle. She craned her neck and studied the page, as though she were reading along.

Giulia has betrayed us. I was afraid this would happen, that a stranger would show up and threaten everything I've worked for. I shouldn't have brought her into our house. But what choice did I have? The news about Parissi Island was catastrophic. So many souls dead. That castle, that beautiful place, now a Nazi outpost. It sickened me then, it sickens me now, to think of those soldiers sleeping in those bedrooms, pounding away in their ugly boots.

And then Giulia arrived. My children welcomed her. They had no idea what the world had become, what danger was at our doorstep. They only knew that a pretty young woman on a strange boat had arrived. They are so desperate for company. And she was hurt, the injury to her foot quite bad. When she

pulled through, it made the children so happy. Marilene espe-
cially. She had no idea of the threat Giulia brought with her,
the threat that the Nazis would come after her. Giulia wanted
to leave, but I convinced her to stay. I explained how leaving
was even more dangerous. If she continued to Anzalea, the
Germans would surely have recognized her and sent her to
Poland with all the others.

So we saved her life. And now she has betrayed us, and
everything again is at risk. God forgive me, perhaps it would
have been better if she'd perished on that strange boat of hers.
What nightmare has she inflicted on my family? How could
she turn on us after all we did to save her? I am not a foolish
man, but I behaved like a fool. How did I allow myself to trust
her? We will pay for her duplicity and my bad judgment in...

"That's where it ends," Emilio said quietly as he closed the
book and lowered it to his lap.

Tori looked down at her hands. The lighthearted mood
between them had dissolved. She shivered.

"That must be Marilene's father's notebook," she said. "He
was a doctor, she told me all about him. But I don't understand.
What could have made him so angry at her? To regret saving
her life..."

"I couldn't say..."

"Could she have turned them over to the Nazis? But why
would she do that? After they'd saved her?"

Emilio shook his head. "It's impossible to put ourselves in
their shoes. People make a lot of questionable decisions when
they feel unsafe."

"You think she felt unsafe?"

"Sure, she did," he said. "For one thing, she was a Parissi.
One of the three nieces. Patricio was famous, he was the heir to
a fortune, a legendary Italian personality. And very much anti-
Nazi. Parissi tried to keep his island private, but he had supply

boats coming in all the time, and no doubt some of the boatmen took photographs that they sold to newspapers. There is a very famous one, the three nieces all dressed up. The Nazis would have recognized her in an instant."

"I know that picture!" Tori said. "Marilene gave it to me. Giulia must have left it behind, and Marilene took it when she left Italy."

She paused. "Go on," she added. "You said that for one thing, she was a Parissi. Was there another thing? Another reason she'd feel threatened?"

He studied her for a moment. "Tori... do you not know that your grandmother was Jewish?"

Tori felt herself shudder in surprise. "What?"

"Giulia's mother—that would have been your great-grandmother—was Patricio's sister, Olivia. She was disowned by their father for marrying the family's Jewish tailor. Patricio lost contact with her. He didn't know she died until Giulia and her sisters came to the castle and told him."

"Olivia," Tori murmured. "My mother's name was Olive. Giulia named her daughter after her mother." She shook her head. "I had no idea she was Jewish. Why wouldn't Marilene have told me?"

"Maybe she didn't know," Emilio said. "She was a child and quite sheltered on that island, according to this notebook."

Tori looked back out at the water. The news about Giulia made her story more complicated. And it raised new questions. Marilene's family had taken such a risk, hiding her grandmother. The Nazis would have wanted her, both because she was a Parissi and because her father was Jewish. Giulia had to have known what a liability she was to this family. They had rescued her, and Marilene's father had treated her injury, which must have happened as she was fleeing from Parissi Island. What had she done to betray the Ciani family—and why would she have wronged the very people who had saved her?

Planning her trip here to Italy, Tori had thought the worst of her grandmother. She'd developed a whole picture in her head —cold, mean, and unspeakably selfish, for abandoning her daughter. Still, Tori had held out hope that she was wrong, that there was a reasonable explanation for why Giulia had stayed away. But this revelation from Dr. Ciani's notebook made the odds of such an explanation very small. And the picture in Tori's head seemed increasingly likely to be accurate. Had she betrayed someone who had helped her? Did Tori even want to know the truth?

She turned back to Emilio. "How do you know all this?"

He smiled. "Everyone around here knows this. Anzalea was built around the Parissi family. They were what kept everyone in business. The markets supplied the island with food, the port was busy all the time accepting shipments of furniture, bedding, and garments to ferry out to the island. Mostly to Parissi Island but to some of the smaller islands in this area, too. Travelers who were going to the castle to work often stayed in our town for a night until they were summoned. Entertainers—musicians, singers, performers of one kind or another—traveled through here on their way to be part of the castle's festivities. Builders, electricians, plumbers—they all stopped in Anzalea. Parissi Island was like a thriving city, and our community thrived because of it.

"My family, too—we owned a little market connected to the house," he added. "Where the breakfast room is now—that was a dry goods market. My grandfather had a boat, and it was my father's job to take supplies out to the island. They'd meet up with the boathouse workers there and learn all about what was going on. My father did that for years, until Parissi Island was invaded."

He looked down at his notebook. "Funny, right?" he said. "This notebook Pietro Ciani kept—see how it only has one page, the page with the writing? I've seen this before. People were so

uncertain back then—on the one hand, they wanted to memori-
alize things, and on the other hand, they were scared. Can you
imagine what would have happened if the Nazis landed on his
island and found this page? Pietro wouldn't have been able to
deny that he knew Giulia was a Parissi and a Jew—and the fact
that he was hiding her in his home would have been disastrous.
These dual drives to keep records and to keep everything
hidden. So much quiet, so many secrets. It's not natural. I think
—now, I don't know this for sure—but I suspect he wrote pages
from this notebook, then thought better of it and tore them out
to hide, so no one would know what he'd done until years in the
future. Maybe he was planning to hide this page, too. Maybe he
never got around to it."

Tori took the notebook and ran her fingers along the ripped
edge inside, where the missing pages were. "You think he did
that?" she asked.

"It's possible. You know, there was a housekeeper at Parissi
Island. Signora Russo, her name was. She's a hero now. Nobody
knew it at the time except a very few people, but she was a spy
for the Resistance. She would send messages about the German
forces to the Americans moving northward from Sicily. And it
wasn't until recently that this was discovered. She'd had all
kinds of information about the castle—who the guests were,
what life was like, how the household was organized—that she
hid in closets and under floorboards. That's how much of the
castle's history was learned. From Signora Russo's hidden
messages."

Tori looked out toward the water again, feeling hot tears
stinging her eyes. Once again, the emotion she felt surprised
her. She didn't become emotional like this at home. But it was
heartbreaking, that there were heroes like Signora Russo, who
gave their lives to help defeat the Nazis. And like Marilene's
father, who put his family in danger by taking Giulia in when
she'd washed ashore after fleeing the Nazi invasion of Parissi

Island. And then, it seemed, there were people like her grand-mother, Giulia. People whose worst instincts rose up when they were most fiercely tested. People who could betray those who had helped them.

She felt Emilio pat her hand, which was resting on the bench near him. "Don't despair, Tori," he said. "You've uncovered a tiny puzzle piece. The puzzle may look far different when you see the whole thing."

She looked back at him wryly, grateful for his attempt to cheer her up but not buying his argument.

"I mean it," he told her. "I've been on this earth for a long time. Much longer than you. And I learn something every day. And one of the things I've learned is that it's not what we say that tells the story. It's what we keep secret. Take my father, for instance. Have you met him back at the hotel yet?"

She shook her head.

"You will," he said. "Now, this is a man who went through the war, who was living right here on the mainland around the time that Parissi Island was stormed. And yet he has never spoken about those years. We know only that he ended up in Switzerland, where he met my mother, and they went on to live in England, where my sisters and I were born. I've spent a life-time wishing he'd tell us what he went through. How did he manage during the war? Was he even in Italy during the Nazi occupation? He never says a word about it. I think he fears reliving it. But by holding it in, I believe he relives it every day."

"I'm sorry," Tori said.

"I don't tell you this to make you feel bad for us," he said. "All in all, my father's life was more good than bad. I tell you this only to give you something to take with you. It's what we hide that causes all the misery. At least, that's what I think. If you want to know someone's story, if you want to know the sources of someone's choices, don't listen only to what's said. Learn what they hide.

"Give Giulia a chance," he said. "There's still much that's hidden."

They arrived at the dock, and she put the notebook back into her bag, then followed Emilio off the boat and onto the dock. The little town was alive in the twilight, the bars and cafés hopping, the lights outside each establishment twinkling.

"I'm going to have a drink, see who's out and about tonight before I turn in," he said. "Join me?"

She shook her head. "No, thank you. I'm tired and need to get some sleep. And I need to call home. I miss my daughter."

He nodded and tapped her shoulder. "Don't go to bed hungry," he said. "My daughter can send up a nice meal to you. Tell her I said so."

"Thank you," she said. He waved and headed toward the strip of restaurants, and Tori began the short walk along the piazza and over to the hotel. Though she had found the town so charming last night, it didn't hold the same magic now. She was touched by what Emilio had said, about how people's secrets were more important than what they shared. Was he right? Were the secrets the key to understanding people? The key to understanding what Giulia had done? And why?

If that was so, then she had to get back into the archives. Tomorrow and maybe multiple times. Because the boxes there held secrets. And those secrets could be the key to learning about Giulia and maybe even finding her whereabouts.

She walked into the hotel, determined to convince Emilio to sneak her again into the archives.

There were still at least a dozen more boxes she needed to open.

TWENTY-ONE

SEPTEMBER 1943

"And the grand staircase was..." Pietro said from behind his desk, his chin lowered as his small eyes peered at Giulia, over his glasses.

"To the left of the kitchen if you were facing the front hall," Giulia answered, her voice even and steady, as though she were reciting something innocuous, a grocery list or an inventory of freshly sewn clothing ready for pick-up at her father's store.

"And how many steps to the grand staircase?"

"I never counted."

"Ten? Fifteen? Twenty?"

"Maybe fifteen."

"And how wide is the staircase?"

"Pretty wide."

"The same as our stairs here? Twice as wide? Three times?"

"Maybe twice. Or two and a half."

It was five days after she'd arrived, and a routine had started to take shape. In the mornings she'd go outside to the backyard to sketch, adding details to the wedding gown as she remembered them, depicting it from the back and in profile, as well as from the front. Sketching the gown from memory transported her back to those long, dreamy days in the castle: sewing dresses to help her mentor, Savio, with his masterpiece; meeting her sisters for splendid meals in the formal dining room; and sneaking away to the main or rear boathouse to see Vincenzo.

Sometimes as she was sketching, she'd be interrupted by Luca, who brought her that strange, weak coffee and sat down beside her for a moment to look at her drawings. She liked being with him, but she was also relieved when he left to wrestle with Massimo and Matteo. He made her feel anxious, with his penetrating eyes and serious nature. While he was playful with the children, he wasn't playful with her, not as Vincenzo had always been. She wasn't used to seeing a young man who smiled only when he was entertaining children, but mostly seemed to carry the weight of the world on his shoulders.

While she was outdoors, Cellina would call everyone in for breakfast, including Signor and Signora Brambilla and Signorina Ottavia. Cellina believed in big morning meals, so there were plenty of breads, pastries, cheese, fruit, meats, and egg dishes on the table. When everyone was finished, Signorina Ottavia would take the children upstairs to the large, sunny playroom on the third floor for their morning studies, Cellina and the Brambillas would clear the table and start in on the morning chores, Luca would find a quiet spot outside to read, and Giulia would go with Pietro to his study.

Having learned that Giulia was a skilled dressmaker, Pietro had informed the children that he'd hired her as a seamstress, to sew and repair clothing and bedding, so the family no longer had to order those items and withstand the high costs and delays involved in transporting them from vendors in Rome. They believed she went into his office every morning to choose fabrics, threads, buttons, and other supplies and prepare orders to be ferried on the regular supply boat to the mainland. But what she was actually doing was answering his endless list of questions about her uncle's island and castle.

He wrote down her answers about the stairway. "Okay, now let's talk about the tower," he said. "Did your uncle use the grand staircase to get there?"

"Yes."

"And how many flights up?"

"Up three flights."

"And then?"

"You walked down a long corridor and through a doorway, and then up another small set of stairs, until you came to the circular landing."

"And that led?"

She sighed. Pulling herself up from her chair, she limped to the window behind Pietro's desk. Her foot was showing signs of healing, and Pietro had wrapped it in a thinner, lighter bandage. It was hard for her to even remember the stinging, stabbing pain she'd felt that first morning on the island, or the sickening sensation of oozing blood when she put the merest bit of pressure on her toes. Her bad foot could bear her weight now without causing her any pain, and she no longer needed a cane to walk, although she moved much more slowly without it. Pietro had said he thought they could remove the bandage for good before long.

"And that led?" he repeated.

"To the doorways," she murmured as she looked outside, the shutters open to let in the daylight. Across the patio, Luca was sitting on the stone bench, reading his book. He loved fantasy novels, she'd found out. Stories of sorcerers and of spirits that lived in the clouds and the ocean. And he loved mythology and mathematics and the complexities of the natural world—the stars and planets and the tides. He liked to figure things out, to understand how things worked together and why things fell apart.

Even the wedding gown she was sketching filled him with questions: Why eight layers of tulle and not seven or nine? Why four folds by the hip and not three or five? Why opalescent beads and not opaque? What made the dress so harmonious to the eye? The symmetry of it, the shape, the drape, or something else? She loved his questions, even as she searched her mind for answers that would not come. She was someone driven by instincts, feelings, intuition. His need for concrete facts fascinated her, as her reliance on passion and raw emotion seemed to intrigue him.

"How does this all come so naturally to you?" he'd asked her yesterday morning. "Where are the *rules*? Did you memorize the rules?"

"There are no rules," she told him.

"How can that be? The world turns on rules. Science is in your blood—your uncle, your older sister, too. Your family exists for rules."

"Not all of us," she'd said. "Not my father, and not me. We go by feelings, not rules. We sense what to do."

"But didn't your father teach you to sew?"

"I suppose I learned by watching him. But mostly he taught me to trust myself. My teacher was the world. The way the grass sparkles when the sun comes out at just the right moment following a rainstorm. The way the surface of the sea dances to the rhythm of a passing boat..."

"Giulia," Pietro scolded. "I must ask you to pay attention."

"I'm sorry," she said, turning from the window, her hand drifting down to her collarbone. "The tower? There were two doors. One that went into a storage room where my uncle kept his research supplies. He was working on a medical device that would grind together minerals and botanicals. He believed the blend would be curative. We hoped it would cure our father's illness. He had a bad heart."

"And the other door?" Pietro said, evidently uninterested in the medical device or her father.

"That went to his bedroom. He worked there, too. My sister, Annalisa, worked with him there. She was helping him."

"He worked and slept there. So it was a large room?"

"I think so. I only saw it once." She remembered how Annalisa had brought her and Emilia there one morning because they yearned to see the inside of the tower. It was so unusual, with the curved walls and complete absence of corners and edges. So different from what she'd always thought a room had to be. Everything was different at the castle. So much to be amazed at.

"But it was larger than a normal bedroom, if it had a bed and a desk and workspace, yes?"

"I think so."

"Giulia, concentrate, please. This is important. Was it bigger than your bedroom here? How much larger would you say? Twice as big? Three times?"

"Three times. I'd say... three times."

She heard her voice break and cleared her throat. Didn't he understand how hard this was for her? This was the place where she and her sisters had spent five glorious weeks, ensconced in what felt like a fairy-tale castle. This was where she and her sisters had been part of an elegant, enthralling world, a world they'd never before imagined. And now she was helping with research to prepare the spies whose aim was to kill the invaders and destroy what had been left behind as the castle's guests fled. Beautiful mahogany beds and gold-trimmed tables and glowing chandeliers would be shattered. Sheet music and sculptures and unfinished manuscripts—not to mention the remnants of her uncle's painstaking research—would turn into rubble.

It wasn't that she didn't understand the importance of Pietro's work. The Nazis had to be defeated. It was simply that her heart was breaking for a world that was no more. For a future she'd embraced with her heart that was disappearing. Or had already disappeared.

"That's all for today, Giulia," Pietro said, clearly aware that he was losing her and wasting his time. "We'll continue tomorrow."

She nodded and left the study, feeling guilty. She didn't like to be the cause of Pietro's frustration, because she liked the Ciani family. Their island was pleasant, even similar to Parissi Island—a place of tranquil isolation, removed from the real world. Theirs was a simple life, and a very appealing one. Pietro and Cellina appeared to have a strong, loving marriage, something she'd never seen before since she'd grown up with only a father. Her papa had never stopped missing his wife. Even though he'd been a healthy man in his early forties when he was widowed, he never yearned for another woman's touch, at least as far as Giulia and her sisters could tell. He kept pictures of their mother all around their small house, and never stopped reminding his daughters of how important it was to think of her, to speak of her, to light candles and recite a prayer every year on the anniversary of her death and the death of their stillborn sister. Their life was infused with a constant sadness for what had been lost, what might have been.

In this house, by contrast, marriage was synonymous with happiness. Pietro and Cellina were fast friends, and their relationship had a playfulness that Giulia found beautiful. There were times when Giulia would see Pietro come into the kitchen and surprise Cellina with a kiss on her cheek or tickle her ear with a feather. One evening as the women were clearing the dinner dishes, a waltz came on from the record player in the living room. Pietro took the dirty plates from Cellina's hands, put them back on the table, and then led her to the living room to dance. The little boys erupted with laughter, but the couple didn't mind. They were skilled dancers. Giulia imagined that if life were different, if there'd been no war, Pietro and Cellina would have had a fine life, going to dances and parties. When Pietro took Cellina in his arms, they looked as young as teenagers. Cellina's complexion glowed and her eyes sparkled.

And one night when Giulia went downstairs for a glass of water before bed, she noticed the door to Pietro's study open, and she caught sight of the two of them by the desk. Pietro was seated, reading the newspaper, and Cellina was standing behind him, rubbing his back and massaging his shoulders. Then he turned and drew her to his lap, and she slid her arms around his neck. Giulia had never seen a middle-aged couple behave so tenderly toward one another, and it captivated her. Luca had told her that Cellina had attended classes to be a doctor, too, but she'd given up her medical studies when the family left Rome. Pietro had promised her she would return to her studies after the war. The two of them seemed to want nothing but happiness for each other.

It was the kind of love she hoped to have for herself someday.

That evening, as usual, the family and staff gathered in the living room, as Signor Brambilla closed the window shutters so the lights of the house wouldn't attract attention. Pietro took a children's storybook from the bookcase and began reading, as the pajama-clad boys climbed into their mother's lap on the sofa. The story was about a boy who learns he's a prince, which makes him feel newly responsible for others. He then leaves his home and travels to a remote village to save all the people and animals from an approaching storm.

Pietro paused his reading to explain that the story was about accepting responsibility and sacrificing when necessary for the greater good. As he spoke, Marilene came to sit on the carpet so she could put her head on her father's knee. Even though the children were isolated, Giulia knew that their parents made them feel loved and secure, and that this would serve them forever.

And she saw anew what was missing in her life, what her wild behavior had been all about. She'd laughed with boys all the time, glad that she was the prettiest one in the family. She liked meeting new people, being the center of attention. She had enjoyed her silly flirtations with Vincenzo. But now, she wondered if a deeper longing had made her behave so frivolously. She wanted to belong to someone. She didn't want to be an outsider. She wanted a family of her own. To make up for the motherless childhood she'd had.

She looked at Luca, wondering if he also wanted what the Ciani family had. If he thought connection could be the answer to his grief over his father's murder. If the cure for losing love was finding it again.

Then he turned her way, and their eyes locked for a second. She saw in his gaze that he was feeling, thinking, what she was. Her heart sped up.

The moment was over too soon, as Pietro turned the page and continued with the book. She wondered if Pietro had noticed the two of them focused on one another, and if that was why his voice now sounded harsher. She looked down, embarrassed. She suspected that whatever she and Luca were feeling, Pietro would want it to stop. He would never want emotions to get in the way of his work. And she had to admit that she was intimidated by him, as he had all the power in the house. She was scared to cross him.

She folded her hands on her lap, trying to listen to the rest of the story. In the coming days, she knew, Pietro would ask her about the hidden staircase in the castle that she'd used to escape. He'd ask where it was located, how big the doorway was, how many steps, how long the distance from the stairway to the back door and from the back door to the boathouse where the *pattino* was stored. He'd ask her about the construction of the dock, its stability, and the perimeter of the railing—was it wood or iron? And as she murmured her answers, her heart would break a little more. And her memories would grow tainted by the realities of this awful world where they all had to live.

"What are you making me today?" Marilene said the next day after the family had eaten lunch and Giulia had gone back outside to the stone bench to work on her sewing. Pietro was adamant that his children believe Giulia was staying on as a household employee. He had instructed her to spend at least three hours each afternoon making garments for the children.

Giulia didn't mind. She enjoyed crafting clothes. She loved that she could choose from among the beautiful fabrics she'd seen in her closet, which Cellina had ordered with the intention of learning to sew and making outfits for the family herself. But she didn't have the patience for it and was happy to hand off the job. She never touched the sewing machine she'd ordered.

Giulia smiled as Marilene sat down on the grass in front of her. She liked the girl, who was assertive yet sweet, and so accepting of her unusual upbringing. The little boys were having their afternoon rest, so the garden was quiet.

"I'm thinking of making you a special dress," Giulia said, pointing to the red tulle fabric alongside her.

"Can you really do that? Did you sew special dresses when you lived in the castle?"

"I did," Giulia said. "Even a wedding gown once. I've been sketching it from memory. Want to see?" She pulled out her notebook from the basket and showed the drawing to Marilene.

Marilene ran her fingers over the page. "That's so beautiful. Whose was it?"

"Nobody's yet. But I gave it to my older sister, Annalisa, to take to New York. She's hoping to get married in it. Then maybe we'll pass it down, sister to sister."

"For you to wear when you get married?"

"I suppose. And our younger sister will wear it, too, some-day." Giulia spoke firmly, refusing to let herself think that this might not happen.

"Oh, that's nice. You're lucky to have sisters." Marilene put the notebook back in the basket and picked up the red fabric. "But why would I need a dress? Where would I wear it?"

"I don't know," Giulia said. "But this fabric is too pretty to do anything else with. Don't you ever have parties or special days here? Like birthdays... when's your birthday?"

"Not until the end of April," Marilene said. "When's yours?"

Giulia paused, thinking about the big birthday celebration her uncle had been planning for her next week. She'd teased Vincenzo, that he wouldn't be allowed to come to the party since he was an employee and not a castle guest. But she'd promised him that she'd sneak a big piece of Signora Russo's special birthday cake down to him at the boathouse after the party was over and everyone was asleep.

"Later this month," she said. "The thirtieth."

"That's less than two weeks!" Marilene said. "For real? How old will you be?"

"Eighteen."

"Wow, eighteen! Oh, Giulia, we must throw you a beautiful birthday party here, with music and presents and your favorite food for dinner that Mama and Signora Brambilla will make and then a delicious birthday cake. And I will wear this dress you make, and you must make a special dress for yourself, too. Do you think you can do it? Make two special dresses by then?"

Giulia laughed, charmed by Marilene's good nature. Her ability to be joyful in this situation, with no friends, no school, no going to the movies or attending parties except for this simple one she was planning, touched Giulia deeply. "I think I can do that," she said. "If you help me. I can teach you stitches and maybe we can also use the machine your mother keeps in the attic. What do you say?"

"Oooh, yes! A party with party dresses! Oh, Giulia, I'm so lucky you're here! I'm so glad Papa gave you a job that you love, so you can stay here forever with us!"

Just then a shadow appeared on the grass. Giulia looked up and saw Luca standing behind her. Marilene noticed him, too, and she jumped to her feet.

"Luca!" she exclaimed. "You're not going to believe it! Giulia's birthday is coming up! She's going to be eighteen!"

"Is that right?" Luca said. "My goodness, such an old lady!"

Giulia felt her cheeks grow hot. She remembered how the two of them had locked eyes last night, and wondered if he remembered it, too.

"Eighteen's not old!" Marilene said. "But it is an important age! We're going to throw her a wonderful birthday party. And Giulia's going to make party dresses for her and me!"

She looked toward the kitchen. "I should tell Mama all about this. Because we have to think of a present, and there's not much time. And Signora Brambilla needs to start planning. Luca, do you know where my mother is?"

"Upstairs with your brothers, I believe."

"I have to go talk to her," she said. "I'll be back soon. Giulia, don't start making those dresses without me!"

"Don't worry, I won't," Giulia called as Marilene bounded inside. She gathered up the fabrics so she could go inside. She felt jumpy around Luca after last night. She was sure that Pietro would disapprove of their growing closer. Besides, even though Luca seemed kind and friendly, there was often a touch of condescension in the way he'd talk to her. Such as the way he'd teased her about her age. *Such an old lady.*

"Wait, don't go," he said. "Please. Sit with me. There's something I'd like to discuss with you."

She hesitated, not knowing what he could want to talk about. But no matter what it was, she couldn't deny the fact that she felt drawn to him. And she had no reason to leave, especially since she'd promised Marilene she'd stay put. She rested her fabric basket on the ground, and they both sat on the bench.

"What did you want to talk about?" she asked.

He breathed in. "Pietro tells me you get upset when you tell him about the castle. He says you become distracted. And sometimes you look like you're close to crying."

She turned away, embarrassed that the two men would be discussing her. And she felt defensive, too. How could Luca not understand how hard it was for her to describe the castle to Pietro?

"Does that surprise you?" she asked, a touch of hostility in her tone. "I don't see why. It's my uncle's home and I'm being asked to help destroy it. It means something to me, that castle. Being there—it was... it was the most wonderful five weeks of my life."

"The most wonderful? And why was that?"

"Because..." She paused, hoping to find the right words. "Because my uncle, my mother's brother, created it. He loved us, my sisters and me, simply because we were her daughters. And he felt close to us and protective of us for that reason alone. And my sisters and I... we were so proud of reuniting our family. Our father with our uncle. Because... well, I don't know if you know our story...."

"Of course, I do," he said. "The Parissis are famous. Everyone knew about them. And not for the nicest reasons. Patricio's father, Francisco—he was a fierce anti-Semite. And a loyal Fascist. Did you know that?"

"Well, we knew he hated Jews. Which was why he disowned my mother when she decided to marry my father. But my uncle, Patricio—he was shattered when his father did that. He was a good man, but a very sad and lonely one, when we arrived at the castle. A recluse, everyone said. He never came down from the tower. But meeting us, his sister's daughters—it transformed him. He became a new man, a loving man, and we were the ones who changed him. Just by showing up. There was a concert one night, his first appearance at an event in the castle ever. He cried when he came into the concert hall. We'd made him so happy. We cried, too.

"And then... it ended," she said. "And it's so sad, to know what Pietro aims to do. I understand why he's doing it. But still..."

"It has to be that way," Luca told her. "As Pietro said last night when he read the children's story, sacrifices are necessary."

She bristled at his tone, which sounded patronizing. She wasn't trying to be immature or selfish. She wanted to be understood. "I'm willing to sacrifice. I just never knew that one day, I'd be giving information that would be used... to kill people. Even evil people. I'm sorry if this sounds childish to you, but I wish so much that I had left Italy... before. That was our original plan, my sisters and me—to get my father medicine and then to leave for America. We knew that things were getting more dangerous for Jews. More and more of my father's customers no longer wanted to do business with him. We thought we had time, though. We didn't realize things would happen so quickly."

He looked at the sky, then turned back to her. When he spoke, his tone was kinder. She was glad she had expressed herself in a way that moved him. She sensed a small but important change in him.

"Tell me more about your parents," he said. "Your father... how did he come to marry the daughter of a man like Francisco?"

"He was their tailor," she said. "That's how they met. But how they fell in love... that's a different story."

"What kind of story?"

She sighed, not knowing if she was strong enough to share this special story without falling completely apart. "You have to understand that my father loved being Jewish," she said. "Not only the religious part but the traditions, the stories, the embracing of life. 'Choose life'—that's what Judaism demands, he would tell us. 'Choose life.' That's what got him through the loss of my mother, through all the days and years he was so sick as his heart failed. He kept alive because that was what he had to do. He would tell us to do that, too. Even now. Forever. Choose life."

She looked down at her hands. Sitting here, she could hear her father's gentle voice.

"Tell me more about your father," he said.

"About being Jewish?" She smiled. "There was one story that he said my mother loved so much. I don't remember how it went. I just remember the end. It had to do with the love that can happen between two people from different backgrounds. Like my parents. Like how someone can change their whole life when they find someone to love. The bit I remember, it's like a poem but it's more of a promise: 'Wherever you go, I will go, and wherever you stay, I will stay. Your people will be my people and your God my God.' It's about how love transcends everything. How it unites even what seems destined to stay apart."

"That's beautiful," Luca said.

Giulia nodded. "My father would go to her house, the family's huge house in Rome, to measure her father for clothes. And that's when he would see her, my mother. And tell her his stories. One night when his work was done, he was leaving to travel back to his home. And he didn't want to say goodbye to her, because he didn't know when he'd see her again. He didn't think he stood a chance with her, a Jewish tailor.

"But that night she followed him out, and in the moonlight she whispered, 'Wherever you go, I will go.' She remembered that line from the story. And he told us that from that night on, he knew he would never stop loving her. And he never did. Even in death, she was his love."

She looked at Luca, drawing strength from her family's story. "And if there's one thing I want in this world, it's what my parents had when they met and started their family," she said. "And what Pietro and Cellina and their children have. And that's why I can't stay here indefinitely, as everyone else seems to want to do.

"I'll give Pietro all the information about the castle that he wants to carry out the attack," she said. "I've made my peace with that, as hard as it is for me to do. But then I have to go find my family. My future is with them."

Luca dropped his head and shook it, looking down at his clasped hands.

"What?" she asked. "What's wrong with what I said?"

"You have an opportunity here to be of even more help. After you finish with the castle, there'll be more to do. How can you talk of leaving? How can you avoid doing your part?"

Giulia tried to answer, but she didn't know what to say. She felt her mouth move, but no words came out. She had a right to refuse becoming further involved in these matters, didn't she? Who was he to judge her, who was he to scold her when she'd opened up so much to him...

There was a shout from an upstairs window. "Giulia!" Marilene called from the window. "Come in! Mama wants you to look at the sewing machine and see if you can work it."

Suddenly she regretted how much she'd revealed. To this stranger. But then she wondered if it was she who needed to try to understand.

Because as she started to leave, he took her wrist. "What your parents had, that's what mine had," he said. "And what you want when you think back on them... I want it as well. But Giulia, we're not put on this earth to think about our last triumphs. Our pretty past. We're put here to think about what we can do next. What we must do next."

She shook her hand free of his and ran inside.

TWENTY-TWO

MAY 2019

Wednesday

By mid-morning the next day, she had purchased another ticket for the castle—this time from a man she guessed was Emilio's father. He'd been at the front desk of the hotel when she'd finished breakfast on the patio. He was quite elderly, his face lined with wrinkles, and his neck, too, above the first button on his white shirt. And where his hairline had receded, she could see age spots dotting his scalp. Still, he was a handsome gentleman. His hair, combed away from his face, was silvery white, and his eyes were a clear blue, his teeth even beneath a short, well-groomed mustache. When he spoke, his voice was soft, and his English, though labored, was precise and elegant. When he smiled and handed her the ticket to the castle, she recognized the same warmth that she'd seen in Emilio, and she supposed he'd been as sociable and outgoing as his son when he was young.

With her ticket tucked into her pocket and Pietro's notebook deep inside her shoulder bag, she set out once again for the piazza. It was another beautiful day, and she was wearing a white linen sundress and wedge sandals with straps that crossed over her ankles. It was such a fun summer outfit, one of her favorites. She loved how white felt so light and carefree in the summer. She loved the simple V-neck style, which felt casual yet neat. And most of all, she loved how its silhouette framed her body while still feeling airy. It always filled her with admiration and delight, how even a simple garment could have such a strong and important impact on the wearer.

At the dock, she waited for the ferry to return from its earlier run and start to load the next boatful of passengers. The piazza was once again busy, with many people standing in line to get to the island, and she found a place on a bench to sit under an overhang and wait. In the distance, she could see the ferry gliding through the aqua water, looking so small and insignificant with the massive, still castle behind it. But as moving as it all was, she knew she couldn't stay here much longer. She was scheduled to stay for another week but thought maybe she should go home sooner. Especially since, after what she'd learned about Giulia, she wasn't entirely sure that she wanted to meet her. Despite Emilio's urging that she keep an open mind.

Even more important, she was needed at home. She'd spoken to Molly after she returned to the hotel last night and had some dinner—a delicious chicken dish with capers, pine nuts, and white wine that Emilio's daughter had sent up. She'd timed the call for three forty-five in the afternoon back home so she could catch Molly in Marilene's car, during the half hour between the end of school and the start of ballet class. Although she was beginning rehearsals for the recital as a member of the corps and not as the lead, Molly had sounded stoic. That was to be expected; Mademoiselle Diana ran a tight ship, and complaining was not tolerated. Tori had said she was sorry about the ballet casting, and she knew it must be disappointing, as Molly had wanted the bigger role.

"It's okay," Molly had said stiffly. "I can handle it."

"Of course, you can," Tori said. "But that doesn't mean you don't feel sad—"

"I'm fine, Mom," Molly had said. "Fine. We don't have to talk it all to death. It's fine."

"Okay," Tori said and went on to ask what was going on at school and with her friends. She hadn't wanted to harangue Molly or make her feel bad by continuing to harp on about the casting decision. But she kept hearing Emilio's voice, and what he'd said on the boat yesterday: *It's not about what we say that tells the story. It's what we keep secret.* She had to wonder: what was Molly keeping secret?

On the ferry, Tori enjoyed the cool breeze and the sight of Parissi Island coming closer. When they docked, she stepped off the boat and proceeded up the stone staircase with the other visitors. She was sure Emilio would be here—he'd said he was working today. But she didn't see him in the lobby or any of the galleries on the second floor. She had to find him. She still had the notebook, so he'd have to let her back into the archives if only to return it to the box. But that wasn't the only reason she wanted to go back. She wanted to learn more.

She wandered around the museum, studying more exhibits about Parissi and his guests, and reading menus of sumptuous meals and daily agendas for the staff. There were lists of staff members and their room assignments, and she took a guided tour of the staff quarters behind the kitchen. At one o'clock, she bought herself another lunch of fruit, bread, and cheese and ate at a table on the patio. But all the while, she kept a lookout for Emilio.

She was gathering her trash, getting ready to go back inside the museum, when she heard her phone buzz. Sitting back down at the table, she reached inside her bag and pulled it out.

It was Jeremy.

She froze for a moment, her breath static inside her chest.

She hadn't expected to hear from him. And though he'd been on her mind from time to time, she'd mostly been consumed with thoughts of Molly and Giulia. She supposed she had intentionally focused extra hard on the search for Giulia so that she didn't have to think about all she'd lost when she'd turned Jeremy down. About how lonely she'd feel when she returned home and it hit her that he was no longer part of her life. She'd hoped that night when he'd said goodbye that he'd change his mind and agree to let their relationship remain as it was. But the realist inside her said that was not going to happen. He was not going to compromise. Not this time.

The phone continued to buzz, and she knew she should answer it. But she was scared this was the final break-up call, the moment when he'd make it official that they were over.

Pressing the fingers of one hand to her lips, she used her opposite thumb to answer the call. She couldn't believe how much her hands were shaking.

"Hey," she said, trying to sound casual.

"Tori, hi." His voice sounded warm and filled with love, the way it always did, and the realization that she probably wouldn't hear it again after today made her breath stick in her chest.

"Am I catching you at a bad time?" he said. "What is it, like almost two o'clock there?"

"Well..." she hesitated, as it struck her that he knew she was away. "Wait... how do you know that? I mean, you know where I am?"

"I ran into Marilene downtown yesterday evening. I was going over to set up the equipment at Danny's for our set, and she was picking up Molly from her ballet class. I guess she had spoken to you a couple of hours earlier. I asked how you were, and she... she told me everything."

"Oh," Tori said. She felt embarrassed. There Jeremy was, setting up for his evening gig at the club, probably after a day planning his syllabus for his summer classes or maybe meeting with the Broadway producers who were hiring him as musical director for their new show. He had been right that night at dinner—he did have his life together. He had designed it exactly as he'd wanted, doing the work he loved. He was ready to add to his life, to make it bigger. To add to his circle, to widen his world, to love more.

And she was in a different place. Her life was a mess. Her family was a mess. Her parents were gone, and the grandmother she'd grown up with was not her grandmother at all. She'd come here looking for connection and identity. Hoping to find her real grandmother, and answers that would make all that had happened in the past make sense. Except that the Giulia she'd somehow hoped to find—a loving grandmother who could explain everything—didn't exist. No, her Giulia was someone capable of a major betrayal, according to Pietro's notebook.

That was so hard to accept. And she believed she had little to offer Jeremy now. He was better off with someone less in shambles. Someone more normal.

"It must have been quite a shock," Jeremy said. "I'm sure you never suspected anything like that. And I'm sorry I wasn't... I mean, with the timing and everything. I'm sorry I wasn't there when you found it all out..."

She felt her defenses rise, making her jaw clench and her chest tighten. She pressed her lips together and looked out toward the water, and up at the beautiful sky that seemed to go on forever. Yes, it was a big shock, what Marilene had told her. But she could handle it.

"I'm fine," she told him firmly. "I can deal with this. For myself, for Molly. And for Marilene, too. I know it probably sounds bizarre, that I came running here to Italy all by myself. I'm sure it sounds crazy to you—"

"No—"

"Really crazy—"

"No," he said. "Not at all."

She paused. "It doesn't?" she said softly.

"Tori, I have no doubt that you're doing exactly what you need to be doing," he said. "And I know you can handle it. You handle a million things on your own that I could never do—your work, and heading up your household, taking care of Marilene, and the way you're raising Molly. Tori, you're the strongest person I know."

She looked down at her lap, feeling all the tension, all the defensiveness, melt off her shoulders. She could hardly believe how good it felt to hear him say that.

"If you need to be there, then it was right that you went," he said. "And I know that whatever you're searching for, you'll find it. And you won't give up until you get those answers. I only called to tell you that, Tori. That no matter what happened between us, I believe in you. Whatever you're searching for, you'll find it. And when you come home, it will be because you were ready to.

"That's the person I've always known you to be," he said. "And it's one of the reasons I'll always love you."

She pressed her hand to her mouth. This was the man she knew him to be. The only person who truly saw her and understood her. And that was why she loved him. Of course, he believed in her. Of course, he had confidence in her. That was the person he'd always been.

"Tori?" he said. "You okay?"

She sighed and then spoke, trying to steady her voice. She didn't want him to hear how much his words had affected her. Or how much he meant to her. Because it wasn't fair to him, to show all that. She had turned him down, and he was moving on. He deserved for her to accept and respect his decision.

"I'm okay," she said. "And... and Jeremy... thank you. For saying that."

"It's the truth," he told her. "Anyway, I should get going, I have to be in the city today. Take care of yourself, okay?"

"I will," she said. "You, too."

She hung up the phone, then stared at it for a few moments. Suddenly all the despair she'd pushed aside that night after he proposed came pouring out. She put her elbows on the patio table and covered her face with her hands. She loved him so much. She didn't know how she would get over that. His decision to walk away had become even more painful with this quick trans-Atlantic phone call.

What was wrong with her anyway? Why couldn't she have said yes that night at the restaurant? Was she missing something, some genetic code that would cause her neurons and synapses to fire like crazy when Jeremy was around, and would induce her to see choosing a partner as a path toward security and stability—and not as an obstacle to it? Did the same genes that produced all the qualities in her—her brown hair, her dark eyes, her artistic talent—did they also have a bit of DNA that made her unable to love fully and completely? Was her need to stay apart something she'd been born with?

Something passed down from Giulia?

She thought about all the brides she had dressed and gowns she had dreamed up in the small workroom at the back of the home furnishings store. Through it all, she'd known there was something to this wedding thing that she didn't understand. What was it to love another person the way her brides loved their fiancés? What allowed a person in love to change their plans, their vision of themselves, their priorities, their whole life? How did they know they weren't sacrificing too much? Or that the card they were playing—the ace of hearts or the jack of diamonds—wouldn't make the remaining ones worthless? How did they march ahead to their wedding day, bold and unwavering, while the thought of marrying troubled her so much, she was willing to say goodbye to the most wonderful man in the world—the man she loved with all her heart, the man who wanted to marry her and be a good, loving father to her daughter?

She lifted her head and looked toward the museum, where so many of Giulia's secrets lay. She wished that Jeremy would call again to say he was willing to wait for marriage. That losing her was worse than having her turn down his proposal. She wished he'd tell her to forget that awful night, that they could go back to the way things were before the velvet box dropped out of the dessert napkin. But she understood why he didn't. He'd made it clear that five years was enough, and he wasn't going to delay the next chapter of his life any longer.

And it was sad, because the chapter they'd written together had been so wonderful. Starting on that magical night when he'd invited her onto the stage. It was warm for spring, and the band had been playing outdoors on the club's rooftop patio. Molly had a sleepover party at her friend's house that evening, so Tori had taken Marilene out for a special evening to celebrate her recent birthday. She remembered looking up, thinking about the juxtaposition of the deep-blue sky and white-hot stars. They glittered so brightly.

She couldn't help herself from wondering whether she could produce that effect in a wedding gown. How could she make the white appear so clear and vivid that it almost became a color never seen before? Would there need to be a darker counterpoint of some kind to set off the white? Maybe she could use satiny white lace atop a translucent, shadowy base fabric. But how could she do that in a way that would highlight the white instead of muting it?

She continued gazing at the sky as the evening wore on, trying to memorize what she was thinking and seeing as the music played. When she looked back down, she saw that Marilene was yawning. She knew she should get her home and tried to spot the server to ask for a check. That's when she realized that the band's lead singer was looking at her from the stage. A moment later, he addressed her as though they were the only two people in the club.

"This next song—somehow it seems written for you," he'd said softly into the microphone. "Would you come and join me up here?"

She couldn't believe this handsome musician with a wide, open smile was addressing her. Why her, of all people? Maybe he felt sorry for her, being there with her grandmother when all the other tables had couples who seemed to be in love. Maybe he'd felt she needed cheering up. She'd waved him away a few times, shaking her head and repeating "No, no, no. Really, no!" But the crowd was clapping, and Marilene was squeezing her hand on the table, and she understood that nothing was going to change until she accepted his invitation.

And to her surprise, she realized that she wanted to accept his invitation. She almost never trusted people off the bat. It took her time to warm up to people, to allow them to connect with her and to believe that they wouldn't... wouldn't hurt her somehow. New people made her nervous, so it had always seemed safer to avoid strangers, and to hold those she had to deal with at arm's length. Often when people stopped trying to get to know her—the other mothers at the ballet school, the brides she fitted who wanted to be friends—it felt like a relief. She'd even been relieved when Molly's father had moved across the country and she didn't have to hear from him except when he sent Molly a birthday card each year.

But there was something so unthreatening about this guy who was now extending his arm toward her. His face was guileless, his smile natural and casual, like an impromptu grin. He wasn't movie-star handsome, at least not in any way she could define. He didn't have huge bedroom eyes or a chiseled jaw. But he had kind, smiling eyes and a tender manner. She knew he wasn't the type to embarrass her or use her to make himself look good. Or make her regret accepting his invitation. There was something about that sincere grin, the way his eyes turned quarter moons when he smiled, and his posture, the way his shoulders were low and relaxed. This was a man who was an open book. And she liked how at ease that made her feel.

She'd risen from her seat, and the crowd erupted in cheers that she'd finally agreed. "What am I doing here?" she'd asked as he met her at the top of the three steps leading to the small, square stage, surprised at how nice her hand felt in his. She hadn't held hands with a man in so many years. His touch was gentle, his fingers warm and solid, the pads slightly roughened, no doubt from his guitar playing. She liked that his skin reflected his work, how committed he was to his art.

"You're here because Jeremy hasn't been able to take his eyes off you all night," the drummer said. "He was coming so close to the edge of the stage, we thought he was going to fall off."

Jeremy, she'd thought. What a great name.

He'd scowled at the drummer and shook his head. "You're here because I think you're beautiful," he said.

He'd gone on to sing a song he'd written called "The End of the Night Sky." It was pretty, she'd thought—tuneful and lyrical. The words—which were now sitting on her dresser at home, she'd had the original music framed—told the story of a guy who has only one night to prove how much he loves the woman he just met, and how it seemed as if the night were conspiring against him, giving way to dawn too fast. Although she'd never considered herself particularly romantic, Tori believed that everything she was feeling at that moment was encapsulated in those dreamy lyrics. Like the guy in the song, she too felt that the evening, the moment here on stage having this lovely man sing to her, was flying by.

As the song ended, Jeremy stopped playing his guitar, letting the keyboard player keep the tune going. He'd moved his microphone between them so she could sing the final line of the chorus with him: "And when the moon drifts away and the night finally ends, please, please still be here." She was reluctant at first—she didn't have a great voice—but he'd sung the line several times already, and she knew the words and melody by heart. And though she couldn't believe it the next day—she'd never done anything like that before—she leaned in at that moment and sang with him, to the cheers of the audience and Marilene's glowing smile.

He told her that weekend, when they went out to a popular Thai place in town for their first date, that he'd never done anything like that before either, and that when they said goodbye and she'd left the stage, he'd felt ridiculous and was sure she must have given him a fake phone number.

"That's what I would have done," he'd said. "I would have thought I was either a conceited jerk or just a big goof. But I saw you and your grandmother were getting ready to leave just as we were about to play that song, and I had to stop you. I had to do something. You were truly the most beautiful woman I'd ever seen."

She'd shaken her head. She wasn't at all beautiful. Her hair wasn't particularly straight or curly but somewhere in the boring in-between, the color a nondescript brown. She was short, and her bottom lip was too thick, her eyebrows not dramatic enough, her face a simple oval instead of a delicate heart shape. It didn't bother her, though. It was fine. And besides, she didn't have time to worry about her looks. She was too busy running her household, taking care of Molly and Marilene, and making a living to ensure they had a comfortable lifestyle. While Marilene earned a bit as a bookkeeper, it was Tori's income—at the store and also through the wedding gown business she ran on the side—that kept them afloat.

"It was your eyes," he said. "I saw you looking up at the sky every few minutes. Those beautiful eyes drinking everything in.

I see it now, the way you soak in the world. What does this girl see, what does this girl know? It was all I could think of that night as we were playing. I wanted you to look at me the way you looked at the sky."

Tori had taken Jeremy's hand at that moment and threaded her fingers with his. She loved that he saw her that way. It was the way she thought of herself, too—someone who yearned to understand... everything. Herself, her life, her background, her upbringing. The world, the universe, the way she interacted with it. Her feelings, her fears, the things she yearned for without even knowing she yearned for them. The things, the pieces of her, that were missing. It felt like the most wonderful compliment she could ever have received.

And here she was, she thought as she sat at a table behind the museum, in this foreign country where she was chasing the ghost of the strange woman who was her grandmother. Alone without the man she loved, the man who had written that beautiful song about the sky and sung it to her. He was the only one in the world who saw her for what she was, and who admired her for it. Other people would have thought she was crazy to be here. Marilene hadn't even completely understood it. She would have been just as happy if Tori had stayed home. But Jeremy did. He understood it. He understood her.

And yet she had turned him down.

She stood and brushed the crumbs off her dress. And suddenly she realized why she liked the dress she was wearing so much. It was the one she'd made last year, the one she'd worn last summer when Molly was away at a dance program and she and Jeremy had rented an Airbnb on the South Shore of Long Island for a week. She loved the way the skirt felt so airy and swayed in the breeze.

One evening, they'd gone to Jones Beach, the huge state park that was crowded with people strolling on the boardwalk or playing shuffleboard or pickleball on the adjacent courts.

There were big signposts along the boardwalk, lit by a spotlight from below, that recounted the history of the park. It had been built in the 1920s, as a refuge mostly for New York City dwellers who wanted to escape the summer. She and Jeremy paused to read each sign, which was accompanied by photos from long ago, the women in flared skirts and sweaters, the men in baggy trousers and button-down white shirts with under-shirts peeking through at the neck. Jeremy had taken her hand, as they contemplated what they might have been doing had they lived in the 1920s, '30s, or '40s and spent an evening here. Would they have danced to swing bands on the plaza just past where the pickleball courts now were? Played shuffleboard? Found seats in the big outdoor amphitheater and listened to a concert? Would they have been the same people they were now? It had been such a fun, playful game.

But now the memory was no longer fun. Nor was the idea of shuffleboard or swing bands or amphitheaters by the board-walk. Not even the white summer dress made her smile now.

Because now everything felt serious. Jeremy was right, she was searching for answers. Not just in this moment, but before, too. It suddenly seemed that for her whole life, she'd been searching for explanations about why she and her mother were the way they were. Answers that might be rooted in what had happened there on Ciani Island and why Giulia had made the decisions she did.

Jeremy understood why she was in Italy, and he had confi-dence she would find those answers. She decided to embrace his confidence.

Because she would never be able to live with herself until she found them.

TWENTY-THREE

SEPTEMBER 1943

That night, hours after her conversation in the garden with Luca, Giulia lay awake in her bed. The room felt warm even though the windows were open, and despite kicking off the quilt with her good foot and readjusting her pillow again and again, she couldn't get comfortable. The air seemed thick and heavy, making it hard to breathe. And although she tried to quiet her mind, she couldn't help picturing him. His elegant, patrician face, with those high cheekbones and angular jaw. His startlingly green eyes that narrowed as he observed her. His weathered skin and hint of a beard. His brown hair with those tousled curls above his forehead that fluttered enticingly in the breeze, making her want to reach out and stroke them back into place.

What was this all about? She'd never thought about a man like this before. The boys she'd known were people to have fun with. Even Vincenzo. She loved him as a friend. But when she thought about Luca, she felt a passion she didn't recognize. And lying here in bed, she began to see herself in a whole new way, too. Who was the silly person she'd been at the castle, who craved pretty clothes and luscious foods, whose idea of doing something daring was sneaking out of the castle to frolic with Vincenzo in the small back harbor? *We're not put on this earth to think about our last triumphs. Our pretty past.* Luca had said this as he grasped her wrist, his fingers slim but his grip firm. A part of her hated how he'd addressed her, as if he were scolding a child who didn't learn her math equations well enough. And yet his words, and his tone, made something rise up inside her. She wanted to be worthy of his attention. She wanted to be a serious person. To think about more than herself and her trifling, momentary pleasures. He made her ashamed of who she had been.

But at the same time, those pleasures—sailing on the water beside Vincenzo, feeling the seawater spray her face, scurrying back upstairs before Annalisa noticed she was gone—those pleasures were familiar and comfortable. They'd fit perfectly with who she was, and they'd kept her from falling apart these last few days. Like strong thread that held together the bodice, sleeves, and tulle of the wedding gown she'd given Annalisa to take to New York. How would she live, breathe, move, exist if she cut the thread that had made her who she was for so long? She couldn't reject the satisfaction of those pleasures, because she didn't know who she would be without them. Yet it seemed Luca was telling her to do just that. He was saying that it was okay to change. That she needed to change.

But could she trust him to value the person she would become? Could she be sure that she'd become someone good? Would she still recognize herself? Or would she lose herself completely by doing what he'd asked?

For the next few days, Giulia avoided Luca as best she could. She began sitting on the front porch in the mornings, instead of on the stone bench in the back garden, where he'd always found her. In the mornings after she'd had her session with Pietro—she was now studying diagrams he'd drawn, confirming that yes, the stairs curved that way, and no, the doorway to the secret stairs was on the opposite wall—she'd open the door to his study to make sure the living room was empty before she'd walk out. In the afternoons, she'd lead Marilene to the attic and lock the door, pretending it was Pietro and Cellina she didn't want to encounter. She explained to Marilene that they didn't want Marilene's parents to know what was going on; it would be a happy surprise when they saw the red dresses for the first time on Giulia's birthday.

At mealtimes, she made sure to take a seat next to Marilene, on the opposite side of the table to where Luca typically sat. She kept her eyes down when she felt him looking at her from across the table, and after the meal had ended, she stayed with Signora Brambilla in the kitchen to help with the dishes.

But even while she'd remain on alert as she sat down before each meal, she'd hold her breath and wait for Luca to arrive in the dining room. Marilene had mentioned on Giulia's first day that Luca occasionally had to travel, and Giulia lived in dread of the day when Luca's seat at the table would be empty. Life was lighter, the mood was easier, when he was around, jostling the little boys and promising them candy before heeding Cellina's plea that he let the boys be seated so that everyone could get on with the meal.

Sometimes as she watched him take his place at the table opposite her and accept a glass of wine and his plate of food, she'd let her eyes linger on his face, glowing gold from the tall candles in their crystal candlesticks. And one evening, as the rain clattered down on the roof, and she watched him unfold his napkin and place it on his lap, her mind drifted, and she wondered what would have happened if they'd met back in her hometown. If he'd grown up near her, if he'd come to her father's shop with trousers to be hemmed or repaired, or a button or zipper to be replaced. Would he have noticed her? Would she have noticed him?

Because she'd ignored so much back then. She'd never want

to focus on the dirty looks that some would cast at her father on the street, or the loss of some customers who didn't want to step into his store, the way his eyes became sunken and red as he contemplated his business records at night. The changes in his customers' attitudes had been gradual, as they lived in a small town far removed from much of the ugliness that Jews in other cities were facing. She'd heard of Mussolini and the Fascists and Hitler and the racial laws, but in their small town, the rules governing where Jews could live, work, or go to school seemed more theoretical than actual. Her father was Jewish—she knew that the same way she knew he was short, wore glasses, had graying hair, had a sick heart. It was... a characteristic, an element of his background, an interesting point of separation from her mother: she was rich, he was poor; she was privileged, he was a tradesman; she was from the city, he was from the country; he was Jewish, she was not.

But now, she saw that his Jewishness was more than pretty stories and poetry that resonated with her and her sisters. It meant something greater. Luca had said it to her: *We're put here to think about what we can do next. What we must do next.*

From across the dinner table, Luca looked up, and their eyes met, as they had that night while Pietro read from the story-book. His body froze, yet his green eyes were yearning. Whatever she was feeling about him, he was feeling it, too. They were in the path of a storm, as fierce as the one sending pounding rain down right now, making the roof and windows rattle as the large raindrops fell. And they were both powerless to push the storm elsewhere.

The next morning Giulia went downstairs to work on the front patio, carrying her basket with variously sized needles, spools of thread, and pieces of the still-unfinished dresses. Walking was easy now, as her foot no longer required bandaging. The dresses were coming along, too, Marilene's with cap sleeves and a high collar trimmed with lace, hers with bell-shaped sleeves and a shawl collar, both with full skirts reminiscent of the sweeping dresses the women would wear at those magnificent dances at the castle. She still remembered that gorgeous scene as she and her sisters snuck toward the castle on their first night on the island. They'd heard the orchestra playing as they sat in Vincenzo's boat and approached the shore, and they'd seen the dancers through the tall, open windows, their figures lit by gigantic chandeliers. They all seemed to float on air, the women twirling and swaying in their partners' arms. Setting her basket on the iron porch chair, she closed her eyes and swayed in the rain-scented breeze. *One-two-three, one-two-three* she counted as she tilted her head in time with the waltz playing in her mind.

Was it Brahms or Liszt? She couldn't remember. She had known before. She had learned so much in those five weeks at the castle. Names of composers and sculptors and philosophers and painters, titles of paintings and waltzes and symphonies and books. Facts she'd learned so easily because she'd loved the life she'd found there. The life that was hers, as a niece of Patricio Parissi. But now everything she'd grasped with delight was fading away. The castle was becoming a dream, the kind of dream you'd swear was real until the moment you fully awoke. The kind of dream that made you yearn to go back to sleep and reclaim all that beauty...

"Good morning," came a voice from the edge of the patio. She blinked, startled that Luca was coming up the steps, a steaming cup in each hand. "I'm sorry I surprised you. I brought you coffee. Or what substitutes for coffee. Have you developed a taste for it yet?"

Her cheeks grew hot. Still standing, she rifled in the basket as though searching for a particular spool of thread. "Yes, it's... perfectly fine," she told him. "Thank you, I'm just going to do my work... now..."

"I see." He put the cups down on the small nearby table, then slipped his hands into his trouser pockets and tilted his head. "I'm afraid maybe I have something to apologize for. Because I get the impression you've been avoiding me."

She lifted her eyes. "No. No…"

"You haven't been where you usually spend your mornings, in the back garden," he said. "I fear I've said something or done something to make you uncomfortable. We are a small group here. It is impossible to hide. It's better to be direct."

She didn't know what to say, so stayed silent.

"Giulia?" he finally said, his voice almost a whisper.

"No, you haven't done anything wrong," she said. He was right, it was not a large house, and there were so few of them. Calmness and steadiness were needed. It was wrong of her to create problems for this family by letting her emotions overtake her. "I've been thinking a lot. About my life. My sisters."

"I know," he said. "I don't suppose this is the way you planned to celebrate your eighteenth birthday."

She laughed sadly. As though her birthday was anything worth thinking about. Birthdays only mattered to children.

"What would it have been like?" he asked.

She sighed and looked skyward. "As frivolous and ridiculously elaborate as you would have expected," she told him. "Signora Russo was planning to bake a rum-soaked lemon cake, five tiers. With the richest buttercream frosting and a chocolate shell covering the whole thing. And there would have been sparklers sending out bursts of white-gold light, so bright you had to squint to see it. And I was making the most stunning dress. Amber with tiny amethysts and rubies attached to the skirt."

She looked down. "I know you think it's silly. And we were fools to bury our heads in the sand the way we did. And maybe my sisters and I were the biggest fools, for not taking even a moment to think about who we were and what was happening to our people, all over Europe. But that's how we lived."

He walked closer. "I was wrong to make you feel I was judging you."

"No. We were childish, loving the luxury as we did, my sisters and I," she said, her voice trembling. "But it wasn't only about the nice things. It was about our little family and what we meant to each other. I know I can't go back. I understand what you said, that we're not put on this earth... what was it? Not put on this earth to think about our pretty past. But if it makes a person happy... I mean, it meant a lot to my father, to remember reciting that poem to my mother. 'Wherever you go, I will go.' And it helped him, to remember that she told him the same thing. That kept him going all those years without her."

She looked Luca straight in the eyes now, the memory of her father giving her the confidence to stand up for herself. Because she was standing up for her father and her sisters, too.

Luca's expression was soft. "I'm sorry," he told her. "I went too far. It's a serious time. But we can all use comfort, too, I suppose—"

"No, it's more than comfort," she said. She reached into the basket on the chair and pulled out the unfinished sleeve of Marilene's dress. "This isn't merely a piece of clothing for a silly birthday party. What you don't see is that clothing... fabrics... matter."

"Oh?" He put the basket on the ground and then gestured to the chair. When she sat, he sat on the adjacent one.

"It's art," she said, leaning forward and holding the sleeve out toward him. "My mother fell in love with my papa because of his way with garments. His hands. Oh, she'd met so many rich men with soft hands, long fingers. But he wasn't like that. His hands were calloused. His fingernails were short. His fingers were stubby, his eyesight was bad. Even as a young man, his back was hunched from working so many hours. But he was lovely. I was young but I remember my mother telling us so."

"And what made her think that?" His eyes were wide and engaged. She felt strong now, as though she was the one with a life lesson to offer.

"Because he *was*," she said. "She loved to go to the workroom and watch him. The way he could do the smallest things and have such an impact. He could make anything longer, shorter, wider, fancier. So detail-oriented, so focused, so intent on... on creating things. That was how he showed her who he was. That was how he showed love. I felt it every day of my life. When he stroked your cheek, his roughened fingers were so full of love that the touch lingered long after he was on to something else."

"That's beautiful," Luca said.

"It was," she told him, consumed now with this chance to reveal what was tucked so deeply inside her heart. "One night my little sister, Emilia, was quite sick. And he made her a silky pillowcase and a soft blanket. I'd never seen someone look as peaceful as she did when she slept that night. And she got better. Oh, I know it wasn't the bedding that cured her. But it felt like it was. It felt like he knew how to do magic.

"And that's what people don't understand—the things we make from simple cloth... they hold the magic of the person who made them. Before my sisters and I went to Parissi Island, I made my father a pillow from my mother's favorite blouse, which I had kept in my dresser drawer. The night we left, I brought it into my father's room and tucked it under his head while he slept. I cried as I saw his body relax, his head resting so sweetly on it. Maybe it smelled like her. I was so taken by that. Even in his sleep, he could sense her."

Luca sighed. "Giulia, those are beautiful memories," he said. "But I still believe they are a luxury no different from the jewels on your birthday dress at the castle. They are fine, except when it's time to follow your head. To be strategic."

"But you're not being strategic," she told him.

His back stiffened. "I'm not?"

"You are following your heart, too. You are so angry. You are mad that your father was killed."

"Don't I have a right to be?"

"Of course you do."

"But feelings don't change things. Action does." He looked down and shook his head. "I am not as unfeeling as you think. You are right that I'm angry, but I feel more than that. I am sad, too. I miss my father, same as you miss yours."

"Tell me about him," she said.

"No. I can't think about him. It's too hard—"

"Please. I'd like to know. Same as you wanted to know about mine."

He sighed, then began, speaking softly. "He was kind and he was even-tempered and he was idealistic. He wanted to be a newspaper editor because he thought words could matter. He loved my mother, and he loved my sisters and me."

He chuckled. "And he loved American baseball. I don't know why, I don't know how he even learned about it, Lou Gehrig, Babe Ruth, Hank Greenberg—do you know these names? To him, they were heroes. Men who believed they could win, men who had hope even when things looked bleak. 'An American baseball game has nine innings'—that's what he would say, as if to tell us there was lots of time to do things. Even though my sisters and I didn't even know what an inning was.

"He took things in stride, my father did. He had a sister living in Portugal when he got word that she'd died. He knew she was sick but hadn't realized the end was so near. 'I thought I'd get to see her one more time,' he told us that evening. That's it. No tears, no anger. Just a moment to be sad. The next day he went back to work. And a week later, they killed him in the street and left him there to rot. The rats had started to eat his face by the time my neighbor found him and brought him home."

"I'm so sorry," she said softly, feeling bad that she had made him think of something so awful.

"How does a son go on from that?" he said, his voice growing passionate. "How do you decide it's all okay? How do you... how did you put it, that Jewish saying? How do you choose life?"

"I don't know," she said. "I just know... I'm so sorry."

"But we do choose life, in our way," he told her. "We choose what we want to come next."

She nodded, thinking about that saying, that plea: *Choose life*. She remembered the night she and her sisters arrived in Anzalea, the town where they met Vincenzo and asked him to take them to the island. There'd been a storm the day before and the water was too choppy for his rowboat, so they agreed to wait in Anzalea until the sea settled. There was a carnival in town that week, and one evening, Vincenzo brought them there. They rode on a Ferris wheel and ate cotton candy and danced under the stars to the music of a polka band. On that night, she would have sworn she was choosing life.

But now she saw there were many ways to do exactly that.

"Giulia," Luca said. "Teach me about sewing."

"What?" she said. She looked up to see him grinning.

"Teach me to sew. I want to learn what this magic is."

"You don't learn the magic right away. It takes time."

"Then there's no time to lose, is there?"

She looked at him for a moment, then laughed and reached for a scrap of red fabric. She folded it in half and pulled a threaded needle from the pincushion in her basket. "Try this," she said, starting him off on a simple seam. "In and out. Feel the fabric so you can learn to work with it, not against it. Listen to its story. That's the trick."

"Listen to it, huh?" he said with a laugh. "Okay. If that's what it takes..."

"You're good at it," she told him as he started to sew. "Your fingers are long. My father's were short. And still, he could feel—"

She halted, suddenly spying Pietro on the bottom step leading up to the patio. She didn't know how long he'd been there. But he looked furious.

"It's time for breakfast," he said flatly.

She nodded and took the fabric back from Luca, then tucked it and the threaded needle inside her basket. The uneasiness she'd been feeling came back to her. And she knew that Pietro was aware of it. Aware that something unpredictable and dangerous was happening.

The storm she'd been anticipating seemed even closer.

TWENTY-FOUR

MAY 2019

Wednesday

Back inside the museum, Tori closed her eyes and took a deep breath to reorient herself and put the conversation with Jeremy behind her. She couldn't afford to let the day slip by as she thought about how much she missed him, and how encouraging and loving he'd been on the phone.

When she opened her eyes, Emilio was at the security post by the information desk. She rushed over.

"Emilio! I'm so relieved to see you," she exclaimed when she reached him. "I was looking all over."

"And I'm relieved to see *you*," he said. He looked around surreptitiously and then lowered his voice. "You have something to... return, yes?"

She nodded.

"If you want to give it to me, I can return it for you. I'm here overnight tonight, so it will be easy. Just tell me where it goes..."

"No, no," she said. "I want to return it. Because I want to go back in. I have more boxes to go through."

"How many more?"

"Not many. Well, kind of a lot. But I can work fast."

"And you can get through them today?"

"I'll try."

He sighed. "My friend, you are putting me in a very difficult position. Yesterday... well, I couldn't say no, you came all this way. But to keep letting you in... I'll lose my job, or worse..."

"Just this once. Once more. I can't go home without going through the other boxes. I don't know how to find my grandmother yet, and I can't leave thinking she's done something terrible. Remember what you said, secrets are how we know people? I need to find more of her secrets."

"Ah, yes. You use my words against me." He chuckled and shook his head. "Okay. Meet me like yesterday. We will do it once more."

She wanted to hug him, but she didn't know him well enough to do that, even though she felt as though they'd known each other for years. He was a friend, a co-conspirator. So she touched his elbow lightly with gratitude and then ran off.

She spent the rest of the afternoon wandering through the galleries, glad that there was still so much more to take in. At four fifty, she went to the lobby and found him. As he'd done yesterday, he waited until the lobby was empty, then led her down the hallway and unlocked the glass door to the archives.

He pulled on her elbow before she could enter. "Remember," he said. "Tonight I'm here overnight, so I won't be meeting you to go to the boat. Keep your eye on the time. Don't forget to get out of here and down to the dock by six for the employees' ferry. Give yourself plenty of time to get down the steps, okay?"

"I will. And thank you," she said.

"I'll see you tomorrow to see how you did."

"Yes," she said. "I'll find you at the hotel."

She smiled and hurried inside the room, passing the tables and chairs and making her way to the tall shelving units in the back. Reaching the "Ciani" aisles, she found the box from yesterday. She took it off the shelf and placed it on the floor, trying again to pull back the tape carefully so she could close it up again as best she could. She pulled Pietro's notebook from her bag, and slipped it inside the box under the lamps and vase, exactly where she'd found it.

Pushing the box back into its place on the shelf, she pulled out the one next to it. It was very light, much lighter than the first box. She set it down and unsealed it as carefully as she'd unsealed the first one yesterday. She pulled back the flaps.

Inside was a stack of garments and fabric pieces, along with trims and sewing notions—a bag of ribbons, a box of buttons, a circular, bright red pincushion, a set of pinking shears. She pushed those items aside and reached in deeper, then pulled out a dress—a frilly yellow one with big pockets in front outlined with white ribbon. Beneath it were two sets of linen shorts, sized for a child or young teen. She dug in further and pulled out more garments—a white sleeveless cotton blouse sized for a woman and three pretty cotton sweaters with pearl-shaped buttons. Below those was a woman's skirt with a small, floral pattern, the underskirt made of tulle, which gave the garment form and movement. The style of the skirt looked familiar, as though it had a kind of signature—as though it was made by a designer whose work she was familiar with. And that's when it hit her: Marilene had said that Giulia made the family's clothing. These had to be some of the clothes she'd made.

Tori hugged the skirt to her chest, breathing in deeply as though she could pick up even a faint scent of her grandmother. But the skirt merely smelled musty. Still, she reminded herself, Giulia had sewn these clothes for herself and for Marilene and Marilene's family. She'd touched these fabrics that Tori was touching now. She shivered, even though the room was warm.

Then she reached into the box again and pulled out a girl's

red dress. It had the same construction as the floral skirt, with a wide shape and a flouncy appearance. But there was something different about this dress, compared to the floral skirt. It was... heavy, in a way. Bottom-heavy. As though the hem was weighted.

Tori laid the dress on a table and moved the upper layers around, then felt the hem of the inner layer. And sure enough, there was a line of small, solid objects inside. She'd heard that sometimes designers sewed coins into the hems of dresses to keep them from flying up in the wind. And she'd seen "dress weights" online—dense plastic bits you can apply with adhesive to the hem of a dress, to serve the same purpose. She'd occasionally considered using them if one of her bridal clients was planning a beachside wedding, where there was sure to be a good breeze. But these objects were different. They felt like little bits of hardware. Curious as to what these items were and why Giulia would have sewn them in, she carefully ripped a few stitches in the hem of the underskirt with her fingers. She reached inside the folds to pull the object out.

It was cylindrical, about an inch in length, and it looked like brass. The top was rounded, almost like the tip of a lipstick once it's been used a few times. The bottom had the word *Corto* stamped in, with thick lettering.

She had never seen one before, but she was pretty sure it was a bullet.

"Tell me you didn't steal something else," Emilio said, looking at her across the small, round table. "Tori, I am starting to worry about you."

"I didn't steal it," she said. "I'm going to put it back. But I had to show you."

They were seated at one of the busy cafés on the piazza the

next morning, two cups of cappuccino and a basket of *cornetti* in front of them. Tori had made it down to the dock yesterday evening in time to catch the employees' ferry, but just barely. She'd been so busy staring at the bullet that she hadn't kept track of the quickly passing minutes. At five fifty, she'd snapped to attention, pushed the box back into its spot, and rushed out of the room, through the front entrance of the museum, and down the stone stairway. Fortunately it had started to drizzle, so the employees took more time boarding the boat, keeping their footsteps small so as not to slip and slide. That gave her a few precious extra minutes to reach the dock.

She'd called home last night to check in and was glad the conversations with Marilene and Molly were fairly routine, because she was distracted by what she'd found. For a moment, she considered telling Marilene about the bullets, but then changed her mind. She remembered how upset Marilene had become the night she'd first seen the wedding dress on Kelly's postcard, and she didn't want to risk upsetting her that way once again. She didn't want Molly to have to try to help Marilene calm down. It wouldn't be right to now mention the bullets or what she'd read in Marilene's father's notebook. No, it was better to get as much of the real story as she could, and then share it with Marilene when she returned home.

Still, she'd barely slept last night, wondering why Giulia would have sewn bullets into Marilene's dresses. Was Marilene headed somewhere dangerous? But what could Giulia have expected the young Marilene to do with those bullets?

And did this have anything to do with the betrayal mentioned in Pietro's notebook?

Tori had come down to the dock first thing that morning, hoping to catch Emilio the minute he returned after his overnight shift. She'd stayed about an hour, watching three ferries come in without spotting Emilio.

Frustrated, she'd taken a walk to the piazza and soon found herself among the shops, browsing the outdoor racks lined with colorful sundresses, straw hats, floral scarves, and little souvenirs like key chains and picture frames. She reached Gabriella and Francisco's bookstore and decided to stop in. It was beautiful, as Emilio had described it, and the brother-and-sister pair was there. They recognized her immediately and were as gracious and warm as they'd been when she'd had dinner with them on her first night in Anzalea. The store carried a substantial collection of Italian-authored books in English translation, and she bought six novels that Gabriella recommended—three romances that she thought Marilene would like and three young-adult fantasies for Molly. She also bought a beautiful book by a local photographer, with stunning photographs of Anzalea at dusk and in the morning, and of the castle as seen on the dock near the piazza. She was glad to find it as she was quickly falling in love with Anzalea. Gabriella offered to have the presents gift-wrapped, and said she'd drop them off at the hotel that afternoon.

"Say hello to Emilio for me," Gabriella said. "We must all have dinner again before you go." She was certain she saw Gabriella blush slightly as she mentioned Emilio's name.

Walking back to the piazza, Tori searched the café patios once again, hoping to see Emilio. She spotted him at one of the places, having coffee with a group of friends. And she rushed over to his table. He invited her to sit with them, and she waited impatiently as they finished their breakfast. Evidently sensing that she had something on her mind, Emilio had bid "*Arrivederci*" to the group and then ordered more coffee and the *cornetti* for her.

She looked around, not wanting anyone to pay attention to what she was about to display. When she was convinced that everyone at the nearby tables was involved in their own conversations, she pulled the bullet out of her bag. She put it on the table, her hand hiding it from any other pairs of eyes, and slid it toward him. She removed her hand.

His eyes widened, and she could tell he was as surprised as she'd been. "*Cavolo!*" he exclaimed, and she figured that was an expression of surprise. "This is a bullet!"

"I know, right?"

He pulled his glasses out of his shirt pocket and put them on, then picked up the bullet and studied it, turning it over again and again.

"Where did you find this?" he asked.

"It was sewn into the hem of a child's dress in one of the boxes I found yesterday. I think it had to be one of Marilene's dresses when she was little. Marilene told me that Giulia sewed all her dresses when they lived on the island."

"They were sewn into her dress?" he asked, shocked.

"Yes, a red party dress. There were several bullets, all inside the hem. They were sewn in so carefully and securely, I don't think anyone would have noticed who wasn't a dressmaker. But I knew there was something unusual about the weight of this dress. It was heavier than it should have been."

Emilio studied the cylinder and then read the inscription along the bottom rim. "Corto," he said.

"What is that?"

"It's the manufacturer. Yes, I know about these bullets. They were used widely during the war years, by police largely, but also by the German and Italian armies. There's a whole section about it in the museum, down in the basement. And there was a black market for them. A lot were bought and sold illegally."

"But why would Giulia have been sewing bullets into a dress? To protect Marilene in some way?"

"Maybe she was smuggling them somewhere," Emilio suggested.

"Do you... do you think this has something to do with what

Marilene's father wrote in the notebook?" she asked. "The betrayal he described?"

"In what way?"

"Could she have been trying to kill someone? Him, even?"

Emilio considered this. "I don't know. But there is another possibility, my friend. Perhaps your grandmother was part of the Resistance."

Tori looked at him, stunned. "She was... what does that even mean?"

"Some of these smaller islands, they were involved in the Resistance. In the same way that Signora Russo was sending messages to the Americans from Parissi Island, many Italians were also trying to undermine the Nazis to give the Allied forces a hand in moving northward. There was a big attack by the Resistance in March of 1944—an explosion on the Spanish Steps in Rome, where the Nazi police force was stationed. Many Nazi soldiers were killed. In the end, the Resistance paid for it dearly—the Germans set out to kill ten Italians for every German policeman killed. They killed even more, in the end. It was called the Ardentine Caves massacre."

"How horrible," Tori said, shaking her head. "I never knew any of this."

"Many Resistance fighters put their lives in danger to try to end the German occupation," Emilio continued. "It's remarkable what they were able to accomplish. And they depended on a steady stream of ammunition coming their way. That explosion on the Spanish Steps—in that case, the individual planting the explosive was a twenty-two-year-old man who disguised himself as a sanitation worker. Rosario Bentivegna, his name was. But for every Bentivegna, there was a host of others working quietly behind the scenes, ferrying supplies and messages and weapons. Maybe even your grandmother."

"But if she was smuggling bullets, why would Marilene's father have said she betrayed him? Marilene said he was a fierce anti-Fascist. That's why he moved his family out of Rome. He and Giulia would have been on the same side."

"I don't know," Emilio said. "Perhaps the betrayal wasn't political, then. Perhaps it was personal."

"That doesn't make sense either," Tori said. "Giulia had a good relationship with Marilene's family. She wouldn't have wanted to kill Pietro. I guess she did do something that angered him according to the notebook. But even then, why sew the bullets into a dress?"

She put her elbow on the table and rested her chin on her hand. "I don't know what to think."

Emilio sipped his coffee, then placed the cup down and looked out toward the castle. "I believe there's one thing that's certain," he said. "Your grandmother was much more than a dressmaker. She was a complex woman. Maybe that's the most that can ever be said."

Tori breathed in. Emilio was right. Giulia was complex. But Tori had never let complexity scare her. She had been surrounded by complex women all her life. And not only her mother and Marilene. All the brides who came to her in pursuit of the perfect wedding gown—they were complex, too. And fabrics were complex—the way they draped or floated or swirled or tapered, the way they formed pleats or folds or shirring, the way they could accentuate or play down the curves and angles of the body. This was the language that textiles spoke. And she had learned how to decode that language. And how to find the order within it.

Giulia had been the same way. Giulia had understood fabrics. That was why she could so skillfully hide the bullets within the hem. And Tori was Giulia's granddaughter. She possessed the same spirit. The same drive. And the same analytical mind.

"Yes, she was," Tori said. "But not too complex for me. I'm

telling you, Emilio. I'm going to figure out what all this means—the bullets, the betrayal, and Giulia's whereabouts."

She picked up the bullet from the table and held it between her thumb and forefinger. "This isn't going to stop me," she said. "It only makes me even more determined to know the truth."

TWENTY-FIVE

SEPTEMBER 1943

The weather turned hot over the next few days, the clouds holding the thick humidity in place. There was no breeze, no hint of air moving, only an oppressive, steady pressure. Giulia had never felt such moisture-soaked heat before. She was constantly wiping her face with her wrist, taking a cold towel to her neck, hoping desperately for relief that never came. She longed to go to the cove and take the *pattino* for a ride, to feel the spray of the sea on her face, that refreshing sensation she knew so well from those secretive jaunts with Vincenzo behind the castle. Or even just to walk by the seashore and dip her good foot into the water. But the shore was entirely off limits. Pietro had told the family that at dinner two nights ago. He'd blurted something about the sea being too unsettled in this weather and the possibility of a sudden storm surge up to the tree line. The surges in this area came fast, he'd said, and the undertow was strong.

"Not that fast," Marilene had said. "You're making that up, Papa. You're saying things that—"

"It's strong and fast," Pietro said sternly. "This is no time to argue. You all stay away. Every one of you. Understood?"

They'd all agreed. Even the little boys, who nodded solemnly, refraining from their usual giggles and outbursts. Giulia couldn't help but believe that Marilene was right, and that his description of the unsettled sea was an excuse. That the true reason Pietro was keeping them all close to the house was even more serious. Because the atmosphere inside the house felt tense and dangerous, too. Pietro still brought her into the study in the mornings to answer questions about the castle. Now they were up to the servants' quarters and the grounds, including the long, winding stone staircase that rose from the shore up the hill to the entranceway. But she could tell he was distracted, and he dismissed her each day after only an hour.

Whatever the new complication was that troubled Pietro so, Giulia knew it involved Luca. Suddenly he was no longer around in the early morning, bringing her barley coffee and teasing the children. He was often in the study with Pietro at various times throughout the afternoons, and while she couldn't make out what they were saying as she crossed the living room, she heard their voices, low and often heated. Then one night, long past midnight, she was awoken by voices outside her window. When she looked out, the moonlight revealed Luca and Pietro walking into the house with two other men, strangers, carrying large cartons. Giulia wondered if these were some of the "visitors" that Marilene had mentioned on her first evening in the house. But they didn't stay overnight or have breakfast with the family. Instead, they left, empty-handed, a few minutes after they'd arrived. They walked back toward the trees in the direction of the shore.

Luca came out of the house then, and stood on the edge of the porch, looking in the direction of the trees. The tail of his white shirt was untucked and hung down past his waist. He put his hands in his pockets and stayed still for a few moments. Then he stepped back and sat on one of the porch chairs, his elbows on his knees and his head in his hands. She could see his hair grazing his collar as he sat there, motionless.

Her head pressed against the window jamb, she watched him. He seemed to be wrestling with something he didn't know how to handle. She wondered if he'd ever felt this way before, if he'd sat like this before, or if this was the first time. And if it was the first time, she wondered if she was part of the cause. If whatever those two men had brought, whatever they'd said, whatever Luca and Pietro spoke about in the privacy of the study—she wondered if her presence was making things more complicated. Because Luca was making things more complicated for her. Her feelings about leaving the island and going to find her sisters in New York were muddled now. Ever since they'd spoken so honestly about their fathers, ever since she'd guided him in sewing that silly seam, she didn't see how she could ever bid him goodbye.

He lifted his head and looked up at the moon, the fingers of one hand pressed against his lips. She yearned to sneak downstairs and out onto the porch. To ask him what was wrong or maybe just to kneel beside him and hold his hand or touch his shoulder. She ached for him to grasp her hand in return, to reach out and press her to his chest. She even started to walk toward her bedroom door, and once she reached it, she grasped the knob. But then she loosened her fingers and returned to the window. She couldn't be with him. Not now, not on this warm night, not with him looking so worried and vulnerable. It would be too hard to reveal that she'd been watching him. It would suggest a level of closeness she wasn't prepared for.

And it was forbidden, that closeness. Illicit. Pietro had made it clear to them that morning when he saw them on the porch. There were rules in this household, she reminded herself. Rules about the children, rules about what could and couldn't be said, what could and couldn't be done. About who could be seen together, and when, and why. That was the structure that kept this house secure. At that moment, Luca rose and turned to go into the house, and Giulia stepped back from the window and pressed herself against the wall. She stayed that way, her breath quick, her heart racing, as she heard him climb the steps, then enter his bedroom at the other end of the hallway and shut the door.

She climbed back into her bed, thinking of her sisters, her past. For a moment, she wished she could go back to being the girl she used to be when she lived on Parissi Island. The feelings she was having for Luca—they were too grown-up, too foreign. So different from the feelings of friendship that she'd had for Vincenzo. Now she knew what love truly was. Still, the Giulia she'd be if she embraced those feelings, if she left her room right now and went to find him in his bedroom—that Giulia existed on the other side of an imaginary line that she wasn't ready to cross.

Lying on her back, too distressed to sleep, she told herself she'd talk to Pietro first thing tomorrow morning and insist that she had to leave. Surely by now, she'd be safe. Surely no Nazi soldiers would recognize her and stop her. They had more important issues on their minds. Her foot was nearly healed and she could walk without a limp. This was not a good place for her. She had to get out so she could go back to being the Giulia she knew.

She woke with a start in the morning, to the sound of someone banging on her door. Blinking awake, she sat up, realizing from the position of the sun that she'd slept way later than usual.

"Giulia?" It was Marilene who was knocking, probably to bring her to breakfast.

"Come in, Marilene," she called as she climbed out of bed. "I'm sorry I slept so late. I'll be ready to come downstairs right away, okay?"

The door opened, and Marilene came in, her face wet with tears and the tip of her nose red.

"What is it?" Giulia said as she rushed to the girl. "Why are you crying?"

"It's not fair!" Marilene wailed.

"What's not fair?"

"Luca's leaving! He won't even be here for your birthday party!"

Giulia held Marilene by the shoulders. "How do you know? Where's he going?"

"Papa said there's some problem at the winery that he has to check on. He's in his room packing right now!"

A few minutes later, after sending Marilene downstairs and putting on some clothes, Giulia rushed across the hallway to Luca's room. She knew she should have expected this. Something serious had been brewing all week. She wasn't a child like Marilene and the boys, who could be told some story about a vineyard and immediately believe it. She should have known better than to try to imagine that this life, this island, this time, was not going to change. Pietro and Marilene, too, had made it clear that Luca came and went from the island. Luca had told her early on that he was part of the Resistance and had a responsibility to the cause —a responsibility that transcended everything and everyone else.

Still, she felt as surprised and sad as Marilene was. Maybe more so. She realized now that she'd come to rely on their life together, here in this remote place, having wonderful meals and long talks in the garden. What was happening on Parissi Island, what was happening in the world—it had all started to feel more theoretical than real. It was so easy for people to recast events when they wanted to, she thought. To embrace the status quo, and even if it was not ideal, to decide it would last another day.

Yes, her feelings for Luca scared her. But she didn't want him to leave. And she didn't want to stay here without him. She didn't want to be left behind.

When she reached Luca's room, she saw that what Marilene said was true. Luca was packing clothes into a thick black valise on his bed. It looked innocent enough, as though he were going away for a weekend trip. But she knew this was far from a lighthearted excursion.

"So it's happening," she said. "You're leaving."

"As we knew I would," he told her. "This comes as no surprise."

"But I didn't realize..."

"But you had to have realized. With all the talks between Pietro and me. And the men who came last night—didn't you hear them? Surely you didn't see our life here as simply as the children do. We never hid the truth from you."

She looked at him as he closed the valise and pressed the clasps shut. His pale face and tense expression belied his matter-of-fact tone. He was concerned. And afraid.

"Of course, I knew something was going on," she said. "But I hoped it would be delayed long enough for the Americans and the British..." She paused, hearing how childish she sounded. As though if she wished hard enough, the war would end.

"When do you leave?" she asked.

"Tonight."

She paused, not sure if she wanted to ask the next question on her mind. But she had to know. "What exactly are you doing?"

"Our group is planning a series of strikes on sites where the Nazi officers are," he said. "Two buildings in Rome and two in towns in the North, in addition to the strike on Parissi Island. I'm leaving for Rome tonight to help coordinate the logistics. We need to figure out how to transport bullets and explosives to the operatives carrying out the attacks."

"Will you... be in danger?" she asked.

"I'll be fine. I know what I'm doing."

"When will you come back?"

"Two weeks. Maybe sooner. But then I'll have to leave again."

"To do what?"

He shrugged.

She nodded and sat down on the bed. "I thought I wasn't happy here. I thought I wanted to leave. But now... I wish things could stay as they've been. I can't... it feels as though every time I start to feel secure somewhere... it all falls apart. Is that how it always is?"

"For now it's like that. For everyone. But hopefully it won't always be."

He moved the valise to the floor and then sat down beside her. "The one thing I regret is how much time we spent together. It was a mistake. People cannot allow themselves to connect in times like this."

She looked down. He was right. She should have been smarter. She knew what the world was like. She'd seen it first-hand, as she ran down the hidden stairs at the castle and escaped on the little boat. But why had he been so charming, so attentive? Why had he given himself that freedom?

If Annalisa were here, she'd scold her. She'd say that Giulia had once again been foolish, and her behavior irresponsible. And yet this wasn't some random infatuation. The kinds of infatuations she'd had back home... she didn't think she'd ever be capable of that type of feeling again. It was as though this week, on the eve of her eighteenth birthday, she'd become an adult. And that was the most concrete thing a person could do. Thinking she could avoid the realities of the world—it was as foolish as thinking she could go back to being a little child again, when Mama was still alive.

"Can't I go with you?" she said. "Can I help? I don't think I can stay here anymore."

"You know that you can't," he said, getting up from the bed. "And it's not just about your name or the fact that you're a Parissi. You're not a fighter, Giulia. You're not made to be one. You've had so much trouble even giving Pietro information about the castle. You don't have it in you to do what I'm doing. You'd be a liability to me."

"No, that's not true. I could be... I..." She trailed off. Because he was right.

"Sit tight, okay? Give Pietro the information he needs. Help with the kids. Marilene adores you. Be there for her."

She nodded and stood, looking down at her hands clasped in front of her waist. She didn't want to distract him or upset him more than he already was. He had so much on his mind. She clasped her hands tighter, so she wouldn't reach out to him, the way she wanted to. She yearned to feel his strong chest against her body, to soak up his warmth, to have him reassure her that they'd see each other again. And that they had a future together. That one day they could share a life where there was no war, no brutality, no constant threat. She was so scared she'd never see him again.

Suddenly she felt a strong touch on her arms, and she lifted her eyes to see Luca there in front of her, his hands holding her, the sensation tender and luxurious on her skin. Without thinking but simply following her instincts, she lifted her chin and moved her face upward toward his. A moment later his lips were on hers, firm and smooth, his mouth warm and giving. As frightened and distressed as she was, she felt her body relax and release, as if this moment was enough, because it was everything. She placed her hands on his chest and then ran one upward so it was resting on the top of his shoulder, loving the feel of his strong frame beneath her fingers. She pressed herself closer to him, letting her mouth meld further with his, so they were moving and responding as if with one mind, one heart—

"Luca?" came a female voice from the staircase, accompanied by the sound of firm footsteps. Giulia broke away from the embrace and walked to the window.

"Luca, I wanted to— Oh, Giulia. I didn't know you were here." It was Cellina. Giulia nodded, still facing the window. "I thought you were still..." she continued. "I mean, why would you—"

"What is it you need, Cellina?" Luca asked.

"Nothing. I only wanted to make sure you have everything. Enough clothes? The food we wrapped for you?"

"I'm set, Cellina, thank you," Luca said.

"Then why don't you both come down for breakfast? The food is hot. Giulia, okay?"

Giulia took a breath, then turned back toward the other two. "Yes, I'm coming."

"Good. Remember, please, we need to put on a good face for the children," Cellina said. "Luca, they think you have some issue to take care of at the vineyard."

Luca nodded and headed for the door. Giulia started to follow him, but Cellina took her elbow, her eyes a mixture of sympathy and steely resolve. Then she let Giulia go.

That night, after the children were in bed, Giulia snuck out of the house and hid behind the trees to watch Luca leave. She knew Pietro and Cellina wouldn't want her to be there. They wouldn't want her to take up any more of Luca's attention than she already had. Soon a small boat pulled up to the shore, and Luca climbed on board. She watched Pietro hand him his valise. She watched him shake hands with Pietro. Then he sat and the boat quietly took off, their way lit by the moon and the stars.

Slowly, she dragged herself into the house and up the stairs.

When she entered her bedroom, she saw a note on the pillow. She hadn't noticed it before and had no idea when it had been placed there. She unfolded it. The handwriting was Luca's:

> *Wherever you go, I will go.*
> *Wherever you stay, I will stay.*

She lowered herself onto the bed, relishing those words. If only she could be sure they would come true.

With Luca gone, it seemed as if all the light in the house, all the sunshine streaming in through the windows, had dimmed. The adults tried to stay involved in their work and their chores, keeping the routines going for the sake of the children, but the usual upbeat feel of the household was gone. Giulia wondered if the house had always seemed like this when Luca had left. Or were things worse now? Was it because what he was doing was far more dangerous than what had come before? Or was everyone aware of what she and Luca had become to one another? It seemed that perhaps her presence had changed the household. That the closeness between her and Luca had reminded all the adults of what they left behind when they came here to stay.

Her birthday arrived, but it was nowhere near the celebration Marilene had envisioned. She and Marilene had both lost interest in completing the red party dresses, so the garments lay upstairs in Giulia's room, unfinished. Signora Brambilla made a lovely birthday cake, and they all sang to her and congratulated her, but there was something flat and sad about the evening. Even the boys pushed away their slices of cake and whined about their schoolwork and chores until Cellina sent them to bed. For presents, Marilene gave her a new sewing kit with spools of thread in many colors, a gift that she'd chosen from a catalog and had delivered with the food and other supplies last week. Cellina and Pietro gave her a sweet silver bracelet they'd also had delivered, and Signor and Signora Brambilla, along with Signorina Ottavia, gave her a beautiful bouquet of wildflowers they'd picked in the woods behind the house. Giulia was touched by the gifts and all the effort that had gone into the party. But like the others, she wasn't going to smile until Luca came home safe.

Then finally, eight days after Luca had left, Pietro called everyone into the living room at night. "I have good news," he said. "I just got word on the radio. Luca returns tonight!"

"Oh, thank the Lord," Signora Brambilla said, and the boys jumped up and down. Cellina had tears in her eyes, and Pietro hugged her. Marilene ran upstairs to make him a "welcome home" card. Giulia sat down on the sofa and breathed deeply, for what seemed like the first time in eight days. She had been so worried. She had missed him so much.

She started upstairs to help Marilene when Pietro touched her arm.

"Giulia," he said softly. "Come. There's something more I need you to know."

She followed him into his study and when he gestured toward an armchair, she sat down. He sat behind his desk. His expression was stern, and she wondered if she'd done something wrong. She didn't think so. She had been giving him all the information he'd asked for about the castle. She'd been even more forthcoming ever since Luca had left. She'd wanted to be helpful because she knew how much danger Luca was putting himself in. She'd even stopped talking about going to the mainland. She hadn't wanted to cause any more trouble for this family.

"Is something wrong?" she asked.

Suddenly Cellina came in and sat in the other armchair.

Now she knew the news was bad. Cellina had never come into one of their meetings before.

"What is it?" she asked, her voice desperate. "Is it about Luca? Is he okay? Is he hurt?"

Pietro shook his head. "It's not about Luca," he said. He sighed and ran his tongue along the back of his teeth. "Giulia, you are going to have to be very strong and very brave. War is horrific, and nobody remains unscathed."

Cellina reached out and took her hand. And that's when she knew.

"It's my family, isn't it?" she said.

Pietro folded his hands on his desk. "When we got word about Luca returning, we also got word about your younger sister," he said. "Your hometown, Caccipulia, was invaded last week. Many Jews were killed. And the people who were suspected of helping them were killed, too."

"Emilia?" she whispered.

"And your friend, Vincenzo."

"But... but no," she said, her voice gasping. "That can't be. My uncle was going to save them. He said he could get them out of Italy..."

"Giulia," Cellina said. "It's what we suspected. Nobody got off Parissi Island when the Nazis came ashore. Except for you."

"So my uncle? And Annalisa?"

Pietro looked at her. "We're going to avenge this. We're going to do harm to them for what they did. The munitions are here, and we'll get them to our operatives. We'll figure out how to smuggle them off the island. We will get back at them for everything—"

But she couldn't bear to hear more. She left the study and ran upstairs. In her room, she closed her bedroom door, then sank onto her mattress. This couldn't be happening. She couldn't have lost her whole family. How could they have slaughtered her beautiful little sister? And her wise older sister?

Now the war had hit home. Now it was her family, the people she loved.

Suddenly she understood Luca's anger about his father. She was angry, too. She sat up and clutched her stomach, picturing how it had happened. Had they lined them up or shot them randomly? In the head, in the heart? Had her sisters begged for their lives? Had they cried? Had Emilia called out "Giulia!" the way she used to when she got her comb stuck in her tangled hair or stepped on a pin while running barefoot through the store because she hated wasting time putting on shoes? Had Annalisa been calm as she died? Had they thought of her?

And what of their uncle, poor Patricio, who had cried when he'd finally met them, his sister's daughters? He'd barely had time to be with family again. Now he was dead. And what of Vincenzo? He'd saved her life by showing her the back dock and teaching her to sail the *pattino*, only to be killed while saving her younger sister.

Yes, she was angry. How ridiculous she had been, hesitating to help Pietro draw that map. Who had she been protecting?

No more, she thought. No more. Now she had a purpose, as Luca did. She would give Pietro even more details about Parissi Castle, anything she could think of. She would label every square inch for him, so the Resistance fighters would know all there was. And... and the munitions, the bullets and explosives Pietro was looking to smuggle?

She looked around until her gaze landed on the pieces of the red dresses still to be finished, which were on the shelf across the room. She went there and touched a sleeve. She was a good seamstress and she understood how fabrics behaved. Fabrics told a story, that's what she'd said to Luca. Now these fabrics would tell a story, too. A story of one brave daughter of a Jewish tailor, a brave daughter who would finally be of service, of help...

At that moment, the door to her bedroom opened. By the

light of the moon coming in from her window, she saw it was Luca. His hair was tousled and his face was wet from the mist.

"Giulia," he said, and she knew he'd heard the news.

She dropped the red sleeve and ran into his arms. And she grasped him as he kissed the top of her head and murmured her name over and over. She didn't know who she was, and she didn't want to know. She only wanted to leave the world behind and lose herself in all the sensations she was feeling. This was where redemption was; this was where peace and possibility resided. It was as though only now, only with him, could she believe there was something meaningful about life. Because Luca understood her. They were both people who had lost so much so young. They were longing for home, which had disappeared for each of them far too early.

But they could find home in each other, she thought as they moved away from the bedroom door. They could find home in each other's embrace. And maybe then they could find a way out of this nightmare.

Maybe they could find a way forward.

TWENTY-SIX

MAY 2019

Thursday

After saying goodbye to Emilio at the café, Tori spent the rest of the morning roaming the shops on the piazza. She was in no hurry to get back to the museum, as all she wanted to do was to explore more boxes in the archives, and she wouldn't be able to get back in there without Emilio. He'd gone back to the hotel to take a nap and change his clothes for tonight, his second and final night shift of the week. He'd promised to meet her at the dock at four o'clock so they could travel to the museum together. Then he'd let her back into the archives, as he'd done for the past two afternoons. He seemed less reluctant to do so, compared to how he'd been yesterday and the day before. It seemed the discovery of the hidden bullets had piqued his curiosity. When they'd parted ways at the café, he'd sounded almost as eager as she was to learn more about Giulia.

Returning to the center of the piazza, Tori decided to carry out something for lunch before all the shops and restaurants closed for the afternoon *riposo*. She was in the mood to try something new, and opted for a *pane e panelle* from a small outdoor eatery. The English-speaking owner described it as a Sicilian specialty featuring chickpea fritters on a sesame seed roll. She ordered a cappuccino as well, and he wrapped the sandwich for her so she could take it to the park by the dock.

As the shops began closing, she unwrapped her lunch and dug in. The fritter was delicious, the sesame seed roll a perfect accompaniment, and she savored each bite. It was strange, but she felt a new mood overtaking her. Maybe it was the magic of this lovely town, but she also thought it had to do with what she'd learned about Giulia. She still didn't understand why Giulia had never returned to her baby, but the mysteries about her life were increasing. And the more Tori gathered about Giulia, the more she wanted to know. Could the bullets and the words Pietro had written in his notebook somehow tie together with Giulia's decision to abandon her baby? There seemed so much more to her grandmother than Tori had realized when she'd decided to take this trip.

And even if she found out that Giulia had no good explanations, she no longer felt it would be best to go home without ever meeting her. She wanted to know Giulia, no matter what she might find out. Sitting here in the sunshine with the water sparkling ahead of her and the castle rising in the distance, she decided that light was better than darkness, knowledge better than secrecy. In unlocking the mystery of Giulia, she'd finally be able to understand where she came from—and possibly learn more about who she was and why she felt the way she did about lots of things.

But mostly about commitment. And why she'd sooner give up the man she loved than marry him.

And for this reason, it felt like her mission here in Italy had changed. She'd arrived here determined to find her grandmother, confront her, and demand an explanation. If Giulia was alive, she'd decided, then she was going to be found. Now, Tori believed that if she never found Giulia, if finding her was impossible, it would still be okay. Because she was getting to know her. She was learning about her. And as long as she could solve the mysteries she uncovered, she'd go home richer and more satisfied than she'd been when she arrived.

She finished eating and called home to catch Marilene and Molly before Molly had to go to school. Thankfully she was getting used to the time change; in fact, she was getting used to a lot of things about Italy. For the first time since she'd arrived, she spent more time talking about what she'd been doing than asking questions of them. She still felt it was better to save all she'd discovered about Giulia for when she returned. But she did talk about Emilio and the hotel and the food. Even Molly seemed drawn in by Tori's enthusiasm and made Tori promise again to bring her to Italy before long.

A little while later, Emilio showed up, and they joined the line to board the next ferry. Tori couldn't wait to find out what she would discover in the archives today. They reached the island and made their way up the stairs, and she marveled at Emilio's stamina. She wandered around the lobby while Emilio checked in for his shift and put on his vest. At a little before five o'clock he let her into the archives, and she rushed back to the shelves. She pulled out the box from yesterday, then drew the brass bullet from her bag and tucked it into the little pocket in the dress formed when she'd ripped the one stitch in the hem. She pushed the box back into its place on the shelf and pulled out the next closest one.

Gently unsealing that one, she looked inside. It was filled with papers—letters, notes, official-looking documents that seemed to have come from an old-fashioned typewriter, slips of paper with handwritten notes that looked like they were scribbled in a hurry. There had to be hundreds of pages alto-gether—and, she noted to herself wryly, they were all in Ital-ian. How could she know which documents and letters might reveal more about Giulia, or even point to Giulia's where-

abouts? She longed to bring the whole box out to show Emilio
and ask for his help in translating, but she knew he'd blow a
gasket if she took even a small percentage of the contents out
of here. As good-natured as he was, he'd been agitated that
she'd brought out the notebook and the bullet, even though
she'd returned them both. And there were way too many documents for him to translate them all before she left for home
next week.

With a heavy sigh, she tried to sort through all the pages,
putting aside the ones that looked official and hunting specifi-
cally for ones that seemed to be written to or about Giulia.
Halfway through the pile, she found a small, yellowed scrap of
paper. There seemed to be a poem on it, two lines in verse, the
handwriting elegant and precise:

> *Dovunque tu vada io andrò e*
> *Dovunque ti starai io restarò.*

Beneath the verse was one word: *Giulia.*

Tori froze. What was this poem, which her grandmother
had apparently written out? Too curious to wait to show it to
Emilio, she opened her phone and typed the first two lines of
the poem into the search bar on her browser, then asked for the
English translation. A moment later, it appeared:

> *Wherever you go, I will go.*
> *And wherever you stay, I will stay.*

It seemed a simple enough pair of sentences, and yet there
was something formal about it, something lyrical. She was sure
it wasn't just words that had popped into someone's head; they
were words that someone knew, that had significance above and
beyond their literal meaning. She went back to her browser to
type the English words into the search box, to see if they had

some historical significance. But before she could finish, her eyes caught the time in the upper right corner of her screen.

Five fifty-five.

"Oh no!" she hissed, shoving the page into her bag and putting the box back on the shelf. She ran past the tables and chairs, and hurried down the hallway and to the front entrance. Remembering that Emilio was again working overnight, she hurried outside and down the stone stairway. But by the time she reached the bottom step, the ferry had left the shore and started back to the mainland.

She climbed back to the courtyard and knocked on the glass doors. The entranceway lanterns switched on.

"I missed the boat," she said when Emilio opened the door.

Twenty minutes later, they were seated at the end of a rectangular table in the museum's cafeteria, one set of overhead lights shining above them and an assortment of antipasti and warmed-over gnocchi alla Romana, the baked gnocchi golden brown and topped with a mixture of butter, sage, and Gorgonzola cheese.

"One benefit of staying here overnight," Emilio said as he poured red wine from a small bottle into two plastic wine glasses. "You get to enjoy the café's leftovers."

"Thank you," Tori said. "And I'm sorry for burdening you with me tonight." She'd resigned herself to staying until morning, as Emilio had explained there was no alternative. No boat would come back for them tonight; and if they called the police, she could face some tough scrutiny.

"Not a burden, my friend. I'm glad for the company. *Salute*." He tapped her cup with his. Then he handed her an empty plate and some plastic utensils. They both helped themselves and started to eat, Tori amazed at how delicious the café's food was.

"I hope you found something important enough to justify your being stuck here," he said in between mouthfuls.

She scowled. "I don't know if I did or not," she said. She finished the morsel on her fork, then wiped her hands on a napkin and pulled the yellowed paper from her bag. "It seems to be from Giulia," she said as she handed it to him. "It looks like a poem or a verse. Do you recognize it?"

He gave her a look, no doubt because she had again taken something from the archives. Then he read it over and shook his head.

"Maybe I'm just imagining it because I want it to mean something that matters," she said. "But it feels... lyrical to me. A love poem, maybe. I translated it on my phone. *Wherever you go, I will go...* that sounds like love. Doesn't it?"

He shrugged. "Maybe. Maybe not. I'll go where you go... people say that all the time. I've probably said it a million times to everyone I know. My granddaughter, my father... you go to Rome on the eight-fifteen train, I will, too. You want spaghetti, that's fine. We'll eat wherever you want. 'I'll go where you go.'"

She smirked. "Well, when you put it that way. But it... I don't know, it rang a bell for me somehow when I read it. Like something I had heard long ago, in a dream or something. Or something my mother said to me. Something she sang maybe. Although the words aren't quite the same as what I remember..."

She didn't know why but suddenly she felt her eyes welling up. She sniffled. "This is all so crazy," she said. "I never cry. But here I go again. Because I'm starting to believe that I'm never going to find her. I've distracted myself with this little game of hide-and-seek in the archives." She shook her head. "What am I even doing here?"

"You came to look for Giulia. Because you were angry with her."

"Yes, I was," she agreed. "And not just me. There's been so

much sadness and anger around me. My grandmother, at least the one I thought was my grandmother, is also angry. She's so mad about Giulia never coming back. And my mother was angry and sad. I barely knew her growing up—that's what I most remember. Until the day she died, she was angry and worked up. And scared. I guess she never got over being abandoned."

She thought for a moment. "Although maybe there's more to it. It was such a bad time for me when I saw the postcard with the wedding dress. Everything was falling apart in my life. Maybe I was just looking for an excuse to get away. I saw myself being so much like my mother. Not able to let things be. Not able to trust. I didn't want to keep going down that road. I didn't want to be my mother. Considering all that happened."

He raised his eyebrows.

"It's an awful story," she said. "I was eleven, Molly's age, and I was at the town swimming pool, and I wanted to go with my friends to the deep end. I really thought I could do it, even though I wasn't a great swimmer. My mother was always so nervous about me. She'd lost track of me at a department store years earlier, and she never could let that go. And she seemed to become more unhinged when my dad died in a car crash the year before.

"Anyway, I followed my friends to the middle of the deep section, and I couldn't make it across. I honestly thought I was going to drown. A man was standing there with his friend in the pool, maybe in his twenties, and I reached out and put my hand on his arm and said, 'Please help me get across.' He thought it was funny, I guess because I was almost there, so he just let me hang onto his arm as he pulled me to the pool ladder. I guess it didn't look like I was in danger, as the life-guard didn't even notice. But my mother saw the whole thing. And was so upset. She was mad at herself for not being there in the pool with me.

"The next morning she wasn't in her bed when we got up. Marilene called the police." She paused.

"They found her at the bottom of the pool," she said. "She must have been hallucinating, maybe she'd been drinking. The gate to the pool complex had been locked, but she'd somehow gotten past the chain-link fence. She had to have been reliving the moment when I was in the deep end. I know that in her head, she was trying to rescue me. I feel so guilty about that. And I'm mad. Because she never got over being abandoned, and it damaged her for life."

Emilio put down his fork and tilted his head. "I'm so sorry, Tori," he said. "I'm sorry she didn't get help. It sounds like she was a sick woman. It wasn't your fault."

"I know. She didn't think she was sick, though. And often she was fine. But then she'd have these episodes... anyway, it all came to a head when Marilene showed me the museum website. That line in the bio, how Giulia lived peacefully in a suburb of Rome. Peacefully!" Her voice was filled with outrage. "That's why I wanted to find her. I wanted her to know what happened. How she left her baby and how much suffering she caused."

She rolled her eyes at what she'd just said. "I was so self-righteous, blaming Giulia for what she did, leaving her child behind. And yet, I feel like I did the same thing."

"But... but your daughter is not a baby, is she?" he said.

"No."

"And you left her with family."

"Yes, but... but no, actually, I didn't," Tori said. "I left her with Marilene. Just like Giulia did when she left my mother. Marilene's not family. But here she is... she's been taking care of us, three generations of us—my mother, me, and now Molly. We don't belong to anyone. We... forced ourselves into her life. And she had no choice. Because she's a good person, and she wasn't going to abandon us. But we're not hers..."

She put her elbows on the table and dropped her forehead onto the heels of her hands. "Oh, God," she said. "I feel terrible. I never saw us this way before. We belong to no one. We never have."

There was quiet for a moment. Then Emilio slid a clean napkin her way, and she took it as she lifted her head to wipe her eyes. She couldn't remember the last time she'd cried in front of someone she knew. But if she had to do so, he felt like a safe choice to witness her tears.

"Tori," he said gently. "What happened to... Molly's father?"

She scrunched up the napkin and put it on the table. "He lives in California," she said. "He's never been in the picture. I met him at a party in New York a long time ago. He was my friend's cousin. He was nice-looking, fun, smart. In graduate school, studying engineering. Neither one of us was looking for anything serious. Don't get me wrong, Molly's the best thing that ever happened to me. But there was never any way... I mean, Brian and I, we weren't going to be together. That was never going to happen."

"He just left? Does he ever see her?"

She shook her head. "He sends her birthday gifts."

"But he never wanted to meet her?"

"There was no reason for him to. He was never going to be a real part of her life or anything. Why open a can of worms?"

"So he wanted to meet her."

"I don't know. Maybe."

"And you wouldn't let him?"

"No, it wasn't like that. You've got it all wrong. Maybe you have to be in my shoes to understand why I handled it this way." It had been the right decision to keep Brian out of Molly's life. Things were hard enough for Molly, having a single mom. Why make things harder by adding a dad who left New York after grad school and never intended to live anywhere but California?

"Of course," Emilio said. "Forgive me. I have no idea what you've had to deal with."

She looked at him. His eyes were sorrowful. She felt bad for snapping at him when he was simply showing concern. And she appreciated him for that. It had been nice these last few days, having a kind of father figure in her life. She hadn't realized how much she'd missed by not having had a father for so long. Or even how much Molly had missed, by not having one at all.

"I know I have a very unusual life," she said. "I never planned it, our little family—Marilene, Molly, and me. It just turned out that way."

"Has there been anyone else?" Emilio asked. "Since Molly's father?"

She paused, then nodded. "Yes. We were together for five years. It ended before I came here. Maybe that's also one of the things I was running away from. Being alone again. Which is why I feel so bad about Molly now. She's learning to live without him, too."

"She liked him?"

"She adored him."

"And you did, too?"

She looked upward and shook her head. "He's the best."

"Then why did it end? If you don't mind my asking."

"Because..." she paused, then pointed to the poem on the yellow paper. "Because I can't do this, okay? I can't tell someone I'll go wherever they go, I'll stay wherever they stay. Whatever this poem is, wherever it comes from, it has to do with giving yourself up completely for someone else. To making the 'together' part more important than the 'you' part. The 'me' part. And I can't. It's too risky. I've had too many people leave. *We've* had too many people leave to trust like that ever again."

She picked up the paper and scowled. "It's ironic, isn't it?

Giulia's saying in this note that she'd go to the ends of the earth for someone. But at the end of the day, she wasn't capable of that at all. It was a lie. She left the one person who needed her— her baby. And all the damage that happened ever since—it happened because of that. Because Giulia didn't love. She wasn't capable of love. She couldn't have done what she did if she knew how to love."

"The poem in your hand suggests otherwise."

She tilted her head skeptically. "What are you getting at?"

"I'm saying that from what I've learned this week about your grandmother, I don't think she was incapable of love."

"But what about the bullets and Pietro's notebook and how he said she betrayed him?"

"I don't think it's a reasonable conclusion to say she never could love. And I think you are hurting yourself to feel that way. She may have loved very deeply. People often love more deeply than we see. Or realize. It's not something that gets switched on or off."

"Oh, you're a fine one to talk about love," Tori said. "What about you? You're clearly in love with Gabriella. I saw it that night at dinner. And she loves you, too. I saw that today."

"You saw Gabriella today?"

"I was in her shop. She said to say hello to you for her. And the way she couldn't help but smile when she said it—I could tell how she feels about you. So you tell me, why are you so willing to be alone? Why are you telling me one thing and your-self another?"

"We are different, you and me," he said, holding up his index finger as if to make an irrefutable point. "I'm an old man. I had a wonderful marriage, to a woman I fell in love with when I was fourteen years old. We have six children, fifteen grandchil-dren. We had a long, full life together. But you... you are still young. You are still learning what love is. But there's time. You don't learn what love is at a party in New York or even after spending five years with someone. You are throwing away something that you don't even yet know…"

He breathed out and looked at the table. She could see his hands trembling. She had figured he was a widower. But she hadn't known the extent of his grief.

"I'm sorry. Again," she said. "I had no business saying all that. And I know that I'm stubborn and haven't yet figured out many things about life. I guess I was hoping that being here, that knowing about my grandmother or even meeting her, would give me some… guidance. And… and she must have been a wonderful person, your wife. I'm sorry she's gone."

He grinned. "She was the best."

She smiled at his use of her words. Then she grew serious again. "So how do you go on?" she asked. "After that kind of loss?"

"You learn to accept it," he told her. "I think if you live in a place like this, where there's so much history, there are always ghosts. You always live with shadows. Although maybe that's true of everyone. No one can escape what came before or what is inside us. You go on. And at some point, you start to appreciate exactly that. That you have those shadows. Those ghosts. They're even here all around us. They always will be, all the people who died. Oh, the memories my father used to share of making deliveries to this island. The views from the water into the castle, the dancing he could see on the top story through the open windows, the music he could hear. It was a very special time, before the war. And it will never come back.

"Although you know what?" he said. "I think now when my father looks across the water, he sees life. He sees a little of what isn't there anymore. People falling in love, enjoying art, music, dance. And it comforts him. I stay here, in the home he grew up in, and try to find the world my father saw. It will be completely gone in a few years, when his generation is no longer around. The castle will just be a museum, a tourist site people can check off on their list of what to do when they come to this part of Italy. I fear it already is."

Tori sighed. "You've been so good to me this week, Emilio," she said. "And I appreciate it so much. Especially tonight. I can see that I've been on a wild goose chase, fooling myself into thinking I could glean something valuable. When the truth is, I need to go home and straighten out my life. I have a business that I'm trying to build, and Molly needs me. It was frivolous to come here. All I did was delay a lot of thinking that I have to do."

"So you're calling off the search for Giulia?"

"I think so."

He paused. "What kind of business?" he asked, his eyes lighting up. Tori could tell he was glad to change the subject to something cheerful.

She smiled. "Believe it or not... I design wedding gowns. I want to open my own shop."

"Wedding gowns!" he said. "What do you know! Well now, that's a wonderful business. A hopeful business. That makes me happy."

They finished their last few mouthfuls of food and then gathered the trash. Emilio took it to the trash bin. "I take it you're thinking of shortening your trip? How many days do you have left?"

She nodded. "Six."

"When will you leave?"

"As soon as I can get a flight. I'll figure it out tomorrow."

"I'll be sorry to see you go. But don't worry," he added with a twinkle in his eye. "I won't charge you for the cancellation."

They left the café and went into the lobby. Emilio showed her the way to the employee lounge. "There's a small sofa where you can get some sleep," he said. "It's not great but it's the most comfortable option. And set your alarm on your phone. We should be down to the dock by nine twenty to catch the first ferry back."

"But what about you? Won't you get to rest at all?"

"No, I'll be in the lobby watching for unauthorized boats. Of course, there's never been an instance of an unauthorized boat showing up, but they still like to have someone there just in case."

Tori looked at the paper that was still in her hand. "Maybe I should put this back now," she said. "So we don't have to worry about it tomorrow."

"That's probably a good idea," he said, and they turned in the direction of the archives.

"I still wish I knew who she wrote this to. Who she was willing to give up everything for."

"You have no idea at all?" he asked. "Marilene never recalled anyone?"

Tori thought for a moment. "Now that you mention it, she did tell me about someone from Giulia's past. Someone she said Giulia talked about when she first arrived on their island. His family had some kind of dry goods market in Anzalea—you know, like the one your family had. His name was something with a V... Vincenzo maybe..."

She continued walking until she noticed Emilio was no longer beside her. She turned to see him a few steps back, stopped in his tracks.

"What's the matter?" she said.

"Tori," he told her. "My father's name is Vincenzo."

TWENTY-SEVEN

OCTOBER 1943

"The Nazis are getting desperate," Luca said. "They are rounding up Jews in towns around Rome and beyond, and deporting them to the camps. They are growing bolder and more determined as the Americans and British make strides from the South."

It was the night after Luca had returned, and Pietro had whispered to him and Giulia to join him in his study once the children were asleep. Pietro was seated behind his desk, and Giulia and Luca were in the chairs opposite him. The shutters were closed but still, the lamps stayed unlit, for extra security. Two candles on Pietro's desk were the only lights he'd allowed.

The news about Giulia's family had hit them all hard, and lately, smoke could be seen rising from Parissi Island through the rear windows of the house, the very windows where Marilene had seen the beautifully dressed castle guests dancing. Small explosions also sounded from that direction, loud and disarming, especially since Pietro had no idea what all the noise and smoke might mean. Giulia remembered how the twins had greeted her on the first night she'd come, asking her between giggles if she was a Nazi. Life had been growing more somber for the family ever since she'd arrived, and Luca's disturbing assessment would only make things worse. The children were no longer allowed beyond the small patio off the kitchen now, and could only be there for short periods of time so they could get some fresh air. The twins no longer giggled. Despite their parents' best efforts, the children sensed their growing fear.

"What did you hear in Rome?" Pietro asked.

"It's still in the initial stages, but we are planning a strike at an officers' quarters in late October. Grenades and handguns. The bullets that were dropped off here before I left need to be smuggled both to Parissi Island and to Rome. I'm to go back to Rome in two weeks to help complete the logistics. The group on Parissi Island has the map you and Giulia drew and will be ready to receive the ammunition."

"How are we to transfer the bullets?" Pietro said.

"It needs to look innocent," Luca told him. "A shipment or delivery that won't seem suspicious. That's how ammunition is being moved across Italy. Messengers on bicycles, women on foot—people they would least suspect. In baskets of fruit, sacks of letters. Everyday goods being transported to Rome..."

"Like dresses," Giulia said.

Both men looked at her.

"Children's dresses," she said. "The clothes I make, they have smocking and seams and hems and trim. I'm a skilled seamstress, and I can hide the bullets so they're undetectable. And I can transport them to Rome. I'll cut my hair and comb it differently so no one will recognize me. And besides, they won't be looking for me anymore. The Nazis believe all the Parissis and their guests are dead. That's what you told me, Pietro. That means they think I'm dead, too."

Luca looked at her, his eyebrows raised. Then he shook his head. "It's too dangerous. You can't be sure they won't recognize you. No, I can do it."

"But you're leaving soon. Before I can get the sewing done—"

"We'll find someone else—"

"No, it has to be me," Giulia said. "I know how to handle and transport garments. No one will look more like a dressmaker than me. Because I am one."

"She's right," Pietro said softly.

Luca shook his head. "But no—"

"Luca!" Pietro said harshly. "This is exactly what I dreaded would happen when Giulia arrived—"

"What did you dread?" Luca asked.

"You know what I'm talking about," Pietro scolded. "Don't make me spell it out and embarrass you both."

He looked hard at Giulia. She felt her face redden and lowered her gaze.

"Now, we need to keep focused," Pietro said. Giulia could tell his attention was more on Luca than her. "We need to make the best decisions. This is about my children, the next generation. If we let our emotions get in the way, cloud our intentions—Luca, the Nazis are hardly more than a stone's throw away from this house. Have you forgotten that? Have you forgotten your father and all he stood for?"

"Of course not!" Luca stood, and from the corner of her eye, Giulia saw his fists clench. "How dare you—"

At that moment, the door to the study opened and Cellina appeared. "Luca! Pietro! Please," she hissed. "Keep your voices down. You will wake the children. It's enough for tonight. You can talk more tomorrow."

Pietro rose and walked around his desk with heavy footsteps. "Cellina is right," he said. "We will have cooler heads in the morning."

He grasped Cellina's elbow and the two left the study. When they were gone, Luca sat back down. He reached over and touched Giulia's hand. "I don't want you to do this," he said softly.

"But I have to," she told him. "For my family. And for all the others, all who have died. It's what you said when I first met you —there are things bigger than oneself. I was selfish. You were right."

He shook his head. "But we talked about this. You're not a fighter. You don't have it in you."

"But I do," she said. "I do now."

The next two weeks passed quickly, and Giulia was busy almost around the clock. During the day she carried on as Pietro wanted her to, pretending to be the family's dressmaker and a companion to Marilene. She continued to teach Marilene how to sew, helped her with her lessons, and listened to her discuss her history readings or recite the poetry that Signorina Ottavia required her to memorize. But after they'd all had dinner and the children were asleep, she devoted herself to perfecting the art of hiding bullets in the hems and seams and trimmings of children's party dresses and gowns.

It was easy to hide the sight of the bullets, she found, by wrapping them in the folds of the fabric. Harder, she realized, was disguising their weight. But she found that if she used the heavier buttons and closures that Cellina kept tucked away with the extra fabric she stored in the bedroom closets, the weight of the bullets wasn't so detectable. She also used beads and stones for decorating the bodices of some of the dresses, a skill she'd learned when she made the elaborate wedding dress while at Parissi Island. Again, the weight of those adornments would help draw attention away from the hidden bullets.

And late each night, after Pietro and Cellina were sure to be asleep, she would find Luca in his bedroom. It was only then, in his arms, that she would talk about her family. About her grief.

And her guilt. Because she knew he heard her. One night, lying next to him, she recounted a story about her younger sister, Emilia, the baby, with the long hair, round face and big, puppy dog eyes.

"I must have been around twelve, and she was ten," she said. "And she bought this little necklace for herself. It had these silly beads in garish colors, but she was so delighted with it, and she asked me what I thought. I don't know, I guess I was in a bad mood, I used to get so jealous because she adored our older sister, Annalisa, and that made me mad. So that day I told her the necklace was ugly and cheap. And she didn't say anything, just took it off and never wore it again.

"Oh, I feel so bad about that now," she said. "Why did I hurt her like that? Why was I so mean?"

"You were twelve," Luca said. "You were young."

"But I wish I could tell her I'm sorry. I remember her face, that stunned look as she picked up the necklace and studied it. She got hurt so easily. I know I was only twelve, but that's no excuse. I didn't realize I would think of it now. It was a foolish thing to say and it will haunt me forever."

He turned on his side to face her. "Everything we say can last forever, if it happens at a certain time or in a certain way. But we live on. We change and we do better."

"But I didn't do better. I didn't save her. We made her go back to take care of our father. We sent her off to be murdered. She was only fifteen." She thought she might cry but didn't. She felt almost too sad for tears.

"You didn't know what would happen. How could you? You made the best decision you could."

"How do I live with it now?"

He took her hand. "You live a life that matters. That will be her legacy. You are the one who holds all their lives in you. You will be the way they live on. As I will for my father.

"Remember that saying you taught me?" he added. "Choose life? You have to choose life, too."

"But how? My whole family is gone."

"You do. You do what would make them happy. You do what would make them proud."

Later, she snuck back to her room before anyone in the house was awake, as she continued to do each morning. And before she knew it, two weeks had passed, and she was saying goodbye to Luca again. This time, by the light of the full moon, she walked him down to the waiting boat, where Pietro and Cellina were standing. She no longer saw the need to hide how she was feeling, as with every stitch of a hem or seam, she was proving her worth to Pietro.

As they walked, Luca reviewed the plans. Giulia would have the next month to finish all the sewing. And then she would go to Rome, posing as a dressmaker delivering garments to operatives posing as store owners. At that point, Luca would find her. And they would receive instructions either to leave Italy or to return to Ciani Island, depending on how the operation unfolded.

They were a team now, she knew. And they were doing exactly what they needed to do. Because while the world was ugly and cruel, it was only for now. He'd convinced her that it didn't have to stay that way.

Giulia spent the next four weeks finishing up her work and getting ready to leave for Rome. She cut her hair short and noticed, with some relief, that being inside so much had made her hair darker. She made herself two trim suits, one gray and one navy blue, with pencil skirts so she'd look like a chic fashion designer when she arrived in Rome. Then she began packing up the doctored children's dresses. From time to time, she'd feel dizzy, her stomach unsettled, her body feeling not at all like her own. But she convinced herself that she was just scared, tired, overwhelmed, grieving.

Three days before she was to leave, she sat down for a talk with Marilene. "You have to go, too?" Marilene complained. "Why does everyone have to leave?"

"I know it seems unfair," she told her. "But it's for you. To make the world a better place for you to live in someday."

"First Luca, now you. I hate that you'll both be gone. I'll be so sad if you don't come back."

"I will come back. We both will."

"Life used to be fun here."

"And it will be again. I promise, sweet girl."

"Don't you love me? Like one of your sisters?"

"Of course, I do."

"Then don't leave."

"I have to. But I will be back. I will come back to you, Marilene. You can trust me."

On the morning she was to leave, she finished packing and went to her bedroom window to look outside. The beautiful Mediterranean showed no indication of the violence and brutality enveloping the world. But there was more on her mind than the scenery. Because standing there, anticipating the task she'd been preparing for since learning of her family's death, she finally had to face what was happening inside of her.

She was pregnant.

She returned to the bed and sat down, clasping her hands together to help her concentrate. What was she going to do now? She was alone, without her family. She was living in a home that was not hers, with people who were essentially still strangers. She'd been ready to sacrifice her life if necessary to help destroy the Nazis and guarantee the future of her beloved Italy. She had come to believe that was the best way for her to live. It was the best role she was meant to assume: Warrior. Resistance fighter. Partisan.

Yet even that decision wasn't simple. Now she had another life to think about. The child she'd made with Luca.

She didn't want to let Luca down. She knew he was depending on her. All the operatives in Rome were depending on her. She tried again to convince herself that she was mistaken. Maybe something else was wrong with her. Her body had been through a lot. Maybe she was ill. Maybe she was unable to deal with the recent humidity or the rich foods that Cellina and Signora Brambilla served. Maybe her body was catching up with all the changes. Maybe she was simply very tired.

But she knew that wasn't the case. Her body hurt in ways she'd never felt before. She was constantly dealing with nausea but was also very hungry. Her chest was growing, and her waist was thickening. She'd been around pregnant women back when she was young. Women in the neighborhood were often pregnant—two, three, four times. She even remembered when her mother had been pregnant, before she'd died in childbirth, along with the baby, the little girl who would have been her third sister. It had become easy to tell when a neighbor was even in the early stages of pregnancy. She recognized in herself what she'd seen in them.

Two hours later, she was seated in Pietro's study, having asked Pietro and Cellina for a word. Pietro had looked at her warily, and she suspected he was worried that she would say she was too scared to complete her task and wanted to back out. And the truth was, he was partly right. She wasn't scared, but she was backing out. There was no choice. She was feeling weak and ill, and she knew that made her a danger to the others on this mission. If she couldn't be in top form, she needed to withdraw.

But it had to be her secret alone. She could never let Luca know the truth. At least not for a long time. She knew he would worry about her, and that would distract him and compromise his safety. She couldn't tell Pietro or Cellina the truth either, because they might try to reach Luca. They might feel he deserved to know. And she feared, too, that Pietro would be furious with him, for letting this happen. Giulia didn't want to do anything to damage the relationship the two men had. She knew that Pietro had been like a father to Luca, after he'd lost his own.

They finally arrived in the study, Pietro taking his place behind the desk and Cellina sitting in the opposite chair.

"You are to leave this evening," Pietro said. "What's on your mind?"

She looked at him straight in the eye. It was as Luca had said when she'd told him about Emilia and the necklace—there was nothing to do except go forward. In the way she felt was best. And she had a good way forward, she thought. The timing worked. And nobody would be hurt by her lie. Because the person she would name as the father was dead.

TWENTY-EIGHT

MAY 2019

Thursday

Tori could hardly sleep that night—and it wasn't just because she was on a small, scratchy sofa, the tweed fabric of the throw pillow like sandpaper against her cheek. It was also because of what she'd just learned from Emilio. She could hardly believe that all this time she'd been exploring old boxes in the archives and trying to piece together her grandmother's life and possible whereabouts—all this time her actual grandfather may have been living in the very house where she was staying. Of course, she didn't know for sure that Emilio's father was *the* Vincenzo. But if he was, then tonight was a game-changer. If that sweet elderly man back at the hotel turned out to be her grandfather, then he could explain what had happened all those years ago—where Giulia had gone and why she had never come back for their daughter and what the bullets were about and what had happened to make Pietro write those harsh words in his notebook. Surely he could answer at least some of those questions.

She thought about him now, Emilio's father, as she turned to her side on the sofa. She had seen him only that once at the hotel, when he'd sold her a ticket to the castle. He'd looked so frail, his face full of deep lines and crevices. His shoulders hunched. His long face, the skin sagging, his cheeks almost lower than his chin. His hands full of veins when he'd reached to a box on the counter to tear a single ticket from the large roll, his fingers trembling as he handed it to her. He didn't resemble her mother or Molly at all. But did that matter? And if it were true, if he was her grandfather, then he was culpable, too. Why had he left his baby, and where had he gone? Had he been with Giulia all this time? How could he have gone on to start a new family with Emilio's mother, to settle in London and then come back here to live out his days? Had he forgotten that he once had a little girl?

On the other hand, she supposed, maybe he never even knew he'd had a baby. Marilene had said Giulia was alone when the baby was born. What if Giulia never told the man she'd loved that she was carrying his child? What if she didn't know she was pregnant until after she'd arrived on Ciani Island—alone? What if everything Tori revealed tomorrow was going to be a huge shock to him?

She thought again of Vincenzo, the Vincenzo that Emilio had described, the father he remembered from when he was a little boy, who'd tell him stories about seeing the castle in its heyday as he rowed toward the shore to deliver groceries. About the music and the dancing that could be seen through the tall windows on beautiful summer evenings when the air was warm and the sky no doubt was lit by a million stars. How he must miss those days when he sat in his boat and watched the dancing through the windows and dreamed of one day making his way to the castle himself, maybe as an invited guest, a young artist with dreams of creation and fulfillment? Would knowing that he had a granddaughter and a great-granddaughter in America, a beautiful great-granddaughter who loved to dance—

would knowing that help ease whatever sadness he held onto from those awful war years?

Finally, the sun was up. Tori looked at her phone and saw it was only six thirty. Emilio had told her to set her alarm, but she hadn't needed to—she'd slept lightly all night and had awoken more times than she could count. She tried to sleep for about an hour more, and then rose from the sofa and slipped on her sandals. In the bathroom adjoining the employee lounge, she tamed her hair with her fingers and then redid her ponytail. There was a tube of toothpaste and a few wrapped disposable toothbrushes on the counter, presumably for the night guards to use. Grateful for small favors, she brushed her teeth and then went to find Emilio.

He was there in the lobby waiting for her, his clothes disheveled and his eyes baggy. She could tell that he'd probably gotten even less sleep than she had. He led her back into the café and went behind the counter to make two cups of espresso. He seemed to know exactly what he was doing, so she figured this, too, was part of the routine for night guards. She watched him lift the top of a large chest-type freezer and pull out a food-storage container. He removed two pastries filled with what looked like raspberry jam and put them into a nearby countertop oven.

When their food was ready, they took it to a table and, wordlessly, they ate. Tori had never seen Emilio so preoccupied. From time to time he caught her eye and smiled, but most of the time he looked away. She didn't blame him. This all had to be coming as an enormous shock. After all, she had known the story of her missing grandmother for several days now; but the story now facing him, a story about his father possibly having had an entire family before he met Emilio's mother, a family he'd never revealed to Emilio before—that was brand new.

"I'm not unhappy, you know," he said after draining his cup.

"I'm..." He closed his eyes and raised his palms as if to say there were no words.

"We may be wrong," Tori said, not sure if she hoped this would turn out to be the case or not. Either way, she felt bad that Emilio was so troubled. It was exactly how she'd felt that night in the living room when Marilene said, *We have to talk.* No matter how old you were, it was hard to learn that everything you thought you knew about your life and your family wasn't real. Or, in Emilio's case, might not be. The ground felt a little less firm under your feet.

"We shall see, won't we?" he said.

They finished eating, then left the museum and went down the stone staircase and over to the dock. Soon the ferry arrived. Tori followed Emilio aboard. They sat in silence as the boat glided toward the mainland. The sun was clear, and the air smelled fresh, and Tori couldn't help but feel the optimism that always came with a new day.

Reaching the shore, they walked the short distance to the hotel, the streets mostly empty and the staccato click of their footsteps sounding tense on the brick paving stones. They entered the hotel, passing the little courtyard where guests were enjoying breakfast. Inside, Emilio's father—Vincenzo—was sitting on a stool behind the reception desk.

"*Buon giorno,*" he said, looking surprised to see the two of them together.

"Papa," Emilio began, then said a few words in Italian that Tori didn't understand. Vincenzo nodded solemnly and went into the back office, and Emilio motioned for Tori to follow with him. It was more of a very small living room than an office. There was a floral sofa and two upholstered armchairs with wooden legs, and a pretty oval coffee table, the surface mosaic tile. Vincenzo sat on one armchair, and Emilio sat on the other, gesturing for Tori to sit on the sofa. When she did, he leaned forward toward his father, his elbows on his knees and his hands clasped together.

"Papa," he said and then continued in English, which Tori knew was for her benefit. "Our guest, Signorina Cole—Tori—came here to see the island and the new museum, as you know. But she also came to find information about the dressmaker, Giulia, who made the wedding gown on display there."

"Ah, the famous Giulia," Vincenzo said. "She is a big draw for the museum. Many people come to see that gown."

"Yes, but she has a particular reason," Emilio said. "She thinks... no, she *knows*... that Giulia was her grandmother. And she was told by people who knew Giulia well... she was told that her grandfather—the father of Giulia's baby—was a young man who would deliver goods from a market here in Anzalea to the castle before the Nazis captured it. A young man named... Vincenzo..."

Tori watched the old man take in this information. He was silent for a moment, and Tori wondered if he understood what Emilio had said. But then he tilted his head and seemed almost to chuckle. Tori didn't know what possibly could be funny. Maybe the chuckling was nervous energy, discomfort, or shock, she thought. Then he reached over and took Tori's hand. He gently squeezed it, the veins pulsating beneath his skin.

"You are Giulia's granddaughter?" he asked, sounding incredulous.

She nodded. "I'm the daughter of the baby she had after she escaped from the castle."

"*Dio mio,*" he said, looking down and scratching his forehead with his fingertips. "Giulia's granddaughter," he said, his accent thick. "I cannot believe it."

Tori and Emilio watched Vincenzo shaking his head. Finally, Emilio spoke.

"Papa?" he said. "What does this mean? Is what Tori was told... is it true?"

After a pause, Vincenzo lifted his head. "Tori," he said. "*Mi dispiace tantissimo.* I am truly sorry. You see, I am the one who took Giulia and her sisters to Parissi Island when they first came to Anzalea. And I did deliver groceries to Parissi Island. But Giulia and I were always friends, no more. I am not *tuo nonno.*"

Tori looked down. Although she'd tried to keep her expectations in check, she was disappointed. Perhaps she should have known that it was a long shot, her reuniting right here with her grandfather. But she'd been so desperate to find family. To have a pathway that could lead to Giulia. More than she'd realized.

"I see," she said softly.

"You mean... you knew Giulia?" Emilio said to his father. "But you never said anything. All these months with the museum opening and people staying here to go see that wedding dress. And still you kept quiet. Why did you never say anything?"

"Because I didn't want the... newspapers, you know. The publicity," he said. "All the reporters who would have been asking questions of me. Those were painful times, and I'm a private person. You know that, Emilio. I have no need for that kind of..." He paused, evidently struggling for the word. "That kind of curiosity. And Giulia never sought it out either. Heroism doesn't have to be loud. Heroism can be quiet." He turned his head to Tori. "And it's a fact, Tori. Your grandmother was a hero."

Tori raised her eyes. It seemed that this was Vincenzo's way of telling her Giulia was dead. "She was?" she asked softly.

"She was a member of the Italian Resistance," he told her. "She used her sewing skills while she was on Ciani Island to save lives. She helped smuggle ammunition to the fighters in Rome by stitching bullets into children's clothing. It was dangerous, and she could have been arrested or worse. This was your grandmother, Tori. This is your inheritance."

Tori raised her hand to her lips and shook her head, almost in disbelief. "The bullets," she murmured.

Across from her, Emilio smiled and nodded. "I told you there could be more to the story," he said. "You wanted to believe the worst."

"But what about..." she started, thinking of Pietro's notebook, with his accusations of betrayal. Thinking about how Giulia had never come back for Olive. "I still have so much I want to know. Like why she left my mother and didn't come back for her. And why—"

"She didn't come back for her, Tori, because she thought she was dead," Vincenzo said.

Tori stared at him. "What do you mean?"

"She was told while she was in Rome that the Nazis had traced the bullets back to Ciani Island. And they came to the island and killed everyone there."

"She thought..." Tori started. She felt horrible. She had judged Giulia from the moment Marilene had spoken of her. It hadn't occurred to her that this could be Giulia's reason for never coming back. She couldn't imagine what Giulia must have gone through, thinking that the Nazis had murdered her baby. She felt her breath grow short.

"*Aspetta un attimo*," Vincenzo said, touching her hand. "Wait, I have more to say. You see, even though I am not who you want me to be, I do know where your grandmother is. And if you would like to meet her, I can take you there."

She gasped, and it took her a moment to verbalize a response. "You can? She's alive?"

"Very much so," he said. "I just need to make a phone call."

TWENTY-NINE

MAY 2019

Friday

It was an hour and a half drive mostly on the highway, although for the last few miles, they traveled through a small, pretty suburb with narrow row houses bordered by flower and vegetable gardens. At Vincenzo's direction, Emilio parked in front of a cheerful yellow house with flower boxes along the front windows, filled with chrysanthemums, daffodils, and lavender peonies. Emilio went around the car to help his father out, and he grasped Vincenzo's elbow tightly as the three of them slowly made their way up the slate steps to the front door.

Before they had reached the landing, the door opened, and a stunningly beautiful woman with wavy white hair and a perfect heart-shaped face opened the door. Tori couldn't take her eyes off of her. The woman smiled, her brown eyes glowing.

"Vincenzo, my friend," she said.

Vincenzo murmured something in Italian that made the woman's eyes fill with tears.

Tori turned to Emilio. "What did your father say?" she whispered.

Emilio paused, then shook his head, as if what he'd heard was even more surprising than anything else that had happened that day.

Then he turned to Tori and answered. "He said, 'Giulia. It worked.'"

With slender, trembling fingers, Giulia reached up to stroke Tori's cheek. "My granddaughter," she said, her voice delicate and emotional yet melodic as well. "I've longed for this moment. Finally, you've found me."

Holding Tori's hand, she introduced herself to Emilio and then led them into her small, picturesque home, filled with elegant furniture in joyful colors—yellows, blues, and soft raspberry tones. She brought them to the dining table, which was set for lunch, and sat Tori next to her as she poured coffee and picked up the platter of small sandwiches to pass around the table. Tori was astonished at how much Giulia reminded her of her mother during her best days—beautiful and sociable, the kind of woman everyone falls in love with. She still had a million questions for Giulia, but for this moment, she allowed the pure joy of reunion to take over.

As they ate, Giulia made her first revelation—that she had believed for many years that Vincenzo was killed by the Nazis. So she'd been stunned when they ran into each other on a street in Rome some thirty years ago and had been fast friends ever since. Back then, she revealed quietly, she was still filled with sadness and determined to keep her identity a secret, and Vincenzo had honored that request, not even telling his children about her.

But the opening of the museum last year was the beginning of a change in her feelings about how to regard the past. "I heard they had the wedding dress there," she said. "And it made me realize that I'd spent enough time avoiding my past. I kept thinking about those horrific years, yet I remembered the lovely parts, too. The parts that never left me. The love. And I realized that I wanted to see if there was anyone who might remember or know or want to know... me..." She blinked back tears and reached for her napkin, pressing it against her mouth.

"So we came up with a plan," Vincenzo said.

"Yes," Giulia said, her eyes bright again. "I decided to... how do you say it in English? Stack the deck? I posted that comment on the website by the picture. It said the dressmaker Giulia Sancino was still alive. I didn't tell the museum about it or respond to any comments there, because I didn't want just anyone to reach out to me. But I thought that if someone from my family wanted to meet me—maybe they would come to find me...

"And here you are," she added and squeezed Tori's hand.

Tori smiled. "Yes, I am," she said. "And that was very clever. But I wasn't the one who figured it out. It was Marilene—"

"Marilene? My Marilene?"

Tori nodded. "She lives with me. I grew up knowing her as my grandmother. She found the museum website and told me about you."

"Marilene?" Giulia said, her voice catching. "My dear God. I thought she had died. She and the whole family. I can't..." She placed a hand to her mouth. "I can't believe this is true..."

Tori felt her eyes fill. Suddenly her heart ached for this poor woman, her grandmother, who would have done so much so differently if only she'd known the truth. "I know that's what you were told. Vincenzo explained that to me," she said. "But she is alive. She's fine. She brought my mother to America as a little girl. She raised her as her own."

"And your mother?" Giulia asked. "Where is she now?"

Tori looked down.

"Oh, no," Giulia said. "How? When?"

Tori hesitated, thinking that now was the moment she'd been waiting for, the moment to blast Giulia for abandoning her baby and setting her on a course for tragedy. And yet, Tori didn't want to blast Giulia. And she didn't want to hurt her. Giulia had suffered too much already.

"It was a long time ago," she said. "And it was very sad. But you do have a great-granddaughter," she added. "Her name is Molly. She's eleven." She reached for her phone to show her a picture at her last birthday party, surrounded by friends. "This is her. I hope you will meet her. She's the best part of my life."

"Oh my darling," Giulia said. "She is lovely. Molly. I will meet her. Whatever it takes. And I will see Marilene again, too. And thank her for all she did."

"We'll call them later," Tori said. "Or we can video chat, so you can see them both." She sighed as she lowered her phone. "I have so many questions to ask you, so much to tell you. I don't know where to start."

"Of course, you do. And we will have time for all that. But..."

Just then, there was the sound of a key in the front door. "Just in time," she said. "Because for now, my Tori, there is someone I want *you* to meet. He went out for a bit after Vincenzo called to give you and me time to get acquainted. But he can't wait to meet you."

"*Amore mio,*" she called. "We're in here."

A moment later a tall man walked into the room. He was wrinkled and stooped over, but his beauty was unmistakable, even at his age. He had a strong jaw, high cheekbones, and soft white hair. And big green eyes that looked right through you. Just as Marilene had described them. He was the man with Giulia in the photo that she'd seen in the first box she'd opened in the archives.

"Luca," Giulia said. "This is Tori, your granddaughter."

Tori got up and went to hug him, feeling his strong arms around her. And for the first time in a long time, maybe even in forever, she felt completely at home.

THIRTY

MAY 2019

Friday

Tori decided to spend the last few days of her trip at the home of her grandparents. As lunch was drawing to a close, she mentioned that her bags were still in Anzalea, but Giulia said that was no problem as her closets were filled with garments.

"Don't forget, I'm a dressmaker," she said.

Emilio and Vincenzo left after lunch, and Tori wasted no time in getting to know her grandmother. There was so much to talk about—the war, the bullets, Pietro's notebook, and the meaning of the words "Wherever you go" on the paper she'd found. But they'd get to all that later. For now, she wanted to talk about the most important topic of all. And she brought it up as soon as she and Giulia were alone, as Luca walked Emilio and Vincenzo back to their car. She explained how troubled Olive's life had been, and the way she had drowned, which brought Giulia to tears.

"You thought your daughter was dead," Tori said. "And Marilene thought *you* were dead. That was the only thing, she said, that would have kept you away. But Emilio—he said the real story could be more complicated. And he was right."

Giulia wiped her tears with a handkerchief and went on to explain everything. How she'd been told right after her eighteenth birthday that her whole family had been murdered. How sad she was, and how much she wanted to feel less helpless. And how Luca felt the same, having seen his father killed after writing an anti-Fascist editorial. How she and Luca spent a month together on Ciani Island, trying to draw comfort from one another. How she came up with the idea to sew bullets into dresses to smuggle to the Resistance fighters operating in Rome. How Luca left to help organize a major attack on Nazi buildings in the occupied towns, and she was to meet him with the final box of altered garments.

"But then I found I was pregnant," she said. "I told Marilene's parents I had married Vincenzo before I arrived at their home. I couldn't tell them the truth, that it was Luca's baby. I was ashamed that we had been together. Marilene's father had seen the two of us growing close, and he'd tried to keep us apart. He thought that I would distract Luca from his work in the Resistance. He considered it a huge betrayal that we had fallen in love. But we couldn't help it. I couldn't stop it. And I couldn't be sorry."

Tori breathed in sharply. So this was it—the reason Pietro had written such angry words in his notebook. This was the betrayal he'd mentioned. Giulia and Luca falling in love—that's how Giulia had betrayed Pietro. Tori decided not to tell Giulia about the notebook. Her grandmother had been through so much and didn't need to be further upset by Pietro's harsh words.

"Marilene's father arranged for others to smuggle the garments with the bullets," Giulia continued and went on to explain that after Olive was born, she went to Rome to find Luca. And as she was connecting with some of the Resistance fighters to learn what had happened to Luca, she was told that everyone on Ciani Island was dead.

"I thought often about going back, but I couldn't bring myself to do it," she said. "I didn't think I could face that island, knowing what had happened while I was away. I wished that I had stayed, so that I would have been killed, too. I did go back, later on. When Olive would have been six. Before I'd even found Luca again, I went back, hoping to stop the hurt. But there were new owners there, and they had no idea what had happened to the Ciani family.

"They let me look around the house one last time," she said, speaking in just above a whisper. "And before I left, I went into what had been Luca's room. He had written a note to me years earlier, and I wrote the same thing now. It was something my father used to say, a sort of poem: 'Wherever you go, I will go, and wherever you stay, I will stay.' I wrote it for Luca. And for Olive. And for Marilene and her family. And for the six million Jews who died. And all the others who died or suffered. I tucked it under the window seat in his room. I hoped someone who needed to find it, would."

Tori let out a shaky breath. "I found it," she said. "It was in one of the boxes at the museum. I was going to put it back, but I brought it to the hotel. It was in Italian so I had to translate it to understand it. And I knew you wrote it." And at that moment, she also remembered where she had first heard those words. Olive, her mother, used to chant them. Except she'd said them in a more formal way. A biblical way: *Whither thou goest, I will go; and where thou lodgest, I will lodge; thy people shall be my people, and thy God my God...*

Giulia slowly rose and walked over to the window, which looked out to the flower boxes, drenched in sunlight.

"There is so much that doesn't make sense," she said. "Mistakes, misunderstandings. So much that could have been different. If I hadn't been told Olive was dead, I would have gone back to her long before she left with Marilene. But we cannot rewrite the past. War and genocide and brutality—they don't let go. They were my life then. They've been my life always.

"But my darling," she said. "I look at you and I think about your daughter, and I... can't help but think I have finally stumbled on... rightness. And peace. There was something else my father would say, something from his Jewish learning. Maybe a command, or maybe a plea. Choose life. Choose life. For so long, I didn't feel I could. But today, with you here, I'm finally able to."

Tori looked at her. "I'm not sure I know what that means."

"It means that I now have a connection with the generation that came next. After the nightmare. Tori, I became an adult during the war, and your mother was born during it. But you... you are the first generation to have no direct connection. You were born long after it was over. And darling, all of us who suffered and all of those who died—and I include your mother in that—we all stand behind you. Do it for us, if you can.

"Choose life, my love. Choose life."

THIRTY-ONE

That fall, and for many years later, Tori would tell herself that she'd done exactly what her grandmother had asked her to do. She'd chosen life.

She'd chosen life when she stayed in Italy for a few extra days, so she could help her grandparents pack up and travel with her for a six-month stay at her home. So they could reunite with Marilene and get to know Molly. So Molly could know the story of the people who came before, and the way their actions helped ensure that one day she would come to be.

She'd chosen life when she brought Molly to California over the summer, to let her finally meet her father. She'd realized that shutting Brian out of Molly's life wasn't in her daughter's best interest. As Emilio had said, a person's secrets reveal who they are. She no longer wanted to be the person who kept secrets as a way of maintaining control. Brian had always wanted to know his daughter, but Tori had kept her distance, fearing that letting him in would open her up to hurt and disappointment. Still, Molly deserved to know her father and to have a relationship with him. Her role, as Molly's mom, was to help Molly forge that relationship, not deny Molly access to her father. Tori had learned from her trip to Italy that the antidote to mistrust is connection.

She'd chosen life, too, when she'd gone back to see Jeremy's band at Danny's bar after she arrived home. Choosing life meant giving the future a chance. She'd sat at the same outdoor table where she'd sat on the night they met, and before the first set had started, she'd slipped a note to the drummer to give to Jeremy, asking him to invite her up on the stage for a second chance. Two songs in, she saw Jeremy read the note. He'd invited her up to sing, as he'd done that first night, and she accepted. But the truth was, she was asking for a second chance to say yes. And she was sure he knew that's what she meant.

And finally, she'd chosen life when she walked down the stairs of her house, wearing the beautiful white linen suit she and Giulia had designed together, to meet Jeremy near the front window that let in the setting orange sun, so they could exchange wedding vows. And when she'd asked Giulia to let out the seams a bit, to accommodate her thickening waistline. Their twins—a boy and a girl, she'd discovered from the ultrasound at her most recent doctor's appointment—were due next June. By then, she and Molly would have moved with Jeremy into a new house that could accommodate their growing family. And though they'd hoped Marilene would move in with them, she'd decided on an alternate plan. She was returning to Italy with Giulia and Luca. To search for her brothers and find out what had happened to her parents. She'd been inspired by Tori's success in uncovering her own story, and she wanted the same sense of peace that Tori now knew.

The wedding was small, but all the important people were there, including Brianna and her newest boyfriend. And a handful of Tori's clients, including Sheree, who had been married in her beautiful dress with the asymmetrical hem, and Kelly, who had sent the postcard from Italy. Vincenzo, Emilio and Gabriella, along with Emilio's children and grandchildren, watched the ceremony on Zoom from the hotel in Anzalea or wherever else they were in the world. And, of course, Albie watched from his favorite spot on the rug.

The guests also included two newcomers. While she was still in Italy, Tori had called the museum director to let him know she'd located Giulia, and that led to revelations about the anonymous couple who had donated the wedding dress to the museum. It turned out that Giulia's older sister, Annalisa, hadn't died trying to escape from Parissi Castle; she'd made it to New York after all. When she'd died just a year ago, her granddaughter, Mia, had discovered the wedding dress in her attic and donated it to the museum. She and her husband lived in Philadelphia, where Mia was studying for a Ph.D. in cardiology, and were delighted to be invited to the wedding. Tori immediately adored her cousin and knew they were going to be lifelong friends.

Standing in front of them all was the town's mayor, a friend of Marilene's, who'd agreed to officiate.

Tori walked along the makeshift aisle between the rows of guests and gave her bouquet to Molly, then reached for Jeremy's hand. By the time she'd returned from Italy, Molly was no longer disappointed with her role in the ballet production. In fact, she loved being dance captain, and felt it was even more fun than being the star. Tori had to hand it to her. She'd been so worried about Molly's reaction. But Molly was resilient, something Tori would need to remember as she moved closer to her teenage years.

Tori and Jeremy joined hands, as the mayor began the ceremony. The two of them had decided to take a very short honeymoon—just a long weekend in the city—because they had a lot to do, what with the new house and the coming babies. And the new store—Tori's Originals—which would open in January. Giulia and Luca had saved some money over the years, as Luca had worked as a teacher and Giulia a dressmaker, and they'd decided that as a wedding gift, they would cover the first six months' rent of the new store. Giulia had always wanted her own shop. And she thought it fitting that her granddaughter, in partnership with her new husband, would realize that dream.

Looking out the window at the setting sun, Tori felt the twins rustle beneath her waistband. She remembered her first ultrasound appointment back in August, when she and Jeremy had seen those two strong heartbeats, pulsing sparks of light. And now the babies were moving. She expected they'd be like her mother, Olive, who Giulia had said was full of life from the minute she was born. Babies didn't have to choose life. They did it automatically. As for adults, it sometimes took a little longer, Tori thought.

But once they did, the sky was the limit.

As she smiled at Jeremy, she remembered a thought she had had last night just before falling asleep. It wasn't a dream, but more like a vision, a premonition. She saw herself going back to Parissi Island sometime in the future with her family—Jeremy, Molly, and the as yet unnamed babies. And at some point, she would sneak away from the museum and the dock, and go to the edge of the shore. There, she'd take out from her pocket the small, crumbling note she'd retrieved from the last box she'd opened in the archives. She'd carefully unfold it and study the Italian words one last time.

And then she'd rip it up into the tiniest of pieces. So small that they would practically become the wood pulp from which they were made.

And when those pieces were as tiny as possible, she'd fling them up into the sky. There they'd scatter and soar, carried by the sea breeze. And as they slowly rained down on the sand and the water and the rocks, and on the shadows of all the people who perished as they tried to escape the island, and on the earth that would forever hold the memory of the six million Jews and all the others who had suffered and died at the hands of the

Nazis, she would make a promise. The same promise that her great-grandfather, the Jewish tailor, had made to her great-grandmother, the disowned Parissi heiress. The same promise that Luca had written to Giulia and Giulia had left for Luca years later. The promise that said you will not be forgotten.

"Wherever you go," she'd whisper as the tiny pieces of paper rained down. "Wherever you go."

A LETTER FROM BARBARA

I want to say a huge thank you for choosing to read *The Lost Gift to the Italian Island*. If you enjoyed it and want to keep up to date with all my latest releases, just sign up at the following link. Your email address will never be shared and you can unsubscribe at any time.

www.bookouture.com/barbara-josselsohn

I think many authors would agree that when you write a novel, you end up learning as much about yourself as you do about the characters you've invented. And often those discoveries entail revisiting moments in your life that you hadn't thought about in years, if ever.

The Lost Gift to the Italian Island is my seventh book, and I think it's my most personal. As I closed my computer after a day of writing scenes about Giulia—the middle Sancino sister who flees to a remote Italian island to escape the Nazis—I often found myself pausing, as long-forgotten memories popped into my head. Many times, I would find myself recalling a squat, brick apartment building in the Bronx, New York where my father's three aunts—Bessie, Ida, and Rose—lived. My family—my mother, my father, my sister and I—would go there when I was quite young for holiday dinners. My grandmother—my father's mother, the fourth sister—had died years earlier, so Bessie, Rose, and Ida had a special place in their hearts for my dad.

I remember lots of people of all ages—uncles, aunts, cousins, second cousins, third cousins, too, I'm sure—crammed together around the narrow, rectangular dining room table, which held bowls upon bowls and platters upon platters of steaming, fragrant food: roast chicken; brisket bathing in reddish-brown juices; small, tender potatoes; cooked carrots and string beans; and some tan-colored side dishes with strange-sounding names, some of which tasted wonderful and others, not so much. Bessie, Ida, and Rose needed to be coaxed to sit down, as they were busy shuffling back and forth from the kitchen, urging all of us—in their thick, Eastern European accents—to have seconds. I believe it was Bessie's apartment, and Ida and Rose both had apartments elsewhere in the same building. All three were elderly, and Ida and Rose were widows. Bessie's husband, Benny, loved being fussed over by his wife and his two sisters-in-law.

My memories of those days are more like snapshots than movies. I was so young and our days there were a blur of people and food, talking and laughter and embraces. Stuffed with food and too much rich dessert, my sister and I would crash in the back seat of our car as we left after dark for the hour-long trip back to our home.

What I remember most clearly was the feeling that I was so incredibly loved by these people. My elderly great-aunts lived for those holidays when they could welcome—and feed—the younger generations of their family. Especially the children.

It's been moving and emotional to me, writing this book and automatically reconnecting with my own long-lost ancestors. I hope that reading this story led you to think about the people in your family who came before. If so, please reach out and tell me about them. I love hearing from readers! You can get in touch on my Facebook page, or through Twitter or Instagram. Or simply go to my website and send me an email!

I hope you loved *The Lost Gift to the Italian Island*, and if you did, I would be very grateful if you could write a review. I'd love to hear your thoughts, and it makes such a difference helping new readers to discover one of my books for the first time.

Thanks,

Barbara

www.BarbaraJosselsohn.com

facebook.com/BarbaraJosselsohnAuthor

x.com/BarbaraJoss

instagram.com/Barbara_Josselsohn_Author

tiktok.com/@barbarajosselsohnbooks

REFERENCES

Below is a handful of books and resources I found most helpful in my research about Italy during the Second World War.

Benevolence and Betrayal: Five Italian Jewish Families Under Fascism by Alexander Stille (Summit Books, January 1991)

The Other Italy – The Italian Resistance in World War II by Maria de Blasio Wilhelm (Norton, January 1988)

The Bicycle Runner: A Memoir of Love, Loyalty, and the Italian Resistance by G. Franco Romagnoli (Thomas Duane Books, August 2009)

And finally… about the sacred texts mentioned in the novel…

The verses that Giulia discovers that begin with "Whither thou goest…" are from the Book of Ruth

The command to "Choose Life" is from the Book of Deuteronomy

ACKNOWLEDGMENTS

Writing a historical novel can feel like walking into a dark cave without even a candle. I'm so grateful to all the people in my life who've shown up to offer some light along the way.

As always, my deepest thanks go to my incredible agent, Cynthia Manson, who has such a great sense of story and has steered my career with dedication and wisdom from the very beginning. I'm thrilled to be right where I am, and I never would have arrived here without her guidance, friendship, and unwavering encouragement.

My heartfelt thanks, too, go to my brilliant editor, Jennifer Hunt. Without a doubt, her insight into what makes a novel sing is unparalleled. Her support and expertise have proved invaluable. They always help me keep the finish line squarely in my sights.

Thanks so much to all the publishing, editorial, marketing, rights, and sales professionals at Bookouture—what a remarkable team! And a special shout-out to the PR crew led by Kim Nash, Digital Publicity Director. You are all so accomplished at what you do—and thoroughly wonderful people to boot! Thanks, too, to all my fellow Bookouture authors. You are such wonderful storytellers, and I love reading your books!

I am enormously lucky to have a wonderful circle of author friends, whose talent blows me away each and every day: Jimin Han, Patricia Dunn, Marcia Bradley, Jennifer Manocherian, Veera Hiranandani, Patricia Friedrich, Diane Cohen Schneider, Ines Rodrigues, and Diana Asher—I am awed by you all! A very special acknowledgment, too, to my newest author friend and fellow Bookouture author, Gosia Nealon, whose Second World War novels are beautiful—you must read them! I was thrilled to meet Gosia in person last summer and can't wait to meet up again!

An extra shout-out to Ines Rodrigues for reviewing and helping me refine the Italian words and phrases in the book. So often, the Italian choice was the very best way to go! And thanks to Dr. Barbara Fisher and to Russell Fisher for teaching me about career milestones for a musician, which was essential as I was developing the character of Jeremy.

I'm deeply appreciative to Kerry Schafer, who lives up to her company's name, Author Genie. She is a graphics and social media whiz and also a fabulous novelist.

Thanks to Westchester Reform Temple in Scarsdale, N.Y., and to the entire clergy team, led by the always inspiring Rabbi Jonathan Blake. I am always moved by your words, and by the teaching that goes on there every day. And thanks so much to the Scarsdale Adult School for its fascinating and important class, "Italian Jews Under Fascism," taught by the incredibly knowledgeable Andrea Glover, professor and cultural historian.

To all the wonderful writers affiliated with the Women's Fiction Writers Association, the Writing Institute at Sarah Lawrence, the Scarsdale Library and its Writers Center, and Westport Writers Workshop, and all those students who have trusted me with their work: thank you for your friendship, willingness to share, and love of story in all its forms. I learn from you all every day.

And a special thanks to all the online bloggers and reviewers I've come to know over the last several years. I am so appreciative of what you do and how you do it! You have all become cherished friends.

Like my earlier book *Secrets of the Italian Island*, much of *The Lost Gift to the Italian Island* was inspired by the beautiful

North Fork of Long Island. Thanks to Scott Raulsome of Burton's Books of Greenport, Jessica Montgomery of Shelter Island Public Library, and Janet Olinkiewicz of Floyd Memorial Library in Greenport for being so welcoming. And much appreciation to Rosemary Nickerson for opening her beautiful home to us. What a beautiful place to write! Thanks, too, to Mark Fowler and Jessica Kaplan, owners of Bronx River Books in Scarsdale, N.Y., my hometown bookstore, for doing so much to support local authors.

Thanks to Dr. Brittany Glassberg and to Ben Pall for your continued help, enthusiasm, and expertise on aspects ranging from medicine to travel to technology!

And finally, I am beyond grateful for my wonderful family: my husband, Bennett; our three children—David, Rachel, and Alyssa; and our newest addition, our mini schnauzer Albie. Whatever lessons about family are in my book, I learned them right there in the home we all built together. You guys mean the world to me, and I love you more than I can say!

PUBLISHING TEAM

Turning a manuscript into a book requires the efforts of many people.

The publishing team at Bookouture would like to acknowledge everyone who contributed to this publication.

Commercial
Lauren Morrissette
Jil Thielen
Imogen Allport

Data and analysis
Mark Alder
Mohamed Bussuri

Designer
Debbie Clement

Editorial
Jennifer Hunt
Sinead O'Connor

Copyeditor
Jenny Page

Printed in Great Britain
by Amazon